K L CREAR

Lila Glover Wants a Lover

First published by Crear Publishing 2024

This novel is entirely a work of fiction. The names, characters and incidents portrayed in it are the work of the author's imagination. Any resemblance to actual persons, living or dead, events or localities is entirely coincidental.

K L Crear asserts the moral right to be identified as the author of this work.

Designations used by companies to distinguish their products are often claimed as trademarks. All brand names and product names used in this book and on its cover are trade names, service marks, trademarks and registered trademarks of their respective owners. The publishers and the book are not associated with any product or vendor mentioned in this book. None of the companies referenced within the book have endorsed the book.

First edition

ISBN: 978-1-7392765-4-6

To my friend Lorraine,

The world is that little bit darker now without you in it.

You left us too soon, but you will never be forgotten.

"If you're sad, add more lipstick and attack."

– COCO CHANEL

Contents

Chapter 1

Somehow, I had managed to find myself on the worst first date ever.

Even the goat's cheese tart starter, which was pretty inedible, still managed to be not quite as cheesy as the man sitting across the table from me. He was leering at me, probably thinking it was seductively, but with a little sprig of spinach wedged in the gap between his two overly white, overly large front teeth.

His name was Christopher, or "Toffer" as he preferred (just kill me now). I had met him on Tinder. Why, oh why had I not swiped left?

He was 34 years old and worked as an accountant - the very same profession my philandering weasel of an ex-husband did. In the past I had always thought accountants were reliable sorts, though maybe a little dull and of course obsessed with the figures on their spreadsheets. This was true to a point with my ex-husband Duncan: he had been into attractive figures, just not the ones on a profit and loss account; and more interested in spreading sheets in the bedroom than the spreadsheets on his laptop - always desperate to make our double divan look as pristine as possible after an afternoon romp with his latest floozy whilst I was toiling away, blissfully unaware, at work. I had learned a very valuable lesson from dearest Duncan: don't fully commit your heart to a man; if they don't own it, they can't destroy it.

It looked as if Toffer was cut from the same incorrigible cloth as my ex. Maybe I should have learned from my past and plumped for a nice traffic warden instead. And somehow young Toffer managed to be even more oily than my odious ex. Quite a feat in itself.

"I've always had a thing for the older ladies."

He looked intently at me as I tried to avert my gaze from the side salad stuck between his front incisors.

"Always found them to be so confident and self-assured, if you know what I mean?"

He served up a wide wolfish grin before spearing a king prawn on his fork and sucking it down with more noisy smacking of lips than was strictly necessary.

"They know what they like, and they aren't afraid to ask for it."

He was right on that score. I knew what I liked, all right, and that certainly wasn't him.

I gave a tight-lipped smile but chose to remain silent. I knew exactly what he was getting at, the randy little sod, and as I pushed my half-eaten tart around my plate, I considered my options. I could leave the restaurant right now with him, go back to his for the night and make all his sordid little dreams come true. But let's face it, that was never going to happen, not in a million lifetimes. Or alternatively I could leave now on my own, which sounded a much more attractive prospect.

I was in two minds. I didn't know how much more I could stomach of toothsome Toffer and his letchy comments. But talking of stomachs, I had ordered the mushroom stroganoff for main, and after the poor performance of the goat's cheese tart I was still bloody ravenous. I felt sure I could battle through another course courageously before I could feign some emergency or attack of explosive diarrhoea and escape screaming into the night and away from "Just call me Toffer" forever.

He had seemed so good on paper: attractive photo – well, he had been smiling with his mouth shut, so that was false advertising for a start. We had many shared interests, namely fine wines, reading and travelling. However, given the fact that he was currently guzzling down a large glass of sweet Liebfraumilch and had already informed me he hadn't so much as picked up a book since being forced to read *A Midsummer Night's Dream* at school, which he couldn't abide as it was full of mincing fairies, I could hazard a guess that fibbing could be added to Toffer's list of favourite pastimes. Another thing he clearly had in common with my rat of an ex-husband: yes, Toffer was not averse to bending the truth.

For a start he had certainly lied about his height: six foot one he claimed, but he was more like five foot seven and a half on his tippy toes. Well at least he would be travelling soon, so that wasn't a lie: travelling home alone in an Uber.

He was still talking, some anecdote or other about a colleague at work, who sounded quite frankly as obnoxious as him. I felt my mind wandering again. When had my dating life become so bad? After the split from Duncan and with our only son Thomas now away at Bristol University, I had initially enjoyed the thrill of throwing myself spectacularly into single life again.

At 49 I felt in the prime of life. If life was there for the taking, I was grabbing it with both hands and on my terms. Things were looking good for me. My career as a solicitor afforded me a comfortable lifestyle and the opportunity to enjoy the finer things in life; and the finer things for me just happened to include à la carte restaurants and dinner dates with dashing younger men.

I wasn't an idiot though; I knew what some people were saying about me: that I was a woman teetering perilously close to fifty years of age dating men in their mid-thirties. It was not the done thing.

I had heard whispered murmurings about me having some sort of mid-life crisis, or maybe I was just lacking in self-esteem. Hah, that was a laugh: I held myself in the highest possible regard, thank you very much. I had to, as when it boiled down to it, I was the person I trusted the most.

I never listened to gossip, as I believed most of it was based on jealousy. In truth I didn't really care what people thought of me. If they were talking about me, they were leaving some other poor bugger alone. Anyway, I never cared what people said; somebody else's opinion of me really was none of my business. And just because I was going to hit the half-century in a month or so didn't mean I had to retire from social life and sail off into obscurity on a boat called Old Biddy.

No, there would be no hanging up my Louboutin slingbacks in favour of a pair of comfortable suede slippers. I would have to be dragged kicking and screaming into the autumn of my life. It was going to be less knitting and more nights dancing till daybreak for Lila Glover.

I had been referred to on occasion as a cougar. I didn't have a problem with that: I already knew my nickname at work was The Rottweiler, so it felt quite apt. I barked in the boardroom, and I purred at the party. And anyway, what fun-loving girl in the prime of life doesn't enjoy a bit of role play once in a while?

In my book, which would undoubtedly be a bestseller, there was absolutely nothing wrong with an older successful woman dating a younger man. I would not be made to feel bad about it in the slightest. I was proud to be me: opinionated, feisty, unapologetically me.

When I was newly single, I had stayed in my own lane, so to speak, dating men of my age or a little older, but truthfully most of them were deadly dull. If their aura had a colour, it would most definitely be beige; more interested in talking about their pension investments or bemoaning their dwindling hair line than dancing till dawn.

Less passion and more passing the time watching the History channel for them. So, after a few mind-numbingly tedious dates I had shaved a few years off my stated age range on the dating apps from 45-55 to 30-42 and never looked back. I still had a lust for life, and so did men in their thirties if you catch my drift.

However, in the last few weeks the dates I'd gone on just didn't seem to hit the mark any more; they didn't come up to scratch. So I had been choosing to swerve dating altogether and stay at home with a takeaway and a good book. And if I did still have a certain itch to scratch, that's where the AAA batteries came in handy.

I glanced over the table to my dining companion, who still hadn't finished regaling me with his long-winded tale. I noted that the wilted spinach must have worked its way loose as his gnashers were now unfettered by wayward foliage. They were shocking in their brilliance, like two bright white tombstones. No human teeth were ever meant to be that shade, surely. I wished I had my sunglasses with me; those things could trigger a migraine.

Maybe I was being a little mean. He wasn't all bad: teeth aside, he had a nice face and lovely thick wavy chestnut hair that was simply wasted on a man. He was a smart dresser, though with maybe a few too many designer logos for my liking. Don't get me wrong, I'm all for a bit of designer smutter myself, but I like to keep the labels hidden inside my clothes. Wealth should be whispered, after all. As Yves Saint Laurent once said, "Fashions fade, style is eternal." But clearly if Toffer had spent a wedge on his outfit, he wanted the world and his wife to know about it.

It wasn't his looks that were the problem: okay, his teeth were giving me serious walrus vibes, but overall he was a decent enough looking chap. With a good personality he would even be considered attractive, but that was where the problem lay: his personality was simply atrocious.

It wasn't just him, though; all my recent dates had fallen way short of what I would consider a success. I would much rather have had a night out on the town with my girlfriends than subject myself to another night out with any of the dreary designer-clad douchebags I'd met of late. At least with my girlfriends I was guaranteed some good conversation. All I was getting from my current date was enough of the ick factor to give me raging indigestion.

Toffer was certainly not rekindling my desire to dive head-first into the dating scene again. If there were plenty more fish in the sea, that water appeared to be full of sewage.

At least I was seeing my friend Charlotte the following day. My legal firm Fluck, Young & Glover were sponsoring a small fashion show at a local hotel to showcase her new business. She had recently started her own fashion brand with her friend Morgan, and it was doing really well. I was keen to support her, let her know how proud I was of them.

"I must stay you're being awfully quiet, Lila; I would get more conversation out of a Trappist Monk."

Toffer honked with laughter at his own joke and looked across the table at me expectantly.

With more enthusiasm than I felt, I decided it was about time I rejoined the conversation.

"I'm so sorry, what were you saying … something about your work?"

Toffer picked up his wine glass and took a hearty swig.

"I was just telling you about my PhD."

I perked up slightly. At last, something potentially interesting to talk about, something with a bit of substance; maybe the night wasn't a complete disaster after all.

"Oh yes, that's very interesting, Toffer. It must be difficult studying whilst working full-time. Is your firm giving you time away from the office to devote to your PhD or do you have to do it all in your free time?"

Toffer was smirking to himself in a most unappealing way.

"No, the firm gives me no time off to study my PhD, it's all done in my own time, a bit of a labour of love you might say. I don't think any boss would pay even minimum wage for me to work on my Pretty Humongous Dick!"

Clearly I was wrong; the evening could get worse, infinitely worse.

Tears were running down Toffer's face he was laughing so hard.

"Damn, I should really get into stand-up. You saw what I did there? You thought I was talking about a degree, and I was referring to my dong the whole time. I'm a comedy legend."

I smiled politely at the middle-aged waiter who was deftly

clearing away our starter dishes, a forced smile etched on his face. He was a pleasant enough looking man, and for a moment I wished he was sitting across the table from me. Anyone would be an improvement on my current date. Hell, let's be honest, at this point in time I would take a Conservative Party candidate with a bad comb-over if they could just hold up their end of a decent conversation.

I sighed deeply and with more restraint than I knew I possessed and forced down the desire to launch myself across the table and wrap my hands around his neck.

"Yes, Toffer, although your sense of humour is exceedingly subtle and nuanced, it didn't completely pass me by."

Though obviously my sarcasm had shot right past him at high speed, as he nodded at me proudly, clearly chuffed with himself.

I said a silent prayer of thanks as the waiter returned and placed a steaming plate of mushroom stroganoff in front of me and an exceedingly rare steak for my date.

Toffer eyed my plate with distinct displeasure.

"Goat's cheese for starter and now mushrooms. Are you a vegetarian?"

I took a forkful of my food and savoured it before answering, as it really was excellent.

"No, not vegetarian; I just try to have a couple of meat-free days a week. It's good for your health and better for the environment too."

He looked unconvinced and sawed into a large piece of his steak, the blood oozing out onto his plate, making it look like a Jackson Pollock painting. He gave me a wink before popping the meat into his mouth.

"Definitely not for me. I'm strictly vag-itarian."

He winked at me as he chewed his food, his mouth slightly open so I could see half-masticated cow stuck between his gnashers again. I couldn't help but wince.

He exploded into laughter once more. He was quite obviously delighted once more by his comedy genius.

I took another mouthful of food. Once my plate was cleared, I was going to be out of here like a marathon runner with their arse on fire.

Clearly though, Toffer was just getting into his stride.

"If we start dating, Lila, that would make you my Sugar Mummy, wouldn't it?"

He blew on one of his chips in a seductive manner, well as seductive as was possible with root vegetables and those teeth.

"I've always secretly fancied being a boy toy. I could do whatever you wanted, and you could thank me with occasional little gifts now and then."

I wasn't often shocked, but this time was an exception. I was rendered completely speechless. A Sugar Mummy? He had to be joking, surely? But this time I actually thought he was being completely earnest. The bloody cheeky little git.

I smiled pleasantly at him. It took a Herculean effort to keep my temper in check.

"I'm sure I could get you a little something if you're a very good boy."

He sat back in his chair, looking for all the world like the cat that had got the cream; obviously thinking he'd hit the jackpot with me: an older experienced woman who was a sure thing in the sack and was going to shower him with gifts too.

Lucky young Toffer. What a treat he was going to have, telling all the young bucks his exploits around the photocopier the following morning at work.

I slowly put down my knife and fork and neatly folded my napkin next to my plate, all the time smiling sweetly at my companion.

"How does a nice big, gift-wrapped box of Go Fuck Yourself sound?"

My chair scraped noisily across the wooden floor as I jumped up from it. In a flash I was on my feet and heading for the door as fast as my black patent stilettos would allow. Toffer would be picking up the tab for dinner. Might teach him a lesson about how not to behave with a lady. Anyway, it was the very least he could do after subjecting me to that fiasco. That was eighty minutes of my life I was never getting back.

Just before leaving the restaurant through its revolving door, I cast a longing glance back at the table I had just vacated: not at Toffer's shocked face, but at my barely touched food. It was a crying shame to have to walk away from that meal. But absolutely nothing would make me endure another minute of the date from hell.

To escape that date, I would happily forfeit my mushroom stroganoff and get myself a vegetarian pizza with extra mushrooms on the way home. But definitely no spinach.

Chapter 2

The spacious conference room of the Wilton Hotel was looking very grand indeed. The underlying dull as dishwater beige décor now boasted an imposing pink and black banner announcing the name of Zaftig & Raven stretched around the entirety of its flaky emulsioned walls.

It was so good to see Charlotte and Morgan's fashion brand up there loud and proud, for the whole world, or at least a small enclave of it in Yorkshire, to celebrate. There was also a makeshift stage area with a runway jutting out from the middle, where the models would strut their glamorous stuff in an array of outfits from the fashion brand.

My eyes darted furtively around the room. It was packed to the rafters with a sea of chattering folk from all age groups and social sectors.

There were smart ladies attired in elegant yet understated twin sets with sensible shoes, set against achingly hip types sporting countless piercings and fashions that screamed "I'm avant-garde and amazing."

I grabbed a small flute of something bubbly from a side table as I spotted my friend poised in a corner talking animatedly to Morgan, her co-owner. I bounded over to them, keen to announce my arrival, yet cautious not to spill my drink.

"Lottie, Morgan, this place looks amazing, really amazing! You've done yourselves proud."

I leaned in to kiss each woman flamboyantly on the cheek whilst leaving a faint smudge of scarlet Dior – my Lila Glover signature greeting.

Lottie was looking fabulously chic in a fitted claret wool crepe dress cinched in with a wide silver belt, just perfect to show off her curves to their fullest. Damn! My best friend had certainly reinvented herself fashion-wise. The sackcloth and ashes fashion of bygone Lottie was well and truly a thing of the past. This confident new creation was most certainly putting the old Lottie to shame. Her dress was a showstopper by itself, most definitely va va voom and hitting in all the right places.

It had taken my dear friend many months of soul-searching and rediscovery to get herself to where she was now. After her rat of a husband had cheated on her with the office floozie, her whole world was changed irrevocably, and it had been one hell of a bitter pill for her to swallow.

Initially upon discovering his infidelity, she had tumbled into a wave of tears, tea and tequila and not stopped until she hit rock bottom. But that was no longer the case. Now like a phoenix she was soaring high, and here today stood proudly, a more confident, beautiful version of my friend.

Of course she had always been beautiful, but until she had believed it herself, it had never truly shown.

I was so proud of Lottie: proud of her strength and her fortitude. Yes, Lottie Potts really rocked. She was finally where she needed to be: fierce and confident and doing it all on her own terms.

However, that being said, I knew that a certain old flame of Lottie's, whose spark had fizzled out before it had ever had a chance to blaze, was soon to be back on the scene. One Leo Knight, entrepreneur and fine-looking specimen, was touching down on British soil from Canada any day now and would be entering Lottie's life again from stage right.

Was he still looking to be Lottie's leading man? And if so, what would that mean for Lottie? I just didn't know. I suppose only time would tell.

It was a testament to Lottie and Morgan's hard work that so many people had turned out to the event. It was a bitterly cold day, and the January sales were in full swing. And even though fewer people like to traipse physically around the stores these days, it would still be a perfect Saturday afternoon to cuddle up at home with a hot chocolate and some online shopping. That's what I would be doing had I not been supporting my friend.

"We're hoping to get the show underway in the next few minutes."

There was a slight tremble to Morgan's voice, revealing how nervous she was. If her voice hadn't given her away, I would never have thought for a second that she could suffer from anxiety. She looked so self-assured and confident.

Like Lottie, her fashion sense was amazing. Her style was polar opposite but no less impressive for it. In short, she looked fierce and formidable, decked out in lace-trimmed black combat trousers and a hot pink vest emblazoned with large outspread raven wings sprinkled with diamanté. It was a head-turning outfit, and from the many young audience members dressed similarly, seated on the white leatherette chairs around the stage, I could see that her fashions were very popular indeed. I didn't think she had anything to worry about, but from her furrowed brow I could tell she wouldn't relax until the show was completely over and could be deemed a success.

"I'm just going to check on the models again, see if they're all in their right places."

Morgan strode off towards the back of the stage, a woman on a mission.

"Models, eh?"

I couldn't help but tease Lottie a little. It was our "thing" to affectionately poke fun at each other.

"Who's modelling your frocks today then, Charlotte, my most fashionable friend? Are we going to be graced by the presence of Gigi Hadid or Cara Delevingne perhaps? Or maybe you're going a bit more old school and plumping for the OGs of the runway and it's Kate Moss in a cagoule or Naomi Campbell in a nylon ensemble?"

Lottie laughed despite herself.

"No such luck, I'm afraid. Our models consist of a gaggle of nervous students from the local college and a few friends and acquaintances Morgan and I have managed to cobble together. At least we don't have to pay them a million quid just to get them out of bed though. These girls are happy to do it for a few free glasses of supermarket plonk and a packet or two of pork scratchings."

"I'm sure they'll be fabulous."

I rubbed Lottie's arm confidently.

"You need an eclectic bunch anyway to show off the fabulously diverse range of fashions your brand offers."

Lottie nodded her head in agreement.

"You're right, Lila. And anyway, we've rehearsed and run through it so many times that I'm sure the poor things are sashaying in their sleep."

She ran her hand through her shoulder-length blonde hair;

it shone like gold under the harsh overhead lighting.

"I know what Morgan means, though; I feel like I've got an army of butterflies fighting in my stomach, I'm so flipping nervous."

Lottie held her hand out so I could see it trembling slightly.

"Look, I'm visibly shaking; I could really do with a stiff drink to calm my nerves."

I rummaged through my huge Mulberry tote.

"You can have a bit of my Allure, if you like?"

Lottie looked perplexed and shook her head.

"You've completely lost me, Lila. What do you mean, have a bit of your allure? I'm not suddenly going to achieve your level of charm and sophistication in the next five minutes; it's taken you nearly fifty years of full-on feistiness, after all."

I laughed and produced a bottle of scent from the depths of my handbag.

"No, I meant have a spritz of my perfume. I've no bottle of vodka on me, so a dab of Chanel will have to suffice. Unless you want to drink it, of course; but thinking about it ounce for ounce, it's probably cheaper than the alcohol they're serving behind the bar here. It's bloody daylight robbery; they should be wearing masks."

My daft humour seemed to be working a treat, as Lottie threw back her head and laughed. I was pleased that I had managed to calm her down a little. She held her wrists out for me to blast with a quick spray of the scent.

She lifted her pale wrist to her nose and inhaled the perfume deeply.

"Mmmm, that's lovely. Well, I smell amazing now. Let's just hope it's a sign of things to come."

I gave my friend's arm a reassuring squeeze. It was time for a bit of a pep talk.

"It's all going to go great."

I reassured her with absolute certainty.

"You're amazing and you've worked so hard; you must be really proud of what you've achieved. I know I am."

Lottie looked up towards the large sign suspended just above the runway. It had gold backing and was rich and opulent looking with embossed letters in deep red standing out from the gold, as if each letter were suspended in midair. The colours were those of my solicitor's firm, and the letters raised out from the fabric spelt out the names of the partners: Reginald Fluck senior partner, Sebastian Young or Seb as he preferred to be known, and me, Lila Glover.

"Thank you so much, Lila, for convincing Mr Fluck to sponsor the show. It's made such a difference."

"Don't worry, he's happy too. He's found out that the press is coming, with the excuse for that decrepit old dinosaur to get his ugly mug in the paper."

The words were barely out of my mouth when I felt a bony figure tapping me on the shoulder. I experienced the sensation of moving in slow motion as I turned around to see the aforementioned old dinosaur facing me with an unreadable expression etched on his cadaverous face.

Chapter 3

"Lila, my dear, I take it that this lovely lady is the Charlotte I've been hearing so much about?"

I had a feeling my mouth was hanging open and I was resembling a slack-jawed imbecile. I shut it swiftly, fearful I would catch flies. I gave my older colleague, aka The Corner Office Crypt keeper, a winning smile.

"Indeed it is, Mr Fluck. Let me introduce you to my very dear friend and co-owner of Zaftig & Raven, Ms Charlotte Potts."

"Delighted, my dear."

Fluck took Lottie's hand is his own bony fingers and furnished it with a kiss.

"So pleased to make your acquaintance finally."

For someone like Lottie who lapped up all the romantic old films, she should have found this gesture utterly charming: rather like a scene from one of her favourite black and white pictures. However, her face looked anything but charmed. In fact, the expression of shock and revulsion would have been more suited to a video nasty. Lottie, though, forever the consummate professional, managed to quell her initial displease and let a warm smile light up her pretty face as she firmly pulled her hand away from the old man's puckered lips.

"It's very nice to meet you too, Mr Fluck. Lila has told me so much about you."

This was met with a few seconds of excruciating silence while I waited for the tumbleweed to go rolling by. Needless to say, anything I had told Lottie about Mr Fluck had been none too complimentary.

I coughed slightly to cover my embarrassment.

"Is your wife with you today...erm...?"

I trailed off, racking my brain desperately to remember his wife's name. Doreen? Deidre? I had met her dozens of times and could picture her so clearly in my head - a quiet, pleasant, mousy type who always looked as if she would rather be anywhere but beside her spouse. I couldn't say I blamed her. But what the hell was her name? It eluded me entirely.

Fluck's beady eyes narrowed ever so slightly.

"Ah yes, my wife. As a matter of fact, she is here today but *Dinah saw* the sign for the Ladies and decided to go and powder her nose; bladder the size of a thimble, that one."

I felt my heart lurch in my chest. Dinah, her name was Dinah. But had I imagined it, or had the old man used my blunder as a pun? Was he, in his own subtle way, letting me know that he had heard every word I had said to Lottie?

I glanced at my friend, hoping for reassurance, but she looked like she'd been smacked in the face with a wet welly. Quite clearly, she had picked up on it too.

Bloody hell! It was one thing to call your boss names behind his back, but quite another to be caught doing it. This was not good. I had some serious sucking up to do. My friend, however, beat me to it.

"Thank you so much for sponsoring us today, Mr Fluck."

Bless her, she was trying to divert him away from the excruciatingly awkward situation.

"I really hope you enjoy the show. But please excuse me, I must go and get things started."

With that, Lottie sensibly made her escape. I wished I could do the same.

"Let me get you a drink, Mr Fluck, whilst you get yourself and Dinah a seat."

I was already unzipping my purse; it was the least I could do.

Fluck's eyes darted around the noisy room.

"Yes, all right then, I'll have a large Scotch, single malt on the rocks, none of the cheap rubbish; and a small sherry for Dinah." He sighed impatiently, his beady eyes scanning the room again. "Why is Young not here yet? As for the press, I see no sign of them either. I was promised a reporter from Leeds Leads would be here to get a picture of our sign and write a few words about our firm being so benevolent to local businesses."

The expression on his weathered old face looked far from benevolent.

"I'd better not have wasted my time; I could just as well be on the golf course this afternoon, you know?"

I felt my throat tighten, and it wasn't just the realisation that I was maybe going to have to sell an organ to afford the round of drinks he had just ordered. Where *was* Seb? Please tell me he hadn't swerved the event, found something more fun to do on his precious Saturday afternoon off. Root canal perhaps? I knew that fashion was seriously out of his comfort zone, at the top of an exceedingly long list of things to avoid. That said, I could really do with a bit of support from my colleague.

Normally Seb was so reliable; almost too reliable, like the devoted family pet that was forever at the door to greet you when you returned home, getting under your feet in their eagerness to please. But thank goodness I spotted him striding towards us, a worried look on his not unattractive face; a face which was rather more pink than usual. I could see he was clearly out of breath: even from a fair distance there was evidently a slight film of sweat gathering on his upper lip.

It was hardly surprising he was feeling a touch warm: although it was early January with a dusting of snow on the rooftops, the temperature in the hotel conference room was verging on the tropical. Probably forward thinking by management, as some of the models would be wearing skimpy numbers and a stiff nipple through stretch satin could prove a little distracting to some. But Seb was dressed like an Arctic explorer: woollen hat pulled firmly down on his head, brown padded coat resembling a sleeping bag zipped right up to his collar, all topped off with a large striped scarf that might have been fashioned from Joseph's technicolour dream coat, possibly knitted by his mother from the confines of her nursing home.

Seb waved enthusiastically upon spotting me and rushed over to give me a swift breathy kiss.

"Sorry I'm late, Lila. I had a nightmare parking, and then I ended up at the wrong hotel, would you believe?"

I believed him. For someone as intelligent as Seb, he could be so scatty at times. Most probably he'd turned up at one of the other bland hotel chains, burst into another conference room that smelt faintly of boiled cabbage and furniture polish, and wondered why he'd ended up in the middle of a slimming club or a gender reveal party for a pregnant stranger, rather than a fashion show.

"I'm just glad you're finally here."

I gestured over to where Mr Fluck and his spouse were now seated, on the front row, facing the stage as honoured guests.

There were also seats reserved beside them for me and Seb.

"You go sit down; I'm just getting drinks from the bar. I'm trying to butter Fluck up as I've already managed to insult him."

Seb laughed pleasantly.

"Trust you, Lila; can't leave you alone for a moment."

"Yeah well, that may be the case, but I don't think calling your boss a dinosaur is a great move career-wise. Anyway, what do you want to drink, seeing as I'm in the chair?"

Seb seemed to be considering his options for a moment, his brow furrowing.

"Just half a soft drink for me, please; lemonade or something."

I rolled my eyes at him to demonstrate how dull I felt his choice of beverage was.

"I'll see if I can get you a straw too, shall I?"

"No thank you, no straw needed as I've already pulled the short one having to give up my Saturday afternoon in the name of fashion."

He gave me a little wink, so I knew he wasn't being serious.

"I could have been playing rugby or engaged in some other manly pursuit if it wasn't for this."

That was his attempt at humour. And to be fair, he could be funny at times; not as funny as me obviously, but mildly amusing. There was about as much chance of Sebastian Young playing rugby in his time off as there was of me knitting him a pair of matching mittens to accompany his scarf. He was most certainly not the sporty type.

I knew that if he had not been here today, he would probably have been sinking a pint in his local with his bearded lodger Adam. Seb owned a large property in Headingley and Adam had lodged with him for a few years, ever since his divorce.

They had been friends since uni, and a shared interest in pub quizzes, sci-fi and home-made shepherd's pie meant that they rubbed along quite nicely.

Seb had never been married. I found that fact strange in itself. He was a nice-looking man after all, fashion sense aside: tall and lean with thick black hair just peppered with a little grey, and sparkling cobalt blue eyes; a little older than me, in his early fifties, but looking quite youthful on it. Must be all the shepherd's pie keeping him so fresh-faced. I might have to give it a try sometime, but I was cutting out carbs now, so would need to rub it into my face at night rather than consume it. It would be a good sight cheaper than my current skincare regime, that was for sure.

Yes, all around he was a good catch. Not for me, of course, but I felt sure there must be plenty of women who would find his woolly wardrobe and love of anything sci-fi positively knicker-dropping.

"Hurry up with those drinks; you don't want to keep the prehistoric Parasaurolophus waiting. I think the show's about to start."

With that he was heading off to the vacant seats. Trust Seb to know his dinosaurs too.

I could see that Mr Fluck was still craning his neck around every few minutes, the sinews bulging, to check if the press had arrived. No such luck; it would appear that the reporter from Leeds Leads had somewhere much more pressing to be. I felt bad for Lottie, but for myself too. Fluck was not going to let the matter drop.

Five minutes later and my purse much, much lighter, I made my way over to my seat, carefully carrying the tray of drinks.

I was just in time as the music was starting up: some easy listening Muzak to warm up the crowd before the show proper kicked off.

I swiftly took my seat and distributed the drinks. Mr Fluck eyed his glass tumbler suspiciously, wary that I might have shortchanged him with a single measure of whisky.

I could see Jacob, Lottie's son, sitting at a small table positioned just off from the stage looking intently at his phone and tapping on it every few seconds. Like teenagers the world over, my son Thomas included, Jacob was obsessed with his technology. However, on this occasion he had a good reason to be studying his smartphone so intently: he was in charge of the playlist for the event – the different pieces of music that the various models would walk to.

Long gone was the need for a sound system or, heaven forbid, a record player. No necessity any more to be recording the top 40 off the radio on a Sunday night, armed only with a double-desk cassette player and cat-like reflexes. That was how I had spent my youth: desperately trying to hit the stop button in the dying moments of the latest A-ha hit, so as to avoid any unwanted dialogue from the DJ.

I would shout down the stairs to my mother to please get me a packet of prawn cocktail-flavoured crisps and a can of Vimto from the kitchen, as I couldn't risk leaving my bedroom for a single moment and missing my favourite song. No, everything was instantly available now, an app for virtually anything.

Jacob had worked hard though, carefully choreographing the music for each part of the show: strong female anthems of empowerment that would suit the different fashions being showcased. Lottie was pleased that it had given him something to focus on.

He was back from his first term at university and was brooding at home a little, getting under her feet. The new term didn't start back for a week or so and he was pining for his new girlfriend, keen to get back to halls and enjoy everything that student life had to offer. So the fashion show had proved to be a good distraction. And he certainly seemed to be concentrating hard enough on his mobile.

He was, however, looking a little dishevelled, even more so than his usual scruffy teenager style. In truth he appeared somewhat green around the gills. I already knew from Lottie that he had been into Leeds the previous night with some old schoolfriends to listen to an up-and-coming band.

It was clear to see from his pallor and the bags under his eyes that it was not just the music he had enjoyed; he had clearly indulged in a fair few alcoholic beverages too. It just went to show you could still get rough hangovers in your youth; not as physically debilitating as in your forties, but dreadful all the same.

Jacob was a good lad though, and I knew how proud Lottie was of him. She was keen for him to return to university and get properly stuck into his course; find his feet and get out from under hers. But she also missed him terribly when he was gone. Her apartment, although much smaller than her previous home, felt large and empty; she was rattling around it on her lonesome. It was great to have your own space, but it could be lonely too.

Suddenly the room was filled with the powerful voice of Chaka Khan as 'I'm every woman' surged out of the many speakers. The audience perked up; in an instant there was a feeling of anticipation fizzing around the room.

The first model was out, striding purposefully down the

runway. She was super tall and statuesque, clad in a tightly tailored cropped satin jacket in the most fabulous plum shade, dark and decadent, with matching wide-legged palazzo pants in an identical hue. The outfit was finished off with a pair of bejewelled training shoes that sparkled like Dorothy's slippers from *The Wizard of Oz.*

I could hear appreciative sounds coming from the ladies in the audience. As soon as the model had completed her walk, including a great hip strut and spin at the end of the runway, the next model was hot on her heels. She was obviously in one of Morgan's designs: an achingly hip leather column dress that was bizarrely teamed with a purple feather boa and pillbox hat. It should have been a disaster, but somehow it worked incredibly well. Not my style of course, but that was not to say I couldn't appreciate it; on the right woman it would have been sartorial perfection.

This model also stopped at the end of the runway, doing a few turns and hair flips to allow the audience to see the outfit from every angle. She sashayed slowly away to the sounds of 'Run the World' by Beyoncé.

Out came the next model, then another, then another. The audience were clearly buoyed up and suitably impressed with the show. Well, most of the audience anyway. I could feel the palpable boredom wafting off Seb. I couldn't say that surprised me: a man like Seb, not averse to an elasticated waistband on his work trousers, was not really the market Lottie was catering to.

I could also feel Mr Fluck's eyes burning into me like laser beams. He had drained the contents of his tumbler and was clearly trying to alert me to scamper off to the bar and refresh his whisky. I studied the hemline of the model closest to me, as if enthralled by the stitching, anything to avoid his eyes.

There was a collective gasp from the audience at the gorgeous confection that was now shimmying down the runway. The model who had previously shown off the leather dress now floated along in the most fabulous dusty pink evening gown with the largest tulle skirt I had ever seen. It was both decadent and delicious, a huge shimmering candy floss.

She swished the skirt back and forth theatrically, showcasing her amazing six-inch-heel, jewel-encrusted cowboy boots. The dress may have been good, but those boots were something else. Great for the cowboy ranch, the cocktail bar or indeed the boudoir. Who didn't love a bit of multi-purpose fashion? I made a mental note to persuade Lottie to put those bad boys aside for me.

Suddenly the music stopped, ground to a halt. It was a rather jarring experience, like when you're at a house party and don't even notice there's a soundtrack playing until it suddenly ends and then the lack of background music is just excruciating in its silence.

Thankfully the music only ceased for a few agonising seconds before it piped up again. However, a few notes in and I felt a lurch in the pit of my stomach akin to being on a rollercoaster ride. Surely this was not on the playlist that Jacob had so carefully organised? I was no connoisseur when it came to modern music, but I was pretty confident that what I was hearing was not a strong feminist anthem. I certainly hoped not.

'Move, Bitch' by Ludacris was blaring out from the speakers. And goodness me, he didn't sound happy; he was effing and jeffing for England.

The shock on the models' faces was mirrored by those of

the audience. This was not a welcome change of pace. The model at the front looked around nervously, clearly at a loss as to what to do for the best. Maybe Kate or Naomi would have known instantly how to deal with this situation, would have styled it out flawlessly; but as for the amateur models, they went into full-on panic mode. As the front one stopped short and turned around, desperately seeking out Lottie or Morgan for advice and reassurance, the girl striding behind her took a tumble, falling unceremoniously off her platform shoes.

Then they all went down like dominoes. It was painful to watch: a paradigm pile-up, a heap of haute couture as they fell stumbling over each other. One twisted her ankle painfully; another, the woman in the fabulous pink evening gown, grabbed desperately at the curtain suspended above, pulling down on the banner displaying the name of my firm.

The embroidered letters, which had looked so dramatic before, now seemed perilously close to disintegrating in front of our eyes, desperate for another dab of superglue to keep them attached. The model hung on to the banner with all her might, determined to keep herself upright; one of her cowboy boots had fallen off in her struggle and was lying forlornly on the runway, like rodeo roadkill.

What on earth was happening? I looked over to Jacob to see what had gone wrong. His chair was empty, his phone lying abandoned on the table next to a can of energy drink and a half-eaten packet of crisps. Where the hell had he gone?

I thought about his pale pasty face, all the signs that he had been out drinking the night before. If I was a gambling woman, which I was on occasion, I would bet he had made a dash to the toilet to be sick. Somehow his show playlist had stopped and reverted to playing a tune from his own collection.

I knew Jacob had very diverse music tastes: everything ranging from heavy metal to a bit of country, even some Harry Styles on occasion for good measure. Somehow, though, we'd ended up with about the least appropriate tune imaginable for an elegant fashion show run by his mother.

From the corner of my eye, I spotted a startled-looking Lottie darting towards Jacob's phone. Her fitted dress made her dash appear somewhat comical, desperate to get to the device and silence it, with Morgan hot on her heels.

There was a sudden ominous ripping sound that seemed to come from the heavens above. Everyone's eyes flew upwards to the curtain that the model was gripping onto for dear life, watching as the banner slowly began to tear. As it did, some of the letters from the firm's logo got dislodged, fluttering down to the runway like gentle butterfly wings, leaving just a few of them still remaining.

My hands flew to my eyes, yet I couldn't help peering through my fingers; frightened to look, yet desperate to see. Of all the letters that could have been pulled off from the sign, why did it have to be those ones?

Now the sign no longer read 'Fluck, Young & Glover, Solicitors at Law; it read 'Fuck You over, Solicitors at Law'.

My heart was in my mouth. I glanced towards my boss. The expression on his face would have been humorous had it not been for the danger behind it. He looked as if his gob had been well and truly smacked. But this lasted only a couple of seconds before his expression changed again, his eyes darting to the left. It might be snowing outside, but his face was thunderous.

I turned to see what he was looking at, steeling myself as to what it could be.

It was then I realised that the press had indeed made an

appearance after all. However, rather than being pleased, Mr Fluck was now desperately holding his arm over his face, clearly not wanting to be seen. No, he was anything but pleased, and desperate not to be associated with the sign. The grin on the reporter's face was as wide as that of the Cheshire cat as he happily snapped away, capturing everything for posterity: from the carnage on the runway to the battered sign hanging forlornly above.

I looked towards Seb in complete horror. He had a half-serene, half-amused expression on his face: like The Mona Lisa if she had had been male and living in present-day Yorkshire, dressed like Doctor Who. He gave me a little wink.

"Drink?"

I nodded at him.

"Yes please, a very large one. Let's get out of here quick."

Chapter 4

Olive Affair was quieter than normal for a Saturday afternoon. Clearly all the usual drinkers were still nursing hangovers from all the booze they'd imbibed over the festive season. Or else their bank accounts, rather like their heads, were feeling a little worse for wear.

It had been a couple of weeks since I had last been here. Then it had been under much happier circumstances - meeting up with my girlfriends for good conversation and even better cocktails, and countless yummy little tapas dishes to help soak up the liquor.

Seb and I had found ourselves in one of the more comfortable booths, and I was now onto my third dirty martini, drinking fast and nibbling slow on a briny olive, like a despondent dormouse.

Seb studied me for a few seconds before reaching over the table and grabbing the hardbacked menu, which was about as thick as an encyclopaedia.

"You're so quiet, Lila. Honestly, I would get more conversation out of a mime artist with laryngitis."

He began to flick through the pages.

"You really need a sandwich or something to eat, to mitigate all that vodka you're so intent on guzzling."

I shook my head gloomily at him.

"No thank you, this olive is about all I can stomach for lunch. I'm far too upset to eat."

"But not to drink, I see?"

His bushy eyebrows were raised disapprovingly. The man clearly had never owned a pair of tweezers.

"It's not all tapas here, you know. They also run to a nice line in home-made pies, proper shortcrust ones with a top *and a* bottom, not just a stew with a flaky pastry hat perched on top."

He clearly took the matter of pastry very seriously.

Pies? Did the man not know me at all? I haven't eaten a pie since secondary school, when my grandmother forced a Fray Bentos minced beef and onion down me with a mountain of lumpy mash. OK, I did like the occasional quiche or tart, but stodgy pies were not really my thing at all. They were the least sexy of any foodstuffs. I could feel my thighs dimpling at the thought of all that lard and saturated fat.

He shut the menu with a firm snap.

"On second thoughts, I'm going to have a chip butty, real nostalgic comfort food; takes me right back to my old mum singing along to the radio while the chip pan bubbled away back in 1980."

I could see his eyes misting over as he recalled this happy family memory. It all sounded a bit too *Coronation Street* for me.

"A chip butty?"

I shuddered physically.

"And you wonder why your abs are more breadboard than washboard."

Seb grinned at me, not at all wounded by my words. He

considered this to be my shtick; my signature way of communicating; to poke fun at him, engage in good-hearted banter.

He had once referred to my teasing him as "Lila's love language". I had quickly shut that down. I was incredibly fond of Seb, but that was as far as it went. In truth, I thought he was just a little too nice for me.

As my mother Veronica would put it, he was one of those "steady away fellows", perfectly nice and all, but never going to set the world on fire. I had to admit she was right on that score. Seb waxing lyrical about the merits of fried potatoes and white sliced bread was never going to tempt me to lose my lingerie any time soon. Oysters and champagne are a guaranteed knicker dropper, but thick sliced bloomer and ketchup certainly are not.

Seb gestured to a passing waiter to get his attention.

"Well, I'm bloody starving. I could eat the arse end of a skunk unshaven. Are you absolutely sure you don't want anything?"

I drained the remnants of my martini in one gulp. The alcohol was taking the edge off my gloomy mood, and I felt a little warm and fuzzy around the edges. Not the worst feeling in the world, and certainly a lot better than how I had felt an hour ago.

I pointed at my now empty glass. It clearly needed replenishing.

"Just more lady fuel for me, please."

Seb ordered me another martini, his chip butty and a garlic and rosemary flat bread. Just in case I saw sense and relented, realising I needed something in my system other than a solitary stuffed olive to mop up all the vodka currently coursing through my veins.

I was still mortified by what had happened at the fashion

show. At least Lottie had since been in touch. I was worried that she was going to be furious with me, but she had actually laughed, already able to see the funny side of things.

And like she had said, there really was no such thing as bad publicity. I wished I could feel the same, but I really didn't imagine Mr Fluck was going to be of the same opinion when the piece written about the firm finally hit the press.

Lottie had been in high spirits for another reason too. She was excited about her "friend" Leo being back from Canada for a visit. I knew it was only a matter of time before the two of them started dating again. I just had a feeling in my gut that Leo would be moving back permanently to the UK sometime soon.

Their relationship had been doomed to fail before, as Lottie had been too recently out of her toxic marriage with her ex, the Dastardliest Daniel. But now things were different; she was in a much better, happier place.

I was convinced that second time around would be the charm for them. My lovely friend was well and truly healed from the emotional wounds inflicted on her through her many years of marriage. Lottie Potts was now her most fabulous self again, and I was truly happy for her.

She had excitedly invited me and Seb to accompany them both for dinner in a couple of days' time. She felt that if we went out as a foursome, it wouldn't seem like such a date for her and Leo. Just a little less awkward. She was still unsure as to where they stood relationship-wise: hopeful for a happy ever after for them both, but not wanting to take anything for granted.

Lottie felt it would be less intense if there was another couple along with them, who were also not an official couple. So that's where Seb and I came into the equation: we were often out on the town together, but most definitely never on a romantic rendezvous.

Of course, that's not to say that Seb didn't want more. He had even come out and told me as much on several occasions. But for me we were strictly good friends. I knew he held a candle for me, one that didn't seem to be fizzling out any time soon. And in return, I was very fond of him. He was good-looking in a lovable, loyal family pet sort of way. And if you could get past his dubious dress sense, he cut quite an elegant figure.

I had occasionally toyed with the idea of us dating, just to see if we would make a good match; but I had always hastily discarded the notion as foolish. To use the most elegant of terms, I didn't want to shit where I ate. I worked with Seb, and we were such good friends as well as colleagues. Was it really worth jeopardising all of that?

The waiter returned with our food. Seb was practically salivating as the chip butty was placed down in front of him. He grabbed a couple of the little packets of vinegar and ripped them open eagerly with his teeth before dumping the pungent-smelling liquid all over his beige food. He picked up his bap and began bolting it down like he hadn't seen solid food in weeks.

A strange feeling came over me briefly, and I crossed my legs awkwardly in my seat. Seeing the way he was devouring his food with such enthusiasm, I wondered for a fleeting moment what he would really be like in the bedroom. Would he tear my lingerie off with his teeth with such wild eagerness? I felt my cheeks flame. What the hell was I thinking? I was the one who was always saying to all and sundry that Seb and I would never be more than friends; and then that image had popped unsolicited into my head.

I pushed away my now empty martini glass. Definitely no more booze for me, thank you very much. That was the trouble with me: one too many alcoholic drinks, and my morals would loosen as quickly as my Spanx would.

I gave my head a little wobble to try and sober myself up. Maybe Seb was right: I needed something to soak up all the vodka. The rosemary bread did look exceedingly delicious, and the tantalising smell was making my mouth water. I picked up the smallest end slice. I would have this little sliver just to be sociable.

Five minutes later and the plate was empty. The bread appeared to have mysteriously vanished. I quickly glanced around the bar, expecting to see David Copperfield sinking a pint of lager and scoffing a packet of salt and vinegar crisps somewhere. Surely, I hadn't eaten it all myself? But it appeared that I had literally sucked down the entire 12 inches, if you pardon the pun.

"I knew you must be hungry."

Seb smirked at me as he blew on a rogue chip that had fallen out of his butty.

"I've clearly had a little bit of a 'snaccident'."

I informed him huffily.

"I blame the booze. I don't even remember eating it all."

I reached over and helped myself to the last chip from of his plate, ignoring his protestations.

"So just the four of us on Tuesday then?"

He drained the last of his lemonade in one gulp.

"You, me, Lottie and this fella Leo?"

I nodded at him fiddling with the stem of my martini glass. The little devil on my shoulder was whispering in my ear to have another.

"Yeah, I reckon they're made for each other; they just need to figure it out for themselves in their own good time. Lottie has been so burned by her ex, Daniel, that she's scared to trust her heart; but I've got a good feeling about the two of them."

Seb nodded and gave me a rather tender smile.

"I think Lottie has always thought the same about us two."

I shut him down instantly with my most withering glare.

"Absolutely not."

Seb smiled slightly to himself and held up his hands in a mock gesture of defeat.

"Well, you can't blame a chap for trying."

I returned his smile, taking in his twinkling blue eyes and kind face. I didn't want to be too sharp with him; I just didn't want to travel down that particular road either. It was full of potholes and banana skins to slip you up and make you fall flat on your arse.

Relationships just never seemed to work out very well for me in the long term. And after my mind wandering off course a few minutes previously and me nearly imagining us getting down to our scanties and sexy time, I wanted to steer well away from that particular avenue.

So I deftly changed the subject, which I was well skilled at.

"I'm dreading seeing Fluck on Monday. He's going to be in a foul mood with me, well even fouler than usual if that's possible."

Seb reached over and gave my hand a reassuring squeeze. I appreciated the gesture, it felt kind and caring. I couldn't help but notice how strong his hands were, his nails tidy and well groomed. I couldn't imagine that he had ever had a manicure; maybe he was just genetically blessed with handsome hands. Some men really aren't; they have mitts like those little sporks you get in fish and chip vans at the seaside.

I dropped his hand as I realised he had been holding mine for a little too long for my liking, and I was beginning to feel somewhat awkward. I rummaged around in my handbag to give my hands something better to do.

I should probably check my make-up, touch up my lippy and give myself the faintest wee sweep of powder and a bit of a freshen-up. I grabbed my compact and gave my reflection a quick once-over. It was fair to say that I was not looking my best. I appeared to have fragments of flatbread stuck to what little was left of my new scarlet lipstick. The woman at the beauty counter had promised it was "invincible" and would last a minimum of twelve hours guaranteed, irrespective of how much you drank, ate or snogged in it. Clearly all lies, as it had barely survived a slice of bread and a few sips of cocktails before disintegrating.

I noticed with horror that one of the crumbs was right at the edge of my lip line, horrifyingly resembling a witchy-like wart. That would simply not do. I was just extracting the bready blemish when a high breathy voice that sounded like it wouldn't be out of place as a sex line operator rang out across the bar.

"Fancy seeing you two here."

Chapter 5

My head swivelled around, keen to establish who was interrupting us. The voice sounded rather familiar, and I had a sinking feeling I knew who it was. And I was right.

Standing in front of us was none other than Jocasta Jennings, the new Paralegal from the firm. All bouncy strawberry blonde hair and pouty lips. She was dressed in an alluring little number, top cut down to her navel, skirt up to her nether regions and smelling like she had taken a shower in Chanel.

It was fair to say she wasn't my favourite person. She had only been at the firm for a few months, but we had never hit it off from the get-go.

It wasn't the fact that at 34 she was 15 years younger than me that I disliked. OK, I wasn't exactly thrilled by the fact; no woman likes to feel they're getting older. But seeing Jocasta sashay around the boardroom handing out case notes like a modern-day Marilyn Monroe made me feel about as ancient as Methuselah's mother.

It was more her faux doe-eyed innocence that really got my goat. She dressed like a 50s pin-up, oozing sex appeal in every outfit she wore. Without a doubt she dressed strictly for the male gaze. She was the type of woman who would purposely wear a wrap-around skirt on a windy day.

Yet she patently portrayed herself to be such a helpless innocent little soul. Fluttering her false eyelashes at all and sundry and coming across like butter wouldn't melt. Wouldn't melt? Hah, it would sodding well sizzle. She wasn't fooling me for a minute. She was quite clearly pretending to be all sweetness and light. She was over thirty, not quite in the first flush of youth after all, recently divorced and already one ex-boyfriend under her belt.

She was now in a new career where she obviously wanted to make her mark; plus the fact that somehow feminism seemed to have completely passed her by.

I reckoned that Jocasta saw other women as a threat that had to be neutralised. I certainly didn't think she had ever heard of "girl code". I knew she was far cannier than she made out. This woman was my adversary, I was convinced of it. Not a girl's girl by any means, and someone I needed to be extremely wary of.

"Jocasta, how absolutely lovely to see you."

My lying voice was the embodiment of thrilled delight as I snapped my compact shut. Shit! The way I could fib, I really *was* a lawyer.

Jocasta's green eyes narrowed slightly as they flicked between me and Seb. Her forehead furrowed as if she found something puzzling and not exactly to her liking. Maybe she was trying to add two plus two in her head; anyway, it was clear from her expression that something wasn't adding up for her.

"Sebastian...Lila, are you two on a date?"

"Absolutely not."

I jumped in quick before Seb could have a chance to answer. I was nipping that straight in the bud.

"We've just been at a work event, a fashion show in the hotel down the road and popped in here for a quick drink."

Jocasta took in the arrangement of drained lipstick-stained martini glasses abandoned on the table with a knowing smile. Damn that waiter, the service really had been below par today. There was a twinkle in her beautifully made-up eyes, all bronze eyeshadow and sparkly highlighter.

"That's interesting to know. Have fun and I'll see you at the grindstone on Monday."

Why on earth would she find that so interesting?

I watched as she sauntered, or rather slithered away to meet her date, a rather oily-looking chap in an expensive suit. Her skimpy outfit gave the whole bar a glimpse at next week's washing.

I turned towards Seb, ready to make a witty remark about gold-diggers, but the words died in my mouth. He was staring at her departing form in the same way he had eyed up his chip butty. I felt a weird churning feeling in the pit of my stomach that I couldn't quite put my finger on. Maybe I was still hungry? Or the alcohol wasn't sitting well. I wasn't sure what it was, but something had just made me feel very off indeed.

Chapter 6

8:50 a.m. Monday morning, and I strode as confidently as I could into Fluck, Young & Glover, taking two at a time the stone steps up to the imposing building in the centre of Leeds.

I was dressed in my favourite cream trouser suit, my blonde hair in a stylish chignon, hoping that if I looked good it might be an omen for the rest of the day. Maybe by now Mr Fluck would have thought things over and be able to see the funny side. It was funny after all, it really was. I had already recounted the fashion show debacle to several girlfriends, and they all found it hilarious, so perhaps he would too. It was always good to dream.

I could see that the thick oak door to his office was slightly ajar. I crept past it, stealth-like on my stilettos like a cat burglar. I thought I had made it safely past when I heard him clear his throat noisily: an unsettling sound like he was digging to China.

"Lila, would you please be good enough to come in here?"

Oh hell. Now I was for it.

Thirty minutes later I was leaving his room after a right old telling off. He was not a happy man, that was for sure. His face had been even more crypt-keeper-like than usual, as the morning winter sun filtered in through the Victorian sash windows and settled in his multitude of wrinkles. Fair to say that none of them were laughter lines. He really did have a face like a blind cobbler's thumb.

Also fair to say that I'd kept my composure well, albeit with a fair amount of grovelling thrown in for good measure. I apologised for the unfortunate incident at the show. It really wasn't anyone's fault though. Just good old-fashioned bad luck.

At least it was over now. I had taken my reprimand firmly on the chin. Promised my boss I would speak to the reporter at Leeds Leads and hope to mitigate the situation. I didn't know what he really expected me to do, as no doubt the story was already online and had been since first thing that morning.

Clearly the old codger was so "old school" that he thought I could sweet talk my way into stopping the printing presses in their tracks. Perhaps shut it all down with a yank on an oily old lever or some such. But at least the confrontation was over and I could get on with the rest of my day.

Maybe even treat myself to something nice for breakfast from the artisan bakery down the street. Perhaps a warm flaky croissant or a *pain au chocolat*? Nothing that would drip on my cream cashmere, of course. I was lost in thoughts of Parisian pastries and strolls along the Seine when I walked slap bang into Jocasta sauntering down the corridor, carrying two mugs of coffee: one for her and no doubt one for our boss, old fart Fluck.

The look of shock on her face I'm sure was mirrored on my own as we barged unceremoniously into each other. Our eyes simultaneously darted to the hot beverages as they sloshed around in their mugs, perilously close to my cashmere and threatening to drench me in a wave of *cappuccino*; but fortuitously the liquid remained safely in the mugs.

"Fuck...that was close."

The relief was evident in my voice as I patted the lapel of my jacket to reassure myself that everything was still pristine. Coffee would be an absolute nightmare to get out of the fabric.

At that moment Jocasta appeared to stumble slightly on her khaki kitten heels, and before I knew it the coffee was on the move again. This time it was headed straight for me. Both mugs hit me full on in the chest, drenching me as the caffeinated liquid mushroomed out all over my navy silk blouse and cream jacket.

I was rooted to the spot in shock and turned speechless towards the younger woman. Was that the tiniest of smirks on Jocasta's face?

My eyes travelled down my ruined clothes and then returned to glare at the woman who was still holding the empty coffee mugs. Was I right? Had she actually just thrown the drinks straight at me?

She was, unlike me now, looking well turned out and spick-and-span in a rather obvious way. Far too good for this early on a Monday morning, that was for sure. I liked to dress to impress and have my make-up on before I braved the day, but the woman looked as if she had been primping with the warpaint for hours.

And she most certainly seemed to favour a certain style for the office. I'm normally not one for shaming a woman's appearance. I like to be in complete favour of body autonomy. Always standing up for our right to wear whatever makes us feel our best in our own bodies. But then again, there is the need to remain professional; and her skirt was, in my opinion, way too short for the office. She should be carrying the briefs, not flashing hers at all and sundry.

Jocasta's eyes were now saucer-wide, her expression one of complete concern for her colleague.

"Li...Lila... I'm so sorry, I just lost my footing for a second there. Your beautiful jacket...here, let me help you with the stain."

She put the mugs down on the edge of her desk and started dabbing at my clothes with a napkin that had been wrapped around the handle of one of the mugs. I don't know what good she thought that was going to do. Quite clearly, she was just ensuring the stain was well and truly ingrained in the material.

I felt my anger bubble up inside me, threatening to cause me to completely lose my cool. I was just glad the coffee had been cool, or I could have been suffering from first degree burns. I took a deep breath before speaking.

"You did that on purpose."

Jocasta shot me a startled look, like a wide-eyed Bambi caught in the headlights.

"No...honestly, Lila, I really didn't. It's just these new shoes..."

She gestured to the delicate footwear adorning her hooves.

"The straps are a little loose and I lost my footing for a second."

I grabbed the soggy napkin out of her hand.

"Leave it!"

My voice was low and even and carried a warning.

"You're only going to make it worse."

My eyes darted anxiously to my watch.

"I have a meeting in twenty minutes, and look at the state of me."

"I'm so sorry, Lila, but don't worry, I'll fix it...just give me five minutes."

And with that she hurried off. Her steps sounded self-assured and now seemingly unencumbered by the looseness of her straps.

Twenty-five minutes later, I was seated awkwardly behind the heavy oak desk in my office. I was a few minutes deep into a meeting with a new client, Mrs Davina Jackson, who was sitting opposite me and looking nervously around the room. Her eyes kept darting about, as if she was on high alert for danger.

Dressed in oversized jogging bottoms and a beige sloppy cardigan, with her greying hair dragged back into a tight bun, she looked like a woman who had completely given up on herself.

It was her first appointment to see me, with the intention of procuring advice on what her best course of action might be. She had recently discovered her husband of over twenty years had been engaged in a bit of extra-curricular activity of the rumpy-pumpy variety with none other than her own sister. She was clearly still shell-shocked, but from the way she was talking it was evident that she had now most definitely crossed the Rubicon in respect of her marriage. Sexual shenanigans with sister dearest were unforgivable.

She had chosen the right person to come and see. Family law was my speciality, and assisting other women to rinse their philandering spouses on a hot wash was usually my favourite sport after badminton. Today, however, I was not feeling my professional best.

I was now wearing what I think is laughingly referred to as a "coatigan": a long garment of either indoor knitwear, or else an appropriate outer garment for braving the Yorkshire winter chills. It was in a lurid shade of green with little open-beaked owls in various hues of brown dotted randomly upon it like hooting lumps of turd. It was by far the ugliest item of clothing I had ever seen outside of Helena Bonham Carter's wardrobe disasters.

This was apparently Jocasta's idea of "fixing it".

The offending garment had been long abandoned in the staff cloakroom, probably once belonging to one of the cleaners or maybe some stylishly challenged weirdo who had just wandered in off the street. It had a faint whiff of mothballs and antiseptic cream about it, and honestly looked as if it had been knitted with the pubic hair from a herd of yaks. And if the ugliness factor wasn't grim enough, to add insult to injury it was flaming itchy to boot.

I suppose it did at least cover the coffee stain. However, I think coffee-soaked cashmere would have still been more visually appealing than this monstrosity. For someone who prided themselves on always looking groomed and professional, I now resembled the sartorial equivalent of a mad bag lady who'd just had a good old rummage at the church jumble sale: the 20p sale item pile that nobody else wanted.

Jocasta had apologised profusely when she returned, scurrying over to me clutching the offending article.

"At least it will cover the coffee stain until home time. Honestly, Lila, I am so sorry for stumbling like that. I really am a silly sausage at times; I can barely put one foot in front of the other without tripping. You'd think by my age I would have learnt how to walk in designer heels."

She had smiled coyly; a look guaranteed to make men swoon the world over but making me more pissed off than I already was. Without a word I had accepted the garment and donned it gingerly, trying my best to ignore the rather pungent aroma emanating from it.

I had managed to make it through the entirety of the meeting with Mrs Jackson, trying my very best not to scratch like a tabby cat with mange. She decided to forge ahead with the divorce, and by the end of our meeting it was encouraging to see a little determined glint in her eye. She no longer looked like the timid downtrodden woman whose sweaty hand I had shaken earlier. Her husband might be in for a bit of a shock. Davina Jackson might not be the little mouse she had first appeared to be.

I was now pretty convinced that Jocasta had "tumbled" off her heels on purpose. All designed to drench me in de-caff. But would she really stoop that low? Maybe I wasn't being fair to her and it was a genuine accident, but I highly doubted it. I had seen that glint in her eye after all.

Why had we got off to such a bad start? It was true that I didn't love the way she dressed, or her breathy girly giggle that always seemed to be a few octaves higher when any men were about.

I also wasn't a fan of the way she hung around Mr Fluck like he was simply fascinating. Even complimenting him on his hair. That was a laugh in itself: his receding hairline went so far back the dinosaurs could probably see it. The only impressive thing about his hair was just how much of it was sprouting out of his ears.

Mrs Jackson was turning the handle on my office door, ready to leave. But thinking better of it, she turned to face me with a warm smile.

"Thank you so much, Ms Glover, for seeing me today. I feel so much better about things now. David won't to be able to take me for a mug any more. He's done it for far too long, and

I'm not going to let him continue."

I returned her smile, genuinely pleased.

"Good for you, Davina, it's time you put yourself first for once."

She nodded in agreement.

"And can I just say how much I love your knitwear? Such a fun fashion choice, especially for a solicitor. I was nervous coming here today, but it put me right at ease just looking at it."

Fun fashion choice? Was she taking the proverbial? But no, obviously bile green knitwear adorned with birds of prey was a sure-fire way to put my client at ease. So my outfit had actually been a success; even though I clearly resembled a fluffy green hairball with winnets of shit dangling from it.

I escorted Mrs Jackson to the main door of the building and shook her hand again before suggesting we meet next in a week's time.

Walking slowly back to my office, I glanced towards Seb's office. The door was open a smidge and there he was. I felt a little wave of affection for him. His red striped tie was hanging loosely around his neck, clashing horribly with the pale green shade of his work shirt. His thick salt and pepper hair was ruffled, as if he had been absent-mindedly running his hand through it.

He was hunched over his desk, his posture terrible, deep in thought, reading some notes. Best leave him to it. I could always catch up with him later; and if I didn't get a chance to, there was always tomorrow night, when we would be meeting Lottie and Leo for dinner.

I continued towards my office, which meant I would need to pass Jocasta again. Being relatively new and rather less senior in the firm, she did not boast an office of her own. Instead, her desk was positioned off from the reception area, with just a small degree of privacy afforded by a large dusty pot plant, and the thick wall of my resentment.

She was studying the screen on her desktop computer. Her shiny strawberry blonde hair cascaded onto her slim shoulders like spun silk. Looking at her, she appeared almost angelic; but then again, hadn't the Devil been an angel before God had the good sense to boot him out of Heaven? Her halo was definitely slipping, as that little smirk was back on her face again.

What was she looking at? It seemed vaguely familiar. Something was ringing distant alarm bells in my head. With a sinking feeling, I realised what it was. She was studying the news page of Leeds Leads. I could now see clearly the press logo at the foot of the screen.

I squinted to read the headline in bold letters at the top of the page of text.

"Farcical fashion faux pas for Fluck Young & Glover at charity show fiasco. Or is the well-established city centre firm sending a clear message to all about their professional conduct?"

Ouch! That sounded so much worse than the actual truth: a monumental fuck-up caused by a teenage hangover, amateur models and cheap signage that disintegrated with a couple of little tugs. It was all just rather unfortunate. But why let the truth get in the way of a good story? And why oh why did my boss have to have Fluck as a surname?

Jocasta suddenly glanced up from the screen and her eyes silently met mine. The sneer was now gone, replaced by something I'm sure she believed resembled concern. Her eyes flickered over me for longer than was necessary. I was still wearing the green acrylic abomination. How she managed not to laugh was beyond me.

"Oh dear, Lila, looks like Saturday was a bit of a disaster. You're having quite a few fashion malfunctions lately, it would seem."

Chapter 7

"Hello, Lila, I must say you're looking very...er... unique today."

Seb was clearly amused to see me resplendent in front of his desk, still dressed in the scratchy lurid green number and tapping my foot impatiently in my high heels.

"Yes, thank you, Sebastian I know exactly what I look like. But it was all Jocasta's fault. That woman has a real problem with me, and I honestly don't know why."

Seb closed the file he had been reading and sat comfortably back in his leather swivel chair, clasping his fingers together behind his head.

"I know I'm going to regret this, and I really shouldn't ask, but go on then, tell me what's happened now."

With a heavy sigh I sank into the chair opposite him to recount my tale of woe.

"The toxic bint literally just threw two cups of coffee all over me, *claiming* she had stumbled. But I tell you, Seb, don't believe that for a second. I saw the glint in her eye, and she did it on purpose. All just to ruin my day and my lovely outfit and force me to wear this knitwear nightmare."

I pulled the offending garment off to display the huge coffee stain covering the décolletage area of my blouse and my ruined cashmere. I managed to give myself a jolting shock of static electricity in the process. It turned out that this outfit wasn't just painful to the eyes; it could actually hurt.

"The woman is just a...a..."

I stuttered, desperately trying to find the right words to describe my dislike for my office subordinate.

"A nefarious nitwit!"

Seb was laughing now, clearly finding the situation highly amusing.

"I'm sorry, Lila, but I must say you're the one that looks like the nitwit in that naff knitwear, not Jocasta."

I felt my eyes narrowing dangerously. It wasn't funny, well not to me anyway. I could see that Seb was eyeing me warily now, realising that I was not in the mood to be poked fun at, and he'd better try a different approach.

He sighed and reached over the desk towards me. For a second, I felt my stomach lurch, thinking he was going to take my hand again; but instead he helped himself to a boiled sweet from the glass bowl that he offered to clients, unwrapped it and popped a green one in his mouth, sucking on it thoughtfully for a few seconds.

A green sweet? I ask you, who chooses a lime-flavoured sweet out of all the delicious flavours he could pick? The man had no taste. We really didn't have a thing in common.

"I really don't think Jocasta would have thrown the coffee at you on purpose, Lila. She does wear some silly little shoes at times, so I think the chance of her stumbling is pretty high. The two of you just need to get to know each other better. You're like two wary lionesses circling each other ready to pounce. I don't know if its jealousy or insecurity or what, but..."

I was flabbergasted. Did he actually think I could be jealous of Jocasta? I most certainly wasn't. Yes, she was younger; and yes, maybe she did have a manner which on occasion seemed to draw people to her more than my own brusque businesslike demeanour. However, I knew I was a good person and nice enough in my own way, but I was certainly harder around the edges and feistier than my colleague, with none of the fluffy bunny appeal that she seemed to have going on in abundance.

My voice was shrill when I finally managed to spit my words out.

"I'm most certainly not jealous of *her*!"

Oh dear, disappointingly my tone now had a definite screechy fishwife edge to it.

"I'm not insecure either. I'm telling you what happened, and she threw hot coffee right at me!"

Seb sighed deeply and helped himself to another sweet, lime again...yuck.

"I don't know what you expect me to say, Lila. I think you're just overreacting a bit and it's not like you got hurt."

All the years I had known Seb, and clearly he had learned nothing about me. You never tell a woman she's overreacting, especially not a woman like me.

My voice was low and steady.

"I just don't trust her, that's all I'm saying; and believe me, I'm a *very* good judge of character. It's the way she looks at me, like she's plotting and scheming all the time. She acts like little Miss Perfect, but I'm not buying it for a single second. I don't know if she feels threatened by me because I'm more senior, or she just doesn't like women in general; but I'm telling you, she's a wrong 'un. She might dress faux from head to toe, but it's not just her hair extensions and false eyelashes; I don't think anything about the woman is genuine and real."

Seb was shaking his head to himself; clearly, he'd had enough of the conversation.

"Look, Lila, I've got a meeting with Fluck in ten minutes, so we're going to have to talk about this later. But I honestly don't think you've got anything to worry about; you're just being a bit paranoid."

This really wasn't getting any better. First, I was overreacting; and now I was paranoid. The bloody cheek of the man.

"Seb, sometimes you need to pick a side, you know. People get killed loitering in the middle of the road."

He sighed deeply and twisted the sweet wrapper around his long fingers.

"Lila, all I'm saying is just rein in your Rottweiler for a minute and let the softer version of you out. I think there might be a bit of good old female rivalry going on here. A younger woman has come along and upset the apple cart a little. She's finding her feet and establishing herself in a firm you've worked in for years, and you're just a bit put out. But you've got nothing to worry about with Jocasta. She's going to be an asset to the firm, and that can only be a good thing for all of us."

I huffed away to myself for a few minutes. But maybe he had a point, and I was being rather unreasonable. Maybe Jocasta and I could start again; bury the hatchet, preferably between her satin-clad shoulder pads.

Seb stood up from his desk and slipped his suit jacket onto his broad shoulders. He gave me a flirty wink.

"And don't you worry, Lila. She may be pretty, but you, my dear, are simply magnificent."

I disregarded his compliment to me entirely and homed straight in on one single word - pretty. It had made my tummy feel strange again.

"Pretty? You think Jocasta is pretty?"

Yes, she was obviously attractive, I couldn't deny that, but I hadn't realised that Seb thought so too. I had seen him staring after her at the bar on Saturday, but I had decided to shrug that off. Told myself he had just been checking out the peach cobbler dessert in the rotating glass display, not checking out her peachy derrière.

Well, she might look attractive for now, but I knew good bone structure, and she wasn't going to age well, that was for sure.

"Well, yes...obviously she's pretty."

Seb straightened his tie and ran his hands through his hair, hoping to make himself look more presentable for his meeting, but instead ensuring he resembled something that had been spat out by a hurricane.

"But it's not just that she's good-looking, she's also sweet and kind and can't do enough to help around the office. She's happy to muck in with all the admin tasks none of us want to do, and she's an absolute asset to the secretaries. She's even hoovered the offices when the cleaner was sick, so she's not stuck up either, which is great."

I muttered incoherently to myself. I really didn't like the way this conversation was going. I couldn't agree with him, I just couldn't. I didn't trust her. I had serious reservations about Jocasta, but it seemed I was in the lonely minority of one. It was clear I was going to need to keep my counsel, so to speak. I was going to have to bide my time and watch and wait. No, I didn't trust the woman, I just couldn't.

I laughed, trying to lighten the mood between us.

"Well let's face it, Seb, you're just too flaming nice. You like everyone; you even grudgingly respect Fluck, and he's about as appealing as a fart at a funeral."

I helped myself to a sweet from his bowl. A strawberry one, like normal people.

"You couldn't hate anyone, even if you tried. You're just a people pleaser. If you had a spirit animal, it would probably be a chicken."

Seb threw back his head and laughed: a lovely warm, low rumble.

"That's more like it, Lila, back to your acerbic best."

He set off towards his office door, and I followed in his wake. He turned to face me before we departed.

"Just don't let Jocasta get under your skin too much. You've got off to a rocky start, the pair of you, and you'll be fine once you get to know each other better. You could be the bigger person, you know, and make the first move to build a friendship."

He gave my arm an affectionate rub, which sent a little tingle coursing through my body. Probably the polyester again.

I smiled indulgently at my friend. He really could be the sweetest man.

"You know what, Seb, I think you're right. I'm going to make a coffee right now, and I'm going to ask Jocasta if she'd like one too, that's what a lovely forgiving person I am."

Seb winked at me affectionately as we made our way down the gloomy corridor: him to go into his meeting, and me towards the kettle.

"That's my girl."

Chapter 8

"That was a really shitty thing to do, Lila. You must have known she would react like that."

It was fair to say that Seb was angry. His jaw was clenched, and a little vein was throbbing away at his temple. I wasn't used to seeing him angry; he was normally the most laid-back person you could ever imagine. Most of the time he made the Dalai Lama look as if he was dealing with executive stress.

I laughed awkwardly, trying to make light of the situation.

"*Shitty* being the operative word here, it would seem."

Things hadn't ended up going too well at the office the previous day. I had started off with the very best of intentions. I fully intended to try and make things good with Jocasta: to hold out the olive branch, so to speak, by holding out a mug of coffee. It was a start, but as soon as I had made my exceedingly kind offer, in my mind, her unreasonable demands had started.

"Thank you, Lila, I would absolutely love a coffee. But if you're not going to Costa, can you make a fresh pot? I simply can't abide that instant rubbish. And I need it piping hot, with just a whisker of my almond milk. Can you make sure you add one and a half teaspoons of my special sweetener too? I keep it in the top cupboard above the microwave. You'll need to stir it clockwise with a spoon for at least forty seconds, so it dissolves properly, and then it will be perfect."

That, in my mind, was taking the piss.

I had nodded sweetly at her. Well, I hoped it appeared sweet. My rictus grin was no doubt as saccharine as the crap she kept in a jar above the microwave. I entered the gloomy little kitchenette with its chipped Formica units and slight whiff of mildew. It could really do with a facelift, but then again, checking my appearance in the back of a teaspoon, it might not be the only one.

Why could Jocasta not just accept the offer of a cup of coffee with a simple "thank you", rather than making me feel I was a waitress taking her drinks order. I half expected her to ask me what the daily specials were. A nice hearty serving of "fuck you" would have been my answer to that.

Sighing to myself, I rooted around in the top cupboard to locate the packet of ground Arabica beans to make the pot of coffee. The foil packet was almost empty. And let's face it, considering I was still sporting a coffee stain on my clothes like a dirty protest, I had no intention of going out to the grocer's shop at the end of the street. I pushed the near empty packet back where I found it and reached for the large trusty jar of Nescafé instead. Unscrewing it, I added a heaped teaspoon to two mugs, one for me and one for Little Miss Entitlement.

I don't know what made me then decide to add white sugar to her brew in place of her sweetener, and a generous slug of UHT whole milk for good measure, but that is exactly what I did. I almost did it on autopilot. I suppose part of me thought she was being a precious plant-based princess with all her demands. I must admit, I felt a little frisson when I passed the mug over to her and she took a hearty swig of her full-fat full-sugar dairy beverage with a satisfied sigh.

How was I to know what a seemingly innocent mug of coffee with cow's milk would do to her bowels? I had no idea she was lactose intolerant. Fair to say, she would have given Usain Bolt a run for his money the way she dashed to the ladies' toilets, one hand clutching her stomach and the other holding her posterior like she expected it to explode at any second. I couldn't help but notice as she raced past my open office door that she appeared to be having no difficulty at all running in her shoes.

It was now the following evening and Seb and I were sitting opposite each other at a table neatly set for four diners, await-ing the arrival of Lottie and Leo. I had picked the venue for the evening, another reason why Seb might not be too happy with me.

It was a new Italian restaurant that I had read about in one of my favourite glossy magazines. It was cool and chic and quite the place to see and be seen, apparently. It was quirkily named The Low Cal Zone, and boasted a delicious menu that erred on the healthy side, with less cheese and cream and more saintly salad and sparkling water. After carefully scanning the entirety of the menu twice, I couldn't find any evidence of them offering a calzone pizza for their diners, despite their name.

There was a somewhat combative air wafting off Seb as he studied the menu, taking in each dish and the exorbitant prices alongside. His expression was as stony as the basket of rye bread sitting between us.

Seb loved to go out for pizza almost as much as his beloved shepherd's pie. He was a man who knew what he liked and liked what he knew. Any time we went to an Italian restaurant, you were guaranteed to hear Sebastian Young order "thick crust" and "extra salami". He also had a habit of losing concentration more than a wayward toddler when the waitress was adding parmesan to his dish; she would be scraping the dregs off the bottom of the bowl before he finally lifted his hand, met her eyes and announced, "That's enough, thank you."

He was nothing if not predictable. And predictably I knew he would no doubt order pizza yet again, or if not that then *pasta carbonara*, or the closest thing he could find amongst the nutritious choices on offer.

He also hated to see anything he thought was "poncy" on a menu: like when salmon was described as "pan fried". He would always grumble at that and ask anyone in earshot exactly how fish was supposed to be fried if not in a pan? An old tin bath perhaps. And that was before considering his dismay at seeing the humble cauliflower zhuzhed up a bit and described as a "steak". For £18.99 he wanted his steak to be all meat and his cauliflower to be under a nice thick cheesy sauce.

So with that in mind, it was never likely that Seb would push himself out of his comfort zone and plump for a nice light *caprese* salad or grilled sea bass, for example. No, that would never pass muster with him. And he looked far from comfortable in his current surroundings; in fact he couldn't have looked less comfortable if he'd had a cockroach planted firmly up his arsehole.

I, on the other hand, was enjoying the ambiance of the restaurant whilst savouring a large glass of Montepulciano, delighting in the toasty rich flavours and beginning to feel somewhat toasted myself.

I hoped Lottie and Leo would arrive soon. I had missed lunch and was ravenous, plus I was beginning to feel a little uncomfortable that Seb was staring at me like he was studying a laboratory specimen under a microscope and was not pleased with what he had discovered.

He was slowly sipping on a long glass of mineral water with a lone slice of lemon. He was probably wise to savour it, as that was likely to be what constituted dessert in this joint. He had no choice but to be on the soft drinks as he was driving me home after the meal, and I was sincerely hoping he would have cheered the fuck up by then.

I picked up the red hard-backed menu once again – even it was skinny – and recommenced reading through the appetisers, even though I now knew them off by heart. I was opting for the grilled vegetable *antipasti* to start, and the Sicilian-style fish stew for main course. I just wished Lottie and Leo would hurry up and make an appearance.

I told Seb what I intended to order, and he physically shuddered. He really needed to open himself up to other culinary choices than cheese, carbs and anything he could buy in a wrapper from the service station.

I coughed to cover up a little rumble from my empty stomach.

"I hope they get here soon, I'm absolutely starving, and I've been looking forward to this all day."

Seb's eyebrows shot up for a couple of seconds in disbelief. Quite clearly, he couldn't imagine anyone looking forward to visiting The Low Cal Zone. He probably found it about as pleasurable as a three-hour boardroom meeting with Fluck. He looked as comfortable in his seat as if he had been strapped to an electric chair. He sighed deeply again; he had been doing a lot of that so far this evening.

"You still haven't answered my question about yesterday, Lila. I asked you about the milk. You know Jocasta always takes almond milk in her coffee; she even has her own carton labelled with her name in the fridge. It has a large grinning almond on it, you can't exactly miss it."

I put the menu down again with a sigh of my own and turned my attention fully to my companion. His face looked so earnest and concerned now. I couldn't help but notice that the pale blue shirt and jumper combo he was wearing looked pretty good on him. Much more stylish than his normal attire. But then again, I suppose if you get dressed in the dark, like he appeared to, by the laws of average outcome eventually you're going to stumble on an outfit that actually works.

He even resembled Hugh Grant a little, well in his geek chic roles anyway. Yes, definitely Hugh Grant with a bit of Jude Law thrown in for good measure. But then, what did I know? My eyesight was probably not to be trusted now, having sunk two large glasses of red wine on a completely empty stomach.

"OK...OK, maybe I should have used the almond milk, but I really didn't think it was going to affect her quite like that. I just thought she was being a bit precious with all her demands, so I made her coffee the way I take mine. I didn't mean for it to end like that."

An image from the previous afternoon popped uninvited into my mind: the normally serene and sophisticated Jocasta racing to the loo like her life depended on it, whilst farting what sounded uncannily like the closing moments from Last Night of the Proms. However, her version was less *Pomp and Circumstance* and more pump and crap your pants.

I couldn't help it, I knew without a shadow of a doubt that I was going to laugh, and I was right. Once the chuckling started, it erupted out of me like the explosive diarrhoea had from my workmate.

"Stop laughing, Lila, it isn't funny."

"Well, I think that's debatable."

"Seriously, Lila, she was stuck in the loo for nearly an hour; and when she finally reappeared, she looked so pale and pasty she resembled a wrung out old dish cloth."

I was laughing so hard now that I had tears running down my face, probably taking my make-up with them. With a huge effort on my part, I managed eventually to curb my snorts and arrange my features into something I hoped resembled concern.

"I know it's bad, and I shouldn't laugh, but you've got to believe me. I really didn't mean to make her sick…I guess I was just being petty, which I know isn't a good act. But I'm going to apologise to her in the morning and make sure she's OK."

Seb nodded. He still had a face like a yard of gravy, but at least he seemed to be softening a little.

"OK, well that's good. Just make things right between you. But I wouldn't dwell too much on the details, as I think she's going to be still really embarrassed about it all."

I kept my head down and nodded. I was worried about catching his eye in case it set me off laughing again.

Finally, Seb's expression softened, and he smiled at me. I was glad to see it. It almost seemed like the dingy dining room had eventually brightened up around us. It didn't last, though, as his face fell when he began studying the menu again; probably already debating whether he should stop for a donner kebab on his way home from dropping me off later.

"Just make sure you do apologise, Lila. I know you think she threw the coffee at you first, which I really don't think she did. But for argument's sake, even if she did, I certainly think you've got your own back on her now. This is where it needs to stop. None of us wants to be in the office with a bad atmosphere because you two can't get on. It's like working in a vortex of misery. Just apologise, say it was a genuine mistake, not that you did it on purpose, and then say you would like to move on. I think she'll be fine with that. She's a reasonable woman, even if you did cause her to shit herself at work."

I couldn't help it, I was off laughing again. Rather like Jocasta and her gurgling bowels, I could hold it in no longer.

Chapter 9

"So sorry we're late. But come on, let us into the joke." Hearing my friend's voice, my head snapped around to greet her. Lottie and Leo were standing by our table, both smiling brightly. I noticed that they were holding hands. This was a very good sign.

"Oh, it's nothing really. Seb just said something that made me laugh."

I jumped up and enveloped my friend in a warm hug, before turning to give Leo a swift kiss on the cheek.

"I'm so glad you're finally here, we're starving. If you'd been five more minutes, we would have ordered without you."

Lottie flushed slightly and I caught a little glance pass between the two. I knew that look all right. They were obviously running late because they'd been indulging in a bit of afternoon aerobics of the bedroom variety.

Leo pulled Lottie's chair out for her and she quickly sat down, introducing Leo to Seb in the process.

Seb grasped Leo's hand and shook it firmly.

"I'm glad to meet you finally, fella. I've only heard good things."

"Me too, Seb. Lottie has told me what a nice guy you are. It's great we can all finally meet up."

A smile lit up Leo's face, showcasing his straight white teeth and his sparkling blue eyes which crinkled at the corners slightly. I gave him the quick once-over. He really was a handsome man. His sandy beard was trimmed shorter than the last time I had seen him, and he was dressed in a smart navy jacket over cream T-shirt and inky jeans.

Lottie looked equally smart in her simple yet elegant black wrap dress. I was touched to see it was the one I had given her for Christmas a couple of years before. It was a timeless little number and it suited her perfectly. Her hair was shining, her make-up, unlike mine, was immaculate and to put it simply, she looked stunning. But I think the most beautiful thing about her entire appearance was her megawatt smile. It simply lit up her face. She was happy, and that was clear for everyone to see.

Lottie was extremely lucky to have found Leo, but the exact same thing could be said of him. They made an impressively elegant couple. I noted them both attracting a few adulatory glances from the other diners.

The waiter who had been hovering by our table as Leo and Lottie arrived sprang into action with notebook in hand and pencil poised. We all ordered our dishes, Leo and Lottie barely glancing at the menu. It was clear that food was the last thing on their minds.

This was such a different Lottie from a year ago. Then the biggest loves of her life were a multi-pack of cheese Quavers and a baked vanilla cheesecake. Now she wasn't simply eating her feelings; no, now she was actually feeling them. And by the look of Leo's biceps through his shirt, there was plenty there to get to grips with.

Twenty minutes later, we were tucking into our starters.

The atmosphere was light and convivial. Seb had thankfully cheered up and was back to his endearing best.

The starters were a success...mostly. Seb wasn't overly enamoured with his hot seared beef and rocket salad. Not one for spicy food, the sauce had nearly blown his eyebrows off. And as for the minute quantity of steak on his plate, he grumbled that he "had seen more meat on a dirty fork".

I couldn't help but notice the little glances shooting between Lottie and Leo. Just looking at them was giving me the warm and fuzzies. My friend had a faint blush to her cheeks that I knew wasn't all thanks to Charlotte Tilbury and some good contouring.

I realised one thing, for sure: I should let Seb choose the restaurant next time we came out to dine. He looked as if he might need therapy after getting a gander at his main course as the waiter placed the oval plate in front of him with an extravagant flourish. From the expression on Seb's face, he might as well have slapped him in the face with the back of his napkin.

True to form, Seb had ordered the pizza, confident that it would be the most indulgent item on the menu. But this was unlike any pizza he had ever seen before. It was fair to say he wasn't impressed. Gone was the thick stuffed crust and three inches of cheese. All he got was the faintest dab of mozzarella, a pinch of *provolone* and a few flakes of parmesan, so sheer he could have watched his favourite *Battlestar Galactica* through them.

"Three cheese pizza! They should have called it "three grams of cheese on your pizza".

He had huffed away for a few moments poking unenthusiastically at his food with his fork.

"That would definitely have been more apt even though I think saying three grams is being a bit generous, is there a shortage of cheddar in Yorkshire I'm not aware of?"

As for the rest of us, we tucked into our meals with enthusiasm. It felt good to know I was eating something light and healthy. I tried as a rule of thumb to stick to healthy eating, but life was really all about variety. And if on occasion I felt the need to dive headfirst into a family bucket of KFC, then I certainly would. It was all part of a well-rounded life. I just tried not to indulge too often, or it would result in a well-rounded Lila too.

Lottie and I made our excuses to the menfolk and headed to the ladies' loo, telling them we needed to have a little "freshen up". In truth, I had been dying to get my friend to myself all evening so we could have a good old chinwag. I wanted all the goss. Never mind the sloshed coffee from yesterday, now I wanted the tea to be spilt.

Lottie was standing by the highly polished mirror, squinting at her reflection as she applied a generous sweep of scarlet lipstick, having lost most of it on her chicken *cacciatore*.

I smiled to myself. I too always squinted my eyes when applying my make-up. It was a strange affectation, but clearly a common one.

"He's so amazing, Lila. We love each other, we really do. Leo said he had from the moment he first saw me, standing outside Ivy's front door. And I love him too, I love him so much."

Lottie's voice was high and happy: a combination of romance and Rioja, no doubt.

"I can't believe I was stupid enough to nearly let him get away. I was so worried about him being younger and what people would think but now I just don't care. And it looks like he's going to be settling down in the UK for good now."

I felt a warm glow flood through my body, and I knew it wasn't from the alcohol either. I might be cynical in matters of the heart, but I knew true love existed and it was clear that Cupid had shot an arrow straight at Lottie and Leo. Maybe one day he would take aim at me too. I could only hope.

My friend snapped her lipstick shut and slipped it back in her leather clutch bag before turning to face me, her excitement evident.

"He's even said he thinks we should move in together."

"That's fantastic, Lottie. I'm over the moon for you."

I let out a little squeal of excitement as I wrapped her in a huge hug. This was the most wonderful news.

"You don't think were rushing into things though?"

Sensible Charlotte was back in the room again, her face dropping a little.

"After Daniel and how that ended, I don't want to make a big mistake; and Leo and I really haven't known each other that long."

"Nonsense, Lottie, your ex was a disaster, and you wasted half your life expecting him to be a decent human being. Leo is a different specimen entirely: he's a gentleman, and you only have to look at his face when he talks to you. He absolutely adores you; it just radiates from him."

I gave her a little cheeky wink.

"At this point you could go at warp speed and you still wouldn't be rushing things. And I could be wrong, but were you two lovebirds messing up the duvet this afternoon? Is that why you were so late getting here?"

She nodded, flushing slightly. It made her appear even prettier, and girlish somehow.

"Oh Lila, I'm so sorry we kept you waiting, but I'm not sorry about what happened. It was amazing! I just have to keep pinching myself to check that I'm not dreaming. After all those years with Daniel, when the closest he ever got to foreplay was to fart before he clambered on top. It was just wonderful."

I half expected her to start twirling around the restroom like a princess in a Disney movie. She looked as giddy as a kipper.

"And you know how I was always so worried about being naked again after being with Daniel? How my stretch marks and saggy tum would turn a man off? All my squishy marsh-mallow parts I like to keep hidden under my Spanx all suddenly on show. Or how there might be new moves that weren't even in my repertoire?"

I nodded back at her. I remembered only too well. I had wisely advised her to down a couple of double voddies before getting down to the deed. A bit of Dutch courage always worked wonders for sexual prowess, in my opinion. Some champagne or liquor turned me into a champion licker, if you catch my drift.

I had also helpfully imparted another top tip. That was to always sit high on the horse, a straight back and good posture in the bedroom was just good etiquette in my opinion. Slouching just wasn't an option, gravity really didn't need any help.

Lottie hadn't finished.

"And my boobs, I was so worried about them once my bra came off. If things got too vigorous, they would be swinging around all over the place and clapping together. But to be honest, I didn't care in the end. By the time we'd finished they could clap away as much as they liked. He deserved a round of applause anyway."

I hooted at this. My girl was on fire tonight, and not just her loins. But I had a question of my own to ask.

"OK, Lottie, but tell me this: we know his bank account is very well endowed, but how about his...?"

I left the last word hanging in the air, but from my raised eyebrows and rapid hand movements she knew exactly what I was getting at.

"I'm not talking about that!"

"Oh, come on, Lottie, all the times I've shared tales of my bedroom antics; it's only fair you spill the beans now. After all, this is the first time you've had anything juicy to impart for years. And I haven't had a date for a while now, so I have to live vicariously through you."

Her face reddened a shade or two more.

"OK...OK...let's just say that at first sight it was pretty impressive, much bigger than Daniel's. But then when I touched it, it almost immediately doubled in size...like when you're kneading dough to make bread."

I couldn't help but laugh. Trust Lottie: even her sex analogies were wholesome.

"So would you say *much* more impressive than old desperate Dan's?"

Her eyes flashed mischievously. Even though Daniel had treated her horrendously, it was clear she still felt a little disloyal talking about him in such a manner. But not enough to actually stop, clearly. She was getting quite a kick out of it too.

"Put it this way, if I carry on the baking theme, Leo is definitely a full baguette, whereas Daniel was more of a dried-up breadstick."

I snorted in that way I often did, which I imagine made me

appear the very height of sophistication...not.

"Yeah, I can imagine poor old Daniel...nobody ever touches the breadsticks. They're always left abandoned on the table. But I'm so happy for you, Lottie. I told you it was about time you tested the bedsprings again, and the fact it's with someone you love is amazing."

"That's what I've been thinking too."

She sighed happily.

"And it's not just the sex; he's just so wonderful, and Jacob loves him too. He's a million miles away from Daniel in every way. I just can't believe how different he is; and you're right, he really does seem to adore me. It's the little romantic things he does that mean so much, like buying me flowers and boxes of chocolates, or even just the fact he holds my hand in public, things that Daniel never did."

"No, old Danny really wasn't one for the romantic gestures, was he? But then again, a serial killer with a wilting bunch of carnations and a half-eaten Mars bar would still be a vast improvement on your ex."

She was blushing again, the colour lighting up her pretty face.

"I know, I have to pinch myself sometimes, because I can't believe this has actually happened to me and I've met someone so wonderful. Ordinary old me, I'm not exactly a *femme fatale* after all. I'm just a plain old middle-aged mum."

"Rubbish! You're talking about my best friend, and I for one know she's an absolute knockout."

I rubbed her arm affectionately.

"Grab life by the lady balls, Lottie. Move in with Leo, live your best life; you deserve it."

I turned back towards the mirror and started to dust powder

on my blotchy face. My tears of mirth earlier had nigh on ruined my visage. I looked like something out of the circus.

"Like I've always said, Lottie, it's better to live in sin than cynicism."

I snapped my powder compact shut and fished around in my silver clutch for my lipstick. It was damage limitation at this point, as I surveyed my appearance in the dimly lit mirror.

"Hell, I don't know why I even bother; my face looks like a melted welly."

"Nonsense, Lila, you look gorgeous, you always do. Like a fine work of art, a masterpiece."

I snorted unattractively at my friend's kind words, dropped my lipstick back in my bag and zipped it up.

"Yeah, I know I'm a masterpiece all right: old, damaged and in need of much restoration. Thank God for the magical powers of MAC."

Lottie laughed at this.

"Oooh, that reminds me, Lila, I was going to tell you all about Jayne."

Jayne was a good friend of ours. I had met her through Lottie, who had known her forever, having lived next door to each other as children. We often liked to go out in a group with our other friend Jasmine. We made quite the formidable foursome: setting the world to rights with sassy conversation and strong cosmopolitans. She was an artist, producing the most fabulous bespoke pieces of jewellery.

Lottie had opened the camera roll on her phone and was staring at it intently.

"She's doing make-up now as well as her jewellery, and she's really good at it."

She passed the handset over to me.

"Here, take a look, it's really impressive."

I scrolled through the photographs: beautiful close-up shots of pouting women, some subtle with beige and rose tones, others striking with hues of peacock blue on eyelids and magenta lips. There was no doubt the looks were impressive and obviously took a great level of skill. The models were simply stunning, another talent for Jayne to add to her repertoire.

A photo popped up on the screen that made my stomach jolt and gave me cause to pause. It was a grotesque image of a face, hard to tell if it was even male or female, battered, bruised and bloody, looking like something from out of your worst nightmares.

"What the hell, Lottie! Who's that?"

She laughed and touched my shoulder reassuringly.

"Calm down, Lila, it's not real; it's all just cleverly applied make-up. Jayne's been on a course for special effects. There's a big demand for it, apparently, and she's obviously good at it, plus she can make a fair amount of money doing it for Halloween events and fancy dress too."

She started tapping at her handset again.

"Anyway, I'm going to forward the pics to you in case there's anyone you know who needs their make-up done."

I felt the relief surge through my body. I had really thought for a second that it was a genuine image of some poor soul.

"Well, there's no doubting that she's talented. We need to arrange one of our girly afternoons soon, with Jasmine too. We all need to get together and raise a few glasses of something fizzy to toast our girl Jayne's success."

Lottie nodded her agreement as she tucked her evening bag firmly under her arm.

"Come on then, we've been in here for ages and I want to

order the most sinful thing on the menu for dessert, and I'm hoping that doesn't mean sorbet. Let's get back to the table; we don't want "our" men worrying we've done a runner on them."

I playfully stuck my tongue out at the reference to "our" men.

"OK, in a min, just let me quickly get your opinion on something first."

I went on to tell Lottie all about my issues with Jocasta. How we really hadn't hit it off, and the fact that she had chucked coffee all over my fabulous outfit. I even told her about the milk mix-up and exploding excrement story. She visibly winced at that part, especially when I described my colleague's dash to the lavatory, running so fast her limbs were as much on fire as her arse.

She turned towards me and I braced myself for her opinion. Lottie always gave the best advice.

"Look, Lila, it sounds to me like you two might actually get on if you gave each other a chance. From what you say, Seb seems to think she's OK and he's a pretty good judge of character. Just start afresh, maybe suggest going out for a quick lunch where you can both chat, just the two of you away from all the distractions of the office."

I had to agree with her. It was the same advice Seb had given me too, and I would be a fool to ignore them both. I didn't have a choice: I was going to have to suck up and play nicely with the mean girl.

"Anyway, how about you and Seb? Any chance of romance there? I know you always laugh it off, but you really do make such a lovely couple, and he's simply the nicest guy...well nearly as nice as my Leo."

Again, I was given cause to pause for a few seconds. After all, Lottie was the sensible and steady one out of the pair of us. She always gave good advice and rarely made a bad decision. But Seb and me? Did the whole world think we were meant to be together? And if we were destined to be, then why had it not happened by now? We'd known each other for years.

I brushed the notion off again like a nuisance bit of fluff. Who knew, Lottie's opinion might be skewed for once, considering she was floating along in her own bubble of love. Clearly the smitten kitten, so of course she wanted the same for everyone else, especially her friends. So, her candy-coated, hearts and flowers opinion could not necessarily be trusted.

I shook my head forcefully, causing my shoulder-length blonde hair, which had looked so chic in my sleek updo earlier, to resemble a half-up half-down disaster. Like Ru-Paul in a bad wig.

"No, Seb and me are strictly just friends. You won't see the pair of us growing old together any time soon. We won't be sharing the same glass of water to put our false teeth in of a night."

My friend shrugged her shoulders and smiled ruefully.

"Well, that's your choice, but I just hope you don't live to regret it. I'm telling you, Lila, Seb's a real catch, and if you don't snap him up at some point, somebody else surely will."

Chapter 10

The following day, I was ready to initiate my charm offensive, befriend Miss Bitchy Britches and make sure the office equilibrium was well and truly restored.

She was busy at her workstation, chewing her bottom lip in concentration and tapping figures into a spreadsheet on her laptop. Her curly blonde hair was piled up high on her head in a loose bun, and designer glasses perched on the bridge of her nose.

I cleared my throat to attract her attention. She looked up from her work, blinking a little like a newborn kitten, her eyes readjusting after staring at columns of figures for too long. She was smiling, but that quickly faded as soon as she realised it was me at her desk. Her hand unconsciously moved towards the coffee mug next to her mouse mat, clearly worried that I was going to grab it and offer to make her another drink.

"Morning, Jocasta, how are you today?"

My tone was bright and breezy, and I was grinning like a loon. If I was going to play nice, then I would be the nicest of the nice.

She eyed me a little warily, clearly wondering why her adversary was being so chipper.

"I'm OK, thank you, Lila; certainly feeling better than I did yesterday. I think it must have been something I ate."

I smiled pleasantly at her.

"Well, I'm just glad to hear that you're better now."

At least this meant we didn't have to address my switcheroo of the milk yesterday. She was obviously even keener than me to forget the unfortunate turn of events, and that suited me just fine.

Jocasta sat back in her swivel chair and eyed me suspiciously. She folded her arms beneath her bust. Defensive body language, if ever I saw it. However, the move only served to accentuate her ample bosom, which was already well and truly on display. I wondered if she had intended to leave quite so many buttons undone when she had got dressed that morning. The cream blouse was teamed with a fitted knee-length black leather skirt, and together they made quite a statement. And that statement most definitely wasn't PG rated.

"I was thinking it might be nice if we popped out for some lunch together, say about 1pm? We haven't had much chance to really get to know each other yet, and I thought it would make a nice change to get out of the office for a bit. There's a new deli that's just opened opposite The Fox & Chicken pub."

My offer hung in the air for a few seconds as I waited patiently for her reply. From the expression on her face, it hadn't been at all what she had expected to hear. She probably assumed we would indulge in a little passive-aggressive office politeness, so we could get it out of the way before trying to avoid each other for the remainder of the day.

Her eyes flashed over me quickly from head to foot. I was confident there was nothing she could find fault with. I was dressed in a smart yet sophisticated manner: ankle-length black and white pin-striped skirt and cream polo neck. OK, maybe my outfit was a little dowager aunt for my liking. I had thought it so chic when I had found it in a little boutique in York, but now after checking my appearance in the office toilets, it had just appeared a tad severe. A little like Miss Havisham without the cobwebs. And if I was Miss Havisham, what did that make Jocasta? Miss Whiplash?

Her face softened and she smiled at me. God, I had to give her credit: she was good. If I didn't know better, I would have believed that there was genuine warmth in that smile. No wonder Seb had been well and truly taken in by her.

"Thank you so much, Lila, I would really like that; everyone has been so nice in the firm, but it would be great for us girls to get to be friends."

"Great, that's sorted then: 1pm for lunch."

As agreed, I arrived at Jocasta's desk bang on 1pm and it barely took us five minutes to walk the short stroll to The Gourmet Delights, making awkward small talk along the way.

We stood two deep in a queue with the all the other hungry customers, waiting to place our order at the counter. My eyes swept around the interior of the shop: it was a new and stylish eatery, all polished surfaces and prints of avocados and smoothies to whet the appetite. And it boasted an impressive array of lunch options: a place designed for the busy worker who desired something more adventurous than a cheese and pickle sandwich wrapped in tin foil.

Within a few minutes, it was our turn to order. I hadn't minded the wait. There were two staff serving: a young woman with spiky blue hair and an even spikier attitude, and a man in his early thirties who was extremely easy on the eye and could give Jason Momoa a run for his money.

Of course, he was younger than me, but then again who wasn't? He had a little hipster edge about him, just enough to make him interesting, but not enough to render him tragic. I was so busy checking him out that I hadn't even bothered to check out the daily specials on the board above his head. He was by far the most delicious thing in the place. But was he available? He'd certainly smiled over in my direction a few times, so it seemed promising.

I told Jocasta to order anything she fancied as it was my treat, so she weighed up the pros and cons between the falafel salad wrap and the halloumi flatbread. Quite the choice.

I knew what I was having: I'd already checked the menu online between meetings, so decided to jump in with my order. I didn't want to miss the opportunity as the look-alike Mr Momoa was staring expectantly at me.

"Could I get the prawn layered salad please, with extra avocado."

He smiled at me, showing a beautiful set of incredibly straight white teeth. His green eyes sparkled; he certainly had the "come hither" charm going on in spades.

"Of course, madam, a prawn salad with extra avo."

He smiled at me again and I nearly melted on the spot. He really was flirting with me, and God was he sexy.

"And how about a drink?"

Well, this was more like it. I had been avoiding dating lately, the way I avoided the Jehovah's Witnesses. After the last few disastrous dates, there were a few too many tossers or "Toffers" around for my liking. But an exception could definitely be made for Mr Sexy Stripy Apron here.

I tossed a slightly smug look in the direction of Jocasta, who was still deciding what to order. I was pleased to see she had heard our exchange and was now looking straight at us.

"That sounds like a great idea, how about Friday?"

Mr Apron's brow furrowed slightly with confusion, and then the penny dropped, and he let out a self-conscious laugh.

"No, I'm sorry…I meant would you like a drink to go with your salad? We have a special lunchtime deal on any freshly squeezed juice: half price when ordering any sandwich or salad from the board."

I laughed brightly, trying to give the impression I had been joking all along; but in truth I was absolutely mortified. There really was no way to style out this blunder. Fortunately, the customers around me had the good grace to avert their eyes to save me any additional humiliation. All except for Jocasta, who seemed to be thoroughly enjoying it all as her hand flew to her mouth to stifle her giggles.

"I'll take a beetroot and raspberry juice please… large."

I tried to avoid seeing my reflection in the polished chrome behind the counter. I could only imagine my face would be as red as the juice I had just ordered.

Chapter 11

Jocasta ordered herself the falafel salad wrap in her customary breathy voice. She really was annoying; way too bloody cheerful for a freezing January lunchtime in Leeds. Yet she sounded for the world like she was full of the joys of spring.

We found an unoccupied table by the window and sat down. I was glad that at least I would be able to gaze out of the window and do a bit of people-watching in case our conversation dried up faster than the left-over Christmas cake I had shoved in my drawer after the work's office party. I had a bad feeling our conversation might become stale even quicker than that.

"Don't feel too bad about what just happened."

She was smiling and rubbing my hand in what I can only assume she thought was a show of solidarity. I wasn't convinced of her sincerity. I could almost feel the waves of pity rolling off her and tumbling to the floor. All I felt was regret. Regret I had ever come into this place, and regret that I had just made a complete and utter tit of myself.

"Chin up, Lila, no one would blame you for chancing your arm. He's probably just your type...or was when you were younger. And I must say he is rather dreamy."

She smirked unattractively again, in that way that just

made me want to slap the smug right off her younger, not unattractive face.

"But you must admit it's funny: it was only the beetroot juice he was offering you, not a taste of his delicious aubergine."

She was wrong. It was anything but funny.

We were clearly at odds over this fact, as she exploded into a fit of uncontrollable laughter. I really wished her head would explode, leaving little splatters of Jocasta all over the interior of the deli, like the abstract paintings that were dotted randomly around the walls.

I fought off the desire to leap across the table and throttle her, rather like Homer would to Bart in *The Simpsons*. To be fair, her face was that golden from all the bronzing powder she caked on it that she wouldn't have looked out of place if we had been having lunch in The Krusty Burger rather than this fancy upmarket deli.

I sat in serene, stony-faced silence and swallowed down my prawns whilst I swallowed down my fury. If I had been out with my friends and had made the same flirting faux pas, I would have been just as embarrassed but after a few minutes the embarrassment would have ebbed away, and I would even have been able to see the funny side of things. Probably never darkened the door of Gourmet Delights ever again, but at least I'd have been able to chalk it up to a funny anecdote for future telling. Plus, I would have taken my friend's jokey jabs firmly on the chin.

I would understand that they were good-natured and not malicious, their teasing coming from a good place, a place of love. But having Jocasta take the piss out of me was, well to be honest, it was boiling mine.

I fixed my gaze on the world outside the panes of glass of the deli window. I wished I was one of those harassed-looking workers, hurrying along in their lunch hour, things to do, people to see and looking just like a marching procession of ants streaming down the street.

The waitress with the spiky hair arrived at our table with our food and quickly passed the plates over to us.

"There you go, condiments and cutlery on the side...enjoy."

From the tone of her voice, it was apparent she couldn't give a flying toss whether we enjoyed our lunch or not. I slowly unfolded my paper napkin, careful not to meet her eye. I had no desire to engage in any conversation with her or to see if she was smirking at me too.

I speared a marinated prawn with my fork and chewed on it unenthusiastically. I didn't have much of an appetite any more. Public humiliation had a way of doing that, working better for weight loss than any diet pill out there.

I decided I'd better say something; it was beginning to feel excruciatingly awkward at our little round table. Now that Jocasta had stopped laughing, the silence felt deafening.

"So, how's your food?"

"Delicious."

She nibbled delicately on the corner of her toasted flatbread. Even the way she ate was royally pissing me off.

"I love falafel, it's one of my favourite foods. I absolutely adore chickpeas."

That just proved we could never be friends. Who in this world ever said they adored chickpeas? For a second, I thought she said chicken pies. That would have made a lot more sense; but chickpeas? Nah, the woman was a wrong 'un through and through.

"I'm loving the job,"

She continued rambling on, even though I hadn't asked.

"Everyone is just so lovely, and Mr Fluck is simply a darling man."

Yep, that put the tin lid on it right there. The woman was a bona fide fruitcake. Fluck a darling man? Give me a sodding break.

She dabbed the corner of her mouth gracefully with her paper napkin – a gesture so refined you would be mistaken for thinking she was taking afternoon tea at Buckingham Palace.

"I'm also loving the fact that you and I are getting to know each other better. I feel like we hadn't really got off to the best of starts, what with the unfortunate accident with my shoe straps, and then you adding the wrong milk to my coffee."

I felt a little pang of guilt, mind you only a little one. Scrap that; in truth it was tiny bordering on the miniscule.

"Yes, Jocasta, I'm sorry about that; I forgot you only took almond milk."

Her green eyes narrowed ever so slightly at the memory, and I could have been mistaken, but her face seemed to pale a shade or two under her layers of foundation and powder.

"You see, I just can't tolerate cow's milk; it makes me shi... I mean it gives me a rather runny tummy."

I began to repeat a mantra in my head to stop the laughter that was threatening to bubble over: "Please don't laugh... please don't laugh...please don't laugh."

Fortunately, she was no longer looking at me and was scrolling through some emails on her phone, clearly trying to find something important. Her tongue was sticking out the corner of her mouth in concentration. It wasn't her best look, and a million miles away from her normal pouty pose.

I speared another prawn from my salad. It suited me fine

that she had ceased her jabbering. I was happiest when she wasn't speaking, but alas it didn't last long.

"Ahhhh, here it is."

Her voice was high and triumphant.

"I was just trying to find this email, and I've got it."

She pointed at her phone screen: a picture of a grand period property set back in its own palatial grounds. It looked impressive.

"It's for a spa afternoon in Harrogate. My boyfriend got it for me as one of my Christmas presents, but now we've split up so I need to take someone else."

I felt a sinking feeling in the pit of my stomach as I realised what was coming.

"It's for a few weeks' time, the end of January. It's already booked and it's non-refundable, but my girlfriend who I was going to take has had to drop out so I wondered if you would like to come with me instead?"

Firstly, I was shocked to hear she actually had any girlfriends; secondly, that she had received a Christmas present from her boyfriend on Christmas Day and was already broken up from him barely two weeks later; and finally, how the hell was I going to think of an excuse to get me out of the whole bloody thing?

"When is it?"

"Last Thursday in January. Give me your number and I'll text you the deets over."

The deets indeed. How old was she, fifteen?

It was on the tip of my tongue to lie and say I was already booked for that afternoon: a family function or the like that I just couldn't get out of; or alternatively that I was just too snowed under with work to slip away to a spa afternoon.

I opened my mouth to let the lies spew forth, but something stopped me. And that was the thought of Seb. I remembered how keen he had been for us to get on. He believed Jocasta was a nice person, since he foolishly always saw the best in people. He really was a good person, much better than me. I felt myself begin to waver. The image of Seb made my resolve weaken.

"Come on, Lila."

Jocasta's voice took on a whiny pleading edge.

"Say you'll come; we'll have such fabulous fun."

Fabulous fun, or fodder for nightmares?

So, with Seb clearly in my mind, I relented. I told Jocasta I would be delighted to go to the spa with her. OK, scratch that, I didn't say I would be "delighted", but I did at least say I would go.

I finished the few remaining leaves of my virtuous salad, and I must say I was feeling quite saintly myself. I had agreed to something that quite frankly I would find about as appealing as halitosis. But I had done it for a good cause, to make my real friend happy.

I wasn't going to enjoy it. I knew that. Firstly, the company was decidedly grim; and secondly, I had never been a fan of spas. I had always found an afternoon of alcohol and good conversation a much better way to relax than seaweed scrubs and shiatsu massage.

To me spas, even the top-end ones, always had a feel of a psychiatric ward about them: people shuffling around in their dressing gowns and slippers, carrying little glasses of orange juice. It really wasn't my scene. But I was trying to get on with Jocasta, so I was going to suck it up, quite literally, even if the orange juice had no vodka in it.

"That's great, Lila, I'm so pleased."

She let out a little squeal of delight that made a chihuahua sitting on the lap of an elderly diner growl and bare its teeth.

"We'll have the best time we really will."

That I doubted very much. I agreed with the dog.

On the bright side, it was still a few weeks away. With any luck something would crop up in the meantime to prevent us going. Maybe Jocasta could break a limb or something. OK, that was mean, I really didn't wish actual bodily harm on the woman. I didn't have any desire to see Jocasta in plaster. Not when a nice crusty cold sore on her over-plumped lip would suffice instead. Yes, I would pray that she had a nice contagious cold sore that would mean we would need to cancel. If Jocasta could just be viral on the last Thursday of the month, that would be perfection.

She was still rambling on, waxing lyrical about the spa and its many amenities, so I arranged my features into a look of concentration; well, I hoped it resembled concentration rather than constipation.

"The place is so fabulous, you're going to love it. All the best people go, even a few footballers' wives, so we could do a bit of celeb spotting."

I stifled the desire to yawn. I had little to no interest in football; that had been my ex-husband's thing. He had worshipped his beloved Leeds United, whereas I couldn't care less about the game, and I cared even less for their wives.

Jocasta was now staring at me a little too intently. I started to worry I had a bit of lettuce stuck between my teeth, Bugs Bunny style, and ran my index finger along my incisors just to check. No, all seemed good, gnashers-wise.

"I think it will do us both good to have a pamper...I hope you don't mind me saying this, Lila, but you've looked a bit tired recently...run down, so I think it may be just what you need."

Run down? The cheeky little moo. She made me sound like a clapped-out old Vauxhall Corsa or the like. Whereas anyone with an ounce of common sense knew that Lila Glover was a Lamborghini. But she hadn't finished. No, she was going to twist the knife a little further, hoping to hit the jugular.

"My mum loves the spa, bless her; I take her quite often. Thinking about it, she's probably around your age and she always says it does her the world of good. The steam room really helps with her rheumatism."

She was looking thoughtful again.

"But maybe the steam room isn't the best place for a menopausal woman; it might trigger a hot flush for you."

Talking of steam, I couldn't believe it wasn't coming out of my ears like an old tea kettle at this point. The bloody nerve of the woman. I was nowhere near old enough to be her mother. But I couldn't deny the words had stung a bit. I should stop by House of Fraser on the way home and invest in another elixir of youth, by way of a pot of anti-ageing face cream. Or maybe I should just drown my sorrows in a deep pan pizza instead. That's all Seb ever did, and he was looking very good for his years.

Jocasta was really starting to needle me, and I was realising with a sinking feeling that the only needle it seemed I needed was from a trained Botox practitioner.

And as for the menopause, that particular gift from the malevolent Mother Nature hadn't made an appearance quite yet. OK, so I had missed the occasional period, and my memory could be as flaky as an apple turnover that had been left out of its tin, but that was all. Oh, and the fact that the thermostat was always turned up too high at work and I could burst into tears at the drop of a hat could all be put down to modern-day living – central heating and stress, I was sure of it.

The fact I now had to clench my pelvic floor for dear life when I felt a sneeze coming on wasn't down to the "change". It was just one of those things, and of course a sensible measure was to repeat the mantra "you sneeze you pees" whenever I suffered from a head cold to remind myself to do my Kegel exercises.

I was beginning to really regret agreeing to this spa day. The thought of poolside pampering, prosecco and this perfumed pillock was less than appealing. The things I did for Seb. But he was my friend, and my friends were important to me. I didn't think I would ever class Jocasta as one, no matter what Seb believed.

Jocasta was still prattling on, but I had long tuned her out. I just caught the end of what she was saying.

"...so we're going to have fun, he's such a lovely guy."

I was confused as to who she could be talking about.

"Who's a lovely guy?"

"Why Seb, silly. Have you not been listening? We're going out on a date tomorrow night."

Chapter 12

"So now you're socialising with *her*?"

I still couldn't believe it, even though I'd heard it directly from the horse's mouth. And that nag's braying words were running through my head like an Olympic sprinter.

Seb was my friend, not hers. I know that seems childish, but I couldn't help it.

He was standing by the open filing cabinet, a pile of hefty documents in his hands. He was wearing his navy-rimmed glasses, the ones that always made him appear a tad more intellectual. The look of shock at seeing me burst into his office like a force twelve hurricane was evident on his handsome face. With a lengthy sigh that spoke volumes, and without uttering a word, he put down the files, shut the drawer and made his way over to me.

He gestured to the chair opposite his, a clear indication for me to park my arse. Once we were both seated, he finally decided to speak.

"So, Jocasta told you?"

I was so riled up by this point that my words just tumbled out, like ice cubes into a nice, chilled martini. And I could have really gone for a bit of alcohol right then.

"Yes, she told me, and boy, didn't she just make a meal of it? So much so she needn't have eaten any lunch. I just don't understand though... why would you want to see her outside work, Seb? I'm your friend, and you know how I feel about her. It's got to be a joke, surely. You are joking...right?"

He sighed, removed his glasses and rubbed the bridge of his nose and then up to his forehead as if he could suddenly feel a migraine coming on.

"No, I'm not joking. As you well know, I've never been considered a gifted comedian."

I fidgeted in my chair like a truculent teenager on the verge of a tantrum. I was getting impatient, waiting for him to tell me what the hell he was thinking.

He polished the lens of his glasses on his sweater sleeve before putting them back on.

His tone was calm, yet businesslike. I had heard him use it many times, often when he was having a meeting with a rather bolshy client, and he was trying to pacify them and coerce them into seeing sense.

"Yes, I'm seeing Jocasta tomorrow night, but it's not a date. I chat to her most days. Like I've told you before, she's a sweet person, and it turns out we have a lot in common. She's a friend, that's all; no romance in it, just mates."

My lips twisted into a smirk.

"You two? A lot in common? Give me a break, Seb, unless you've suddenly started waxing your bikini line and taken to watching *Love Island* of an evening with some roasted chickpeas to snack on. I just can't see it myself."

Seb chose to ignore me. Probably a wise move on his part.

"She's into sci-fi, as it happens, and she loves a good pub quiz. It turns out there's one on tomorrow night in the pub down the road from where she lives. She asked me to go along with her, as the friend she normally pairs up with can't make it. So, I'm going instead as a favour. She just suggested we could grab a late dinner after it finishes, that's all."

It seemed that Jocasta was being let down by a lot of "friends" just lately. I sincerely doubted whether these people even existed.

This still didn't make sense to me. Why was she setting her sights on Seb? My Seb. OK, so he wasn't mine, of course, but I did feel protective towards him, and if I was completely honest a little unnerved by the thought of this workplace vixen getting her French-tipped claws into him.

Something just didn't add up. Yes, Seb was a great guy, but he really didn't seem the type of fella that Jocasta would go for, as friends or otherwise. I wasn't buying the whole sci-fi devotee and into pub quizzes either. I'd seen the magazines she read: *Vogue* and *Cosmopolitan* to name but two. But I also knew the names of the sci-fi mags that Seb devoured monthly, and I'd never once seen an edition of those in her over-sized patent tote. And as for sipping half a pint in her local whilst racking her brain over question four on the general knowledge round, that just didn't ring true to me either.

I cast a roving eye over Sebastian. He was sporting a jaunty argyle sweater over his work shirt. It was maroon with a zigzag pattern. It wasn't quite Giles Brandreth level, but it was pretty dire nonetheless. The knitwear was teamed with straight-legged trousers that were a smidge too short. He looked like an overgrown schoolboy dressed up for tea with the vicar.

It was fair to say that his current garb was about as far from stylish as you could imagine; not likely to grace the catwalks of Paris or Milan any time soon, and about a million miles away from the style of the slimy suitor we'd seen on Jocasta's arm at Olive Affair. That guy had an expensive "wanker banker" vibe to him; whereas Seb, although a solicitor, had more of a laid-back librarian aura.

That other guy was the type to be forever flashing his platinum card; Seb, on the other hand, was more likely to flash his Costco card, and that was only when he needed to buy his beloved bourbon biscuits in bulk.

It wasn't just Seb's outfit that wasn't quite cutting it fashion-wise. His crowning glory was also letting him down royally. While he had lovely thick black hair with just the right amount of salt and peppering, it was rather unruly and could do with a bit of a trim. And it wasn't just the hair on his head that was questionable; there was his monobrow too.

Seb liked to think he was a modern man, even a feminist; but the modern art of male grooming had passed him by completely; in fact, sped past at warp speed. It was fair to say that he cared little about his appearance: a splash of cold water to the face and a quick sweep with a comb through his unruly mop was about all the grooming he did of a morning. It was part of his charm.

"I just don't think she's your type, Seb. She's very high maintenance, a real social climber."

Seb was shaking his head.

"Oh, come on, Lila, aren't we all wanting to better ourselves in our own way? Doesn't that make us all social climbers?"

"Not me, I climbed nowhere; I took the lift directly to the top. Plus, I don't buy her love for all things sci-fi. I saw her face when you were debating who was the best Doctor Who with Donald from Financial Services, and she was fake yawning behind your back, her eyes rolling so much I wanted to give her a slap just to knock them back into place."

I smiled over at him in what I hoped conveyed my depth of feeling for him – friendship, of course.

"If I'm honest, I think she's only befriending you to piss me off."

Seb held up his hand to silence me. Rather like my old headmaster when I had been caught smoking in the girls' toilets and I tried to lie my way out of it by saying I was just holding the lit Benson and Hedges for somebody in the cubicle having a poo.

"You really need to drop this combative attitude, Lila. It's like you're laser-focused on finding fault with her. I'm telling you she's a nice girl, and you've got her all wrong. You just have to let this vendetta go; it's not an attractive trait, and it's beginning to make me see you in a new light. And I don't like that. Just take it from me, Jocasta is a lovely person."

I was smarting from his words. Seb rarely got angry with me. He always seemed to have me neatly placed on my own little pedestal where he could only ever see the best in me, a version that I didn't even know existed. But it appeared that pedestal was shaky now, and I was perilously close to sliding off it completely. I couldn't help it, though; I still needed to chip in with the final word.

"I would agree with you, Seb, if it wasn't for the fact that then we would both be wrong."

His blue eyes darkened like the sea when a storm threatens to take hold.

"Give her a bloody break, Lila! She's not long come out of a difficult marriage, and then the guy she was seeing after that sounds like he was a complete bully, controlling her terribly, as well as cheating on her left, right and centre, the same as her husband did. Cut her some slack; she's had a bad run of things."

That shut me up. I hadn't known all this about her. I knew she had been married before, and I knew she had split up with someone at Christmas. But with regards to her marriage, I was under the impression that she had cheated on him, not vice versa.

Thinking about it, where had I heard that from? I racked my brain but couldn't remember. It must have been office gossip, no doubt. But if what Seb was saying was true, I couldn't help but feel bad for Jocasta. Nobody deserved to be treated like that. I knew that only too well from personal experience; finding out that my ex-husband Duncan had cheated on me had near destroyed me.

I had never shown that to the outside world. To prying eyes, it appeared that I just moved him out and then moved on with my life. But the nights that followed his departure had been the most wretched of my life.

I knew enough was enough now. I had to shut my trap. I had said all I could on the subject of Jocasta, and I had to let it be. Trying to lighten the mood, I told Seb about the spa afternoon.

His eyes brightened again, and a smile broke over his gloomy face, like the sun breaking through after the storm had ended.

"Well, that's more like it. What could be better than that? A chance to relax and have a good chat. It'll do you the world of good, reinvigorate you and with any luck you'll have a new friend after the day is done."

I smiled back at him, suspecting it didn't quite reach my eyes. I still wasn't looking forward to it. And why had Seb said I needed reinvigorating? Did he think I looked like a bag of hot dog crap too?

A few hours later, I was back sitting at my desk. It was after 7pm and everyone else had left for the day. The office was quiet and eerie, the gloom settling on me like a heavy cloak. It was deadly silent apart from the distant hum of a vacuum cleaner. The cleaner always came once the working day was over.

I stared blankly at the files piled up in front of me. I hadn't done any work of any value in hours. My head was chock full of unwanted thoughts that just wouldn't seem to loosen their grip. I had the sinking feeling that I was losing Seb. I knew in my heart that I was being ridiculous; we were great friends, and had been for years. It would take more than this to loosen our foundations. But I just couldn't shake off the nagging feeling of hopelessness.

Was I really jealous of Seb seeing Jocasta? Even if it was just as friends? I hated to admit it, but I was. I picked up my mug of coffee and took a large gulp. It was stone cold.

I had to shake myself out of this. I was being ridiculous. Well, if Seb could go out with Jocasta, maybe I should resume my dating life too.

I picked up my phone and glanced at the screen. No missed calls. No text messages for me to answer. Nothing. That made me feel a hundred times worse.

Sitting alone at my desk in the semi-darkness, it was as if I was the only person that existed in the world. Cast adrift by despair, down and defeated. Lila the loser in love. But this wouldn't do. This wasn't who I was. I was Lila Glover, that stood for something.

I was a powerhouse, magnificent not mousy. And I needed my mojo back. This would require going balls to the wall and bringing the big guns out. I tapped on the screen, finding the app I was looking for: its recognisable logo with the little red flame. I started to swipe right, over and over again.

A couple of hours later, I was finally leaving work. I'd had enough waking hours for one day. I swung my bag over my shoulder and left the building for yet another day. As I walked the short distance to my car, I was humming to myself and there was a definite spring in my step.

I had arranged a date for the following evening. Lila Glover was back on the market. Form an orderly queue.

Chapter 13

"**W**hat can I get you to drink, Lila?

My date looked at me expectantly, his neat dark eyebrows raised in anticipation.

"I'll have a gin and tonic, please."

His name was Mervyn. I know, a pretty bad start, as names go. What was even worse was the fact that *this* Mervyn was forty-one years old. Forty-one, I ask you. That meant that in 1983 his parents must have decided that this particular name would be perfect for their adorable new-born baby boy. The mind boggled. Before tonight, I would have assumed that anyone named Mervyn would have to be pushing at least seventy.

But here I was, Thursday night, out on the town, or at least in a little back street boozer in Headingley, with Mervyn Lewis: 41 years old, 6 foot 2, brown hair, blue eyes, hates cats and works in sales, or at least that was what his profile had stated.

He hadn't elaborated on what his actual work was. To me "sales" could mean anything from working in Poundland to Columbian drug lord. Let's hope it was somewhere safely between the two.

Old man name aside, he was rather quite dishy. He was tall, nearly as tall as he had stated; tanned and muscular, dressed in a white linen shirt with enough buttons undone to expose a smooth toned chest. His long legs were clad in tight-fitting denim that hugged his bum extremely well. And as long as that wasn't a couple of pairs of socks stuffed down the front, it might turn out to be my very lucky night.

He had an air of Jonny Depp about him. And that was never a bad thing. All tousled shoulder-length hair and straight white teeth. OK, the teeth weren't particularly Jonny, probably expensive veneers, but overall Mervyn was quite magnificent.

He had ordered a bottle of lager for himself. That was a definite tick in his plus column. Nobody wanted to be on a date with the guy who ordered a colourful drink with a cocktail cherry in it: rather like a Yorkshire-based Del Boy supping at The Nag's Head.

We took our drinks and found an intimate little table to occupy, safely away from the other customers and the lavatories.

"So, Mervyn, you say you work in sales?"

I always found a bit of work small talk was a good icebreaker.

He took a long swig of his beer and sighed contentedly.

"Yeah, that's right. I do a bit of this and a bit of that. Wheeler dealing, you know?"

He shrugged non-committally.

"I also like to dabble in the stock market, when I get a chance."

Even without the lurid drink, he really was beginning to sound a lot like Del Boy.

I took a small sip of my drink, thankful he had ordered me a double. It had been a while since I had been out on a first date, and I was feeling somewhat nervous. Which was odd for me, as I was normally super-confident on dates.

I knew I was looking good. I was certainly bringing my A

game, wearing my crimson bodycon dress that cinched in in all the right places. I was a walking rhapsody in red. And teamed with subtle make-up and killer heels, there was no doubt I looked hot to trot.

I'd seen him check my pins out whilst I sat down at the table, carefully hitching my skirt up ever so slightly to showcase my long, tanned legs.

"I love your shoes."

He cast his eyes appreciatively over my legs and down to my footwear.

"Very sexy. How high are those heels?"

"Six inches."

"Wow, that's big."

I bit my tongue. I was not going to comment. If I blurted out that I didn't consider six inches to be that big, it might very well have killed the conversation stone dead.

"Are they really difficult to walk in?"

"They're not the easiest, but sometimes it's worth the effort. And you know what they say: the higher the heels, the closer you are to heaven."

I gave him my most angelic smile.

He smiled back at me with a little twinkle in his eyes.

"What size feet do you have? You look like you'd have really dainty ones."

"Seven and a half."

He was nodding his head thoughtfully and let out a little whistle.

"That's quite big for a woman. Even though I'm tall, I've got quite small feet for a man."

Well, I hoped that wasn't an indication of the size of other things; but then again, the bulge in his pants was telling a very different story.

The evening was moving along pleasantly enough. We'd covered all the small talk bases: families, hobbies, holidays we'd been on, holidays we hoped to go on, that sort of thing. Thankfully nothing was concerning me; there were no discernible red flags that would have me running for the hills.

Before coming out, I had of course had a quick Google of him. It was the sensible thing to do. And fortunately, that hadn't thrown up any nasty surprises. So, so far so good.

He had already made me aware that he liked to work out every day and lift heavy weights. He said it was good for his stamina. Ding dong! I liked the sound of that.

I nodded in agreement and informed him, in what I hoped was my most flirtatious tone, that I was a great advocate of daily exercise. My first white lie of the evening. In theory I loved the idea of daily sessions at the gym, but in reality there was always something else I would much rather be doing. Like cleaning out the fluff drawer on the tumble dryer. Genetically I had been blessed with a slim figure, without ever having to put in much effort on my part. It was the only thing I was thankful to my mother for; well, that and the ability to render an opponent dumbstruck and cowering with a perfectly timed withering put-down.

I wasn't going to admit to Mervyn that my fitness levels were rather below par. And in fact, last week I had pulled a muscle in my neck whilst opening a jar of olives for my martini.

And never mind the fact that I'm sure all that swiping right the previous night on Tinder had given me a little rheumatism in my index finger.

I could feel the gin rushing straight to my head. My stomach gurgled to remind me I needed some food in my system to mop up all the booze.

I had spent such an age shimmying into my new dress that I hadn't had time to get some food down before bolting out of the door to meet him. When we had arranged our date, nothing had been mentioned about food, but I was going to need something to nibble on. And maybe later on too, if things went to plan.

"Are you hungry, Mervyn?"

"I could eat."

He glanced around the bar area, trying to locate a menu.

"I think they may have some bar snacks on, you know, like little Yorkshire-style tapas dishes."

Yorkshire tapas. That didn't sound yummy to me in the slightest, in fact it sounded decidedly yucky.

"OK, surprise me."

My voice was a silken purr and I raised one eyebrow suggestively.

"Oh, don't you worry, you'll be getting lots of surprises with me."

He matched my tone with a seductive growl of his own, which made my tummy do a little somersault that wasn't due to my hunger. It had been a couple of months since I'd had any action in the boudoir, and my lady regions were waking up from their hibernation.

He marched off towards the bar. All hunter-gatherer vibe. Within a few minutes he was back.

"It's sorted, I've ordered us three dishes; there was a 3 for £15 special on."

Last of the big spenders. Be still, my beating heart.

"I got us the mushy pea croquettes, mini Yorkshire puddings with gravy and snack-size pork pies with brown sauce for dipping."

Blimey, Gordon Ramsay had nothing to worry about here. I couldn't help but wonder what Seb and Jocasta would be eating for their dinner later. Would they be munching on mini beige foodstuffs too? Or perhaps something more intimate? Images of decadent chocolate mousse with only one spoon, or shared spaghetti à la The *Lady and the Tramp* flooded my mind.

The food was delivered to our table within ten minutes. Just long enough to pull it out of the bottom of the freezer and whack it in the microwave for the requisite eight minutes. It was served on one big oval platter garnished with a few tired-looking lettuce leaves and a mound of grated carrot. It was not a thing of beauty.

The surly barman literally dumped it on our table scattering some carrot in the process.

"Dig in while it's hot."

So, I did. And he was right, it was hot, and not just a little bit hot either. Oh no, my gob was on fire and not with witty repartee this time.

The roof of my mouth was literally peeling away against the furnace of heat from the boiling bar snacks. My eyes watered and I took a huge swig of my gin in an attempt to extinguish the fire. I gulped down half the glass for good measure, and it was a good measure, a generous double. If I didn't slow down soon, the alcohol was going to have me on my back, and not in the way I wanted.

"Maybe would have been best if you'd blown on it first."

Mervyn blew on his own croquette for a few seconds before taking a tentative bite. Clearly, he was as unsure of the gastronomical delights as I was.

If I hadn't been in physical pain from my burning mouth, I would have shot back with a witty quip about my skills at blowing. But I just nodded at him wanly. The stinging in my mouth sadly saved him from my rapier-sharp wit.

A few minutes passed and I felt recovered enough to attempt one of the mini pork pies, delicately dipping it into the ramekin of viscous brown sauce. Seductively I licked the sauce from around the edge of the crust.

Mervyn looked delighted by this display.

"Don't want it to drip."

My voice was laced with so much simpering I would have given Jocasta a run for her money.

"I just love a bit of sauce Mervyn."

"I bet you do, you saucy minx. Anyway, in that outfit you're the one that's definitely bringing all the sauce tonight."

"Why thank you, kind sir."

Oh dear, this was all getting a little *Carry On* film for my liking. Ooh err, Matron, if you know what I mean?

Mervyn was giving me the once-over with hungry eyes, and he was eating me up with far more enthusiasm than he was showing the mushy pea croquettes.

I knew I looked good. OK, so my outfit might be a little much for a Thursday night in a half empty pub, where the only other patrons were a table of old men playing dominoes, drinking halves of mild and eating pork scratchings. But I had always lived by the adage of "dress for the job you want" and tonight I was. Or at the very least, dressing for the job Mervyn wanted.

He was still gazing at me and seemed to be suitably impressed.

"I just love the way you look. You're absolutely gorgeous, but so natural too. If I'm honest, I've never been a fan of the 'fake' look."

I smiled to myself at this. Men could just be so gullible at times. They said they hated the "fake" look but believe me I was very far from natural. From my fake eyelashes to my highlighted roots, I was simply an illusion; my Wonderbra and Spanx just part of my armoury in the fight against the ordinary.

And as for my make-up, did he really believe my eyelids were this natural sparkly shade of gold? Or that my lips were naturally this glossy red?

It was fair to say that Mervyn wasn't the brightest crayon in the box, but he did possess other attributes that more than made up for it. And I wasn't looking for a life partner, after all. I just wanted to live my life and have a bit of fun while I went about it.

The rest of the evening passed in a splendid blur, not surprising really considering the amount of gin I'd guzzled.

The surly barman had to ring the bell for last orders twice while Mervyn was helping me into my leather jacket, or at least trying to as I seemed unable to get my arm through the sleeve successfully. Then he asked the question I'd been waiting to hear: Did I want to go back to his place for a coffee?

Apparently, he only lived around the corner, and it would be an ideal location for ordering me an Uber back to mine. I paused for a moment or two to consider my options. I didn't want to appear too keen, but why the hell not? I fancied him, he was nice, not nice enough that I was in danger of losing my heart, but good company nonetheless.

If I was honest, I didn't want to go home alone tonight. Normally, it wouldn't have bothered me in the slightest. But I had enjoyed the night, enjoyed being out, and enjoyed the attention from a handsome man and I didn't want the evening to end. So in for a penny in for a pounding, with a bit of luck.

The thought of being curled up alone on the sofa with a crime documentary and a chilled chardonnay just wasn't cutting it tonight. No, tonight I needed company. Seb had Jocasta and I had Mervyn. And that was that. I was absolutely fine with my choice.

He had been right about the distance. It was just a quick brisk stroll from the pub to the flat where he lived, an imposing Georgian stone building on an attractive sweeping avenue. The property was divided into four flats, with him on the ground floor.

He ushered me through the rather scruffy entrance hall, past the chipped skirting boards and piles of takeaway fliers, to his front door. It took him a couple of attempts to get his key successfully turned in the lock. I hoped this wasn't an omen for the rest of the night. He had to be just as tipsy as I was.

Once inside, I was pleasantly surprised. I knew he'd claimed to be single and live alone, but you never did know if that was the truth. But a quick surreptitious inspection seemed to confirm that was in indeed the case.

There were no obvious signs of a significant other anywhere. No romantic framed photographs or love tokens dotted around that I could see. I'd excused myself to freshen up, and his bathroom cabinet was bereft of any lady items: no tampons, lotions or potions to give him away. Just a sad-looking can of Lynx, some shaving stuff, paracetamols and a solitary toothbrush in a mug. So, all seemed to be in order.

I returned to the lounge post-inspection and made myself comfortable on his lumpy brown leather sofa, happy to observe that it was suitably free of scatter cushions – another sign there was no lady on the scene, and he was indeed single.

"Would you like a brandy as well as the coffee?"

He questioned from the kitchen, his voice muffled as he

rooted nosily round in his cupboards.

"Yes please."

It was Friday tomorrow, so why the hell not? OK, maybe not technically the weekend, but everyone knew that a minute past Friday lunchtime was just a downward descent to the weekend anyway. Friday afternoons in my experience were always a bit of a write-off.

I heard him instruct Alexa on what music to play. Suddenly the room filled with the dulcet tones of the walrus of love himself, Mr Barry White. It was pretty obvious what Mervyn had in mind by playing this music, but I suppose it could have been worse: he could have whacked on a bit of the Vengaboys or something equally cheesy, and then I wouldn't have had a clue if it was seduction or a skip around the shagpile he was after

He was suddenly beside me, passing me a piping cup of coffee and shooting me an equally steamy look. I thanked him as he placed a short-stemmed glass generously filled with cognac on the nest of tables beside me. As he reached over, his lips trailed butterfly kisses across my cheek. A tingle shot through my body, prompting an electric shock to my nether regions. That was certainly a jump-start all right.

And then we kissed. And it was lovely. He was an excellent kisser: just the right amount of pressure and not too much tongue for a first encounter.

I had learnt by my age that most men in their thirties and beyond had learnt the subtle art of kissing. Probably coached in canoodling by dissatisfied former girlfriends. The days of teenage testosterone and tongue sandwiches were long gone, thank goodness.

He pulled me to my feet, almost spilling my coffee in the

process. Ooh, he was masterful. And before I knew it his hands were running up and down the length of my body, locating the concealed zip on my dress. With one fluid motion it was down, and the dress fell effortlessly to the floor in a silken satin heap.

I was now standing before him resplendent in only my matching satin bra and panties and my high heels. His eyes feasted over every inch of my near naked body as if he was ravenous. His hands ran over my breasts encased in their satin cups.

His voice was deep with desire.

"Exquisite, simply exquisite."

We continued kissing, my hands finding the few remaining unopened buttons on his shirt and quickly rectifying that. Within a couple of seconds it hung loose, showcasing his muscular chest and well-defined abs.

He looked so delicious, he simply had to be fattening.

Before I knew what was happening, he had kicked off his jeans. He had dressed ready for action, as beneath the denim he was going commando, his soldier standing to attention and proudly saluting me. I was glad to see there were no socks in sight, on his feet or otherwise.

This was turning out to be an incredibly erotic night. I was glad I had decided to dip my toe back in the dating scene again. This was beating Netflix and n'er do well criminals any day of the week.

And then, like a scene plucked straight from a romantic movie, he swept me up into his arms as if I weighed as little as a feather, which certainly wasn't the case, and carried me effortlessly to his bedroom, kissing me as he went. I had the distinct feeling this was going to be the best night of my life.

As it turned out, it wasn't the best night of my life; but then again, it wasn't the worst either.

In the grainy light of early morning, things appeared a little less seductively sepia-tinged than they had previously. Less *Dirty Dancing* and more dirty duvet, if you know what I mean.

I blinked against the semi-darkness, trying to refocus my eyes. As his room became clearer, I nearly snapped them closed again, wishing to return to the halcyon memories of the previous night.

There was a major disconnect to what I had experienced last night as to what I was encountering now.

His bachelor pad, which had looked so masculine chic previously in the soft glow of candlelight, now had a distinct air of neglect about it. His bedroom's muted brown and cream shades, which had looked so chocolatey chic under the influence of gin and gentle lighting, now had a grottiness to them which was rather less than appealing.

There were piles of clothes heaped in the corners that could have been clean or in need of a whirl in the washing machine it was impossible to tell. Like a teenager he appeared to favour the floor-drobe rather than actually hanging his clothes up.

I slowly drew myself up into a sitting position, conscious of being naked beneath the bedding. I could hear the excited chatter of young children outside the bedroom window, making their way to school. Bloody hell, what time was it? I really needed to get myself to work.

My head was fuzzy, like a mist of fog had settled in my brain. I gave it a little shake to try and clear it. That did nothing but make me feel a bit queasy and likely to throw up my Yorkshire tapas from the previous night. They hadn't been too appetising going down, so I could only imagine what they would be like coming back up all over his pillowcases.

If I was brutally honest - and considering how brutal my hangover was, that was the best policy - the sex had been satisfactory at best. A definite 7½ out of ten. Not amazing, but not atrocious either. It had been mildly diverting, and considering the amount of gin I had sunk, I knew that achieving the Big O was highly optimistic, if not mission impossible.

But overall, it had been adequate. A solid enough performance. I wasn't over the moon that he had referred to my boobs as "honkers" or his penis as "the ham candle", but I suppose nobody's perfect.

But talking of my less than perfect man, where was he? I really needed to be getting going, but I didn't want to dress and desert him without a single word. I was nothing if not polite.

A few laboured grunts alerted me to his location. He was quite clearly in the bathroom. I heard the distinct plop of poo hitting porcelain.

"Mervyn?"

"Lila, I'll be out in a minute. I just had to nip one off. It's all that beige food we had last night. It's playing havoc with my bowels. I don't know what I was thinking. I normally only eat clean, and my system is revolting against all those processed foods."

He was right. Something was certainly revolting, and that was the smell emanating from below the bathroom door. If his aura had a colour this morning, it would be toxic waste green.

I prided myself on having a robust constitution, but that smell was enough to knock me sick.

I took a quick gander at his bedroom again. He might like to eat clean, but that's as far as it went. I dreaded to think when he had last given the room a good wipe down with a cloth. I was sure the only Mr Muscle that had been in this room was his good self in his boxer shorts.

"Don't rush yourself, but I need to be going or I'll be late for work. Don't worry, I can give you a call later."

I was more than happy to skip the small talk and tea this morning. If this bedroom was anything to go by, I wasn't taking a chance on stopping for breakfast. Last night I would have put money on him being a smoked salmon and champagne sort of guy, but I'd rather changed opinion on that. I think I was more likely to get salmonella than smoked salmon in this gaff.

I jumped out of bed in one graceful movement. Far more graceful than I was feeling, with a grunge band tuning up in my skull.

I had a plan to execute, which was to locate my errant underwear, don my dress and dash straight out of the door. Thankfully I soon found my dress strewn over a tatty armchair in the corner of the room, and my underwear had been kicked across the floor next to it. But where were my shoes? I must have left them in the other room, discarded during the throes of passion.

Worse was still to come. As I grabbed my knickers and was stepping into them, careful not to stagger against the little waves of nausea that kept assaulting me like a slap to the gut, I noticed a scruffy brown something under the corner of the bed base. It looked furry and feral. I recoiled in horror. His room must be even dirtier than I had first thought. It had to be a rat, of all things, with half its body sticking out from the bottom of the unwashed under-sheet.

I screamed: a blood-curdling noise that immediately silenced the children outside the bedroom window. I hated to scream, but I really couldn't help myself. There was only one thing in life that I was truly scared of (well, two if you included upper arm cellulite), and that was rats.

I didn't want to go all girly, but that's exactly what I did. I screamed with as shrill and high-pitched a screech as I once did in primary school when David Johnson called me a "ploppy head" and pulled my pigtails. I just couldn't take it. Spotting a rodent whilst suffering a raging hangover was enough to finish me off.

I heard Mervyn jump off the toilet with an audible gasp of shock, and without flushing it he dashed to my aid like a defecating defender rushing to his damsel in distress.

"A rat, it's a rat!"

The scream that came from me was so high and shrieky I barely recognised my own voice,

"You need to get..."

The words instantly died in my mouth as I clapped eyes on Mervyn in all his morning glory.

Rather like his bedroom, my dashing Greek god from the night before was looking somewhat less appealing in the cruel morning light.

His tanned skin now appeared rather blotchy, like he'd dropped a couple of used teabags on himself. And as my eyes travelled over the rather grubby bedding, I realised that most of his "natural" tan must have come straight out of a bottle and was now staining the sheets like a dirty protest.

This was bad enough, but alas there was much worse still to come.

Mervyn, who had sported such lustrous shining locks the previous night, now appeared to be somewhat receding in the hairline department. And when I say receding, it went back so far that they were probably discussing it on the History channel.

And how on earth had he become so follicly challenged in the last eight hours or so? I'd heard of rapid hair loss, but that was taking the biscuit; in fact, the whole bloody bakery.

Apart from a few strands of a comb-over plastered over his pate, Mervyn was as bald as my lady garden was after I had attacked it with my Bic razor in my pre-date preparations.

"My hair!"

He jumped across the room butt-naked, still holding a piece of toilet roll, and grabbed straight for the rat.

I shrieked again in abject terror.

He was on it in a flash, like a pigeon on a chip and wrestled bravely with the rodent, and within a few seconds he was the worthy victor, holding it aloft like a champion fighter showcasing his trophy.

Only it would now appear that it wasn't in fact a rat. No, it was something far more terrifying. It was his wig. His wig was indeed ratty-looking, but not of the rodent variety after all. My hirsute Jonny Depp was looking far more Danny DeVito with each passing second.

He plopped the brown hairpiece unceremoniously onto his head, where it sat at a bit of an angle like run-over roadkill. It resembled a mangy old housecat stretched out on a radiator.

And rather like a cat, his mouth now appeared to resemble one's arse. What had happened to his lovely dazzling smile? It was then I noticed his teeth, or should I say lack thereof. His false teeth that had been so realistic and appealing last night were sitting on the bedside cabinet where I had been snoozing obliviously next to them for hours. My Jonny Depp was now morphing into Jonny Vegas, right in front of my very eyes.

But the worst and most unforgivable thing was what he was sporting on his feet. He had squeezed his size 9 trotters into my beautiful red stilettos and was stumbling around the room like a pig in a ginnel. And this hog was hobbling around in four hundred quid's worth of designer footwear that I was never ever going to wear again.

It wasn't often I was lost of words, but this had rendered me completely speechless. Coco Chanel was quoted as saying "a woman with good shoes is never ugly." She may well have been right on that score but unfortunately the same could not be said about men, well this man at the very least.

I had to get out of here, this very second if not sooner.

I knew it was Friday, but was it also the 13th? Because I seriously felt like I was stuck slap bang in the middle of a horror movie.

Of course, I had no choice but to wear my shoes to get home. Much as it pained me to put them on, it had pained Mervyn even more. The look of tangible sorrow on his face as he'd eventually prised them off and returned them to me, the rightful owner, had been bordering on the heartbreaking.

It had taken monumental restraint on my part not to bop him on the beak when I had discovered how badly my beautiful shoes had been stretched out of shape.

It hurt my pride to realise how chuffed I'd been to see Mervyn checking out my shapely legs in the pub, because now I knew he had been eagerly imagining how his own hairy ones would look, resplendent in my sexy slingbacks.

I had physically shuddered as I put them on, still warm from the previous occupant. But I had no intention of walking along the mean streets of Leeds in my bare feet, so I had little choice. Second-hand stilettos were still preferable to my naked toes sliding over an abandoned chip wrapper, or worse.

I managed to order an Uber to pick me up from the end of

his street, so as soon as my shoes were firmly on, I was out the door, running like a startled whippet.

There were definitely no "catch up soon" or "we'll have to do it again" pleasantries coming from my vicinity. Nope, I legged it, slamming the door behind me. The only way I would be seeing Merv the Swerve soon would be in my nightmares.

I quietly endured the Uber journey of shame back to my house, trying my hardest to drown out the cheerful wittering from the driver. As I sat in the back of the vehicle, I felt a million miles away from the confident and chic woman from the night before. Sitting shivering in my short dress and smudged make-up, I felt small and timid and very, very alone; as if my moral compass was dented and my dreams along with it.

I had gone out with such high expectations for my date, and it had ended in complete disaster. A farce of comical proportions. But normally this wouldn't have brought me down so much. I had always known that Mervyn and I weren't destined to be soulmates, and even if the date had gone perfectly, we would probably never have met again.

OK, I hadn't expected what had actually happened, and who would? But the confident me would by now be realising that it would make a great anecdote to tell the girls on our next boozy lunch, and I would already be relegating it to the back of my mind, eager to get on with the rest of my day. But I couldn't help it: I felt emotionally bruised, and it was a feeling I just wasn't used to and couldn't shake off.

And then it hit me like a bolt of lightning. I missed Seb.

Chapter 14

Time trotted on as it invariably does, rather like I imagined Mervyn would be trotting in a pair of ladies' pumps to his next unsuspecting victim.

It had been a couple of weeks since my date from hell with him. I now referred to this encounter as "my meet with Merv the Swerve". As swerving away as fast as possible would be my modus operandi on ever seeing that particular gentleman again.

That one night with him had completely put me off arranging any more dates with prospective suitors, fearful that they might turn out to be just as bad or, perish the thought, even worse.

I really didn't feel equipped to throw myself into the dating pool again: too scared I would belly flop right into another nutter. But I knew it wasn't just the fear of all the single freaks out there that walked amongst us, posing as eligible bachelors. No, it was also because I'd come to a startling realisation. And that was the fact that I had feelings for Seb.

I had sidelined him for so long, been convinced we just weren't right for each other; when really I should have recognised what had been under my nose the whole time - that we were meant to be together.

After Duncan, I had locked my heart away, deep within me. I didn't want to face my fears, that was the whole point, why would I want to face something that scared me? And I was scared, scared of being hurt once again.

I didn't need love; all it did was damage you in the end. I was happy as I was, in control of my life and my relationships. I set the rules. There were far too many perils to falling in love, thank you very much. Much safer to settle for casual flings with attractive men. Fun that would never prove fatal to my heart. The very heart which still bore the bruises from entrusting it so completely to my ex.

I had convinced myself that Seb and I would only ever be friends, could only ever be friends.

He was just too nice, too dull, too thoroughly dependable for me. Where was the excitement in that? But now I realised that my self-preservation had built up a wall of excuses. A wall I now wanted to dismantle, brick by brick, until it tumbled down completely.

I had believed I was protecting myself by never seeing Seb as anything but a work colleague and friend. I had placed him in a box I felt comfortable with, and that is where he had stayed, closed in it, for years.

But that was me protecting myself, never giving "us" a chance. I wanted to open that box now, see if love would pop out like a jack-in-the-box; or would it be a metaphorical slap in the face? I needed to take that chance.

I had always thought Seb would be there as my friend, or whatever I wanted, when I wanted it. Things would always be on my terms. I had never envisaged him with a girlfriend, but now I realised how smug and entitled I had really been.

Seb and Jocasta had now been seeing each other for several

weeks. Although it had only started with that informal pub quiz and a bite of food, it seemed they really clicked and then had been out and about to different venues on quite a few occasions.

Seb was of course still his normal lovely self. He hadn't changed a jot in his attitude towards me, but for some reason I felt rather awkward and ill at ease around him.

Never one to lack confidence, I had suddenly become a little tongue-tied and stiff when chatting with him. My laugh appeared false and hollow to my ears. It was as if the power dynamic had shifted and the world had tilted slightly on its axis.

It wasn't just the fact he was seeing Jocasta, although I had to admit I was far from happy about that. It was because I had realised my depth of feelings for him.

I couldn't believe I had been so blind for so many years: always believing he would be forever waiting for me on the sidelines, his life on hold until I eventually decided it suited me, snapped my fingers and he would come running.

I had been such a fool. What is it they always say – you always want what you cannot have. And I did want him, far more than I had ever desired a designer dress or craved the latest "must have" handbag. All those irrelevant meaningless things I had once considered so important.

I was sitting at my desk, aware of the mountain of papers piled up in front of me and yet unable to concentrate my mind on anything but thoughts of Seb.

My workload was building by the day, like the leaning tower of transcripts, and I really needed to focus on it to keep myself distracted from pining away like some lovestruck puppy.

I felt as if I were Snow White, had finally woken from my sleep to the reality of how things really were. But it hadn't been the kiss from my dashing prince that had finally roused me from my slumber; oh no, it had been a 6 foot 2 slaphead wearing my ruby slippers that made me see sense – that Seb was my prince and always had been. But alas, my prince had a princess of his very own and she just happened to be the bitch from across the office.

And speaking, or at least thinking, of the Devil had summoned Jocasta in all her simpering glory.

After the briefest of knocks at my door, without giving me a chance to respond, her head poked around it. The way it jutted through reminded me of the Punch and Judy shows I had watched as a child at the seaside, and I sincerely wished I had a big stick à la Mr Punch to give her noggin a good bash at this precise moment.

"Hello, Lila, just wanted to remind you about the spa afternoon tomorrow. Hope you haven't forgotten?"

Bloody hell, I absolutely had forgotten. I felt a sinking feeling come over me. There was nothing I wanted less than to spend the afternoon half naked being massaged in the vicinity of this vixen, or encased in mud for that matter, as I imagined there would be enough mud-slinging as it was.

I answered her through gritted teeth and a rictus grimace.

"Yes, of course I hadn't forgotten, I'm really excited for it."

I doubted very much whether this excitement was evident on my pained face.

She walked right into my office now, she was carrying a thick cream coloured padded envelope under one arm.

I hated to admit it, but the woman looked good. I'm sure she could barely breathe in her two-piece fitted fishtail suit, cut short and extremely tight. It was teamed with a cream blouse that was verging on the scandalous from the number of buttons undone. The suit was a tartan print, one I didn't recognise, possibly the McSluttish clan.

"Me too Lila, I'm looking forward to it so much."

She let out a deep sigh, as if she had the weight of the world on her narrow tartan shoulders.

"January is such a dire month; it will be lovely to have a bit of a pamper."

I smiled at her stiffly. I really didn't want to get into conversation with the woman I knew I'd be stuck with tomorrow. But for now I just wanted her to piss off back to her own desk.

I wasn't to be so lucky. She thrust the envelope she had been carrying towards me, mere inches from my nose.

"Mr Fluck has asked if you wouldn't mind dropping these important documents off with his clients at Hogan & McKenzie? I would do it myself of course, but he's asked specifically for you to. He wants to have a meeting with me in his office in..."

She paused for a second to glance at the gaudy designer watch hanging from her slim wrist.

"About five minutes."

She let out a little fake, self-conscious giggle.

"I seem to be quite in demand at present."

I could feel my hackles rising. Why was Fluck having a meeting with her? She was a junior in the firm, after all. And when had I suddenly become the office lackey?

Was this Fluck purposely exerting his authority over me in front of a more junior staff member because he was still pissed off with me about the fashion show? Or was it something else? I didn't know, but I certainly wasn't chuffed with the situation, that was for sure. And I certainly wasn't going to let this little madam know the extent of my feelings.

I took the padded envelope from her with a stiff nod.

"Fine, I'll do it now. I was going out anyway, so it's not an inconvenience."

This was a lie; I'd had no intention of leaving my office for the remainder of the day, not because I was feeling lazy, but simply because of a stronger motivation to sit on my arse for the afternoon. However, it made me feel slightly more in control if she thought I wasn't going out of my way to run an errand on her say so.

I left the room, slipped on my warm winter coat and busied myself wrapping my scarf around my neck numerous times in preparation for bracing the elements of a dreary Yorkshire January.

My mind wandered to Seb. I wondered if he was busy. I doubted very much whether Fluck would have insisted on him having to take time out his day to deliver paperwork to another firm.

Then I suddenly spotted him. He was shaking hands with a client and showing them towards the door, making polite small talk as they went. His glasses were perched on the end of his nose in an almost comical way, and I felt a sudden unexpected wave of affection for him.

He ushered the client out of the building, and as he turned to return to his office our eyes locked for a mere second. Not long at all, but long enough for my heart to leap as if I'd just glugged a triple espresso at breakneck speed.

I scolded myself inwardly. Seriously, I needed to get a grip. But I felt like a lovestruck teenager clapping eyes on their crush in the back of geography class. I hoped I wasn't blushing too, as I did back then.

There was something different about him though, something I couldn't quite fathom in the brief moment our eyes connected.

But with a sudden jolt of realisation, I knew what it was. Seb looked good, no strike that; Seb looked bloody great. As if he had just stepped out of an advert for male grooming products. All handsome and rugged and, yes, there was no denying it, stylish too.

Gone were his garish woollen jumpers and half-mast corduroy trousers. Now he was seriously spruced up and dressed in an elegant crisp white shirt with fitted charcoal grey suit that somehow showcased the blueness of his sparkling eyes to perfection.

On second thoughts, never mind the male grooming advert, he could have stepped straight out of a Sunday supplement on elegant male living. He had most certainly had what I think was commonly called a "glow up".

I felt a sudden desire to give myself a sharp pinch to check I wasn't dreaming.

His back was already to me as he made his way down the corridor. But I had to stop him, had to say something, anything. I hated the awkwardness between us, whether it was all in my head or not.

"Seb, you look good...different."

He stopped abruptly and turned on his heel to face me. His demeanour seemed to be tinged with embarrassment.

"Yeah... well... um, Jocasta gave me a few tips on things, told me how I should dress, you know, smarten myself up a little. It took me a while to take her advice; you know me, I'm stuck in my ways, but it was high time I bought a few new things as my clothes were so ancient some were dropping to bits. So I let her take me shopping."

I felt as if I'd been physically punched. Shopping? She had taken him shopping?

I would have felt less hurt if she'd taken him to a Soho strip club dressed in full-on gimp attire. Shopping was and would always be "my" thing. I should have been the one to share that with him, not her!

"You look good."

I had to say it. I had no choice, because the truth was that he really bloody did.

"But I *always* liked the way you looked."

Seb seemed to relax a little, his eyebrows becoming rather less knitted together. But then again that might have been just down to the fact that there was so much less of them now. His monobrow of old, stretching across his face like a slumbering slug, was now divided into two neat arches of well-plucked perfection.

I cast my gaze down to his hands, which always well-presented now boasted the neatest manicured nails I'd ever seen. Quite clearly Jocasta had talked Seb into visiting the beauty salon too.

"Come on, Lila, you've got to be kidding me, you've ripped the shit out of me for years about the way I dress. Saying I've got as much style as Jeremy Clarkson wearing his grandad's hand-me-downs."

I couldn't argue with the facts. I had mercilessly teased him throughout our friendship about his style, his lack of knowledge on all things sartorial. But strangely now, seeing him standing here looking so elegant and dashing, I felt choked with sadness for the Seb I'd lost. And I had lost him. I knew that now.

He didn't seem to notice though and was tugging at the

sleeve of his suit jacket, clearly impressed.

"I never realised that clothes could actually be so smart yet still so comfortable. It always felt like some of my jumpers were so itchy and intolerable that they actually hated me, like they were bearing a grudge."

He let go of his sleeve and smoothed it down carefully, his expression clearly impressed.

"Yes, I wasn't sure to start off, but I must admit I'm beginning to get used to the new more stylish me. I've even had women talk to me as if suddenly they can see me. I've been pretty invisible to women my entire life, and now suddenly... poof, as if by magic, they can see me. It's shocking, really. I never knew clothes could make such a difference."

I felt an ache in my heart for his childlike enthusiasm. He was in his fifties before he had cottoned on to what us women had known since the playground: that fashion could really elevate you; not just your look, but your outlook too.

I smiled weakly. Seb, my devoted loyal lapdog, had morphed into a veritable fox, a salt and pepper-tinged hottie of the highest order, from his elegant tailoring to his sparkling blue eyes, like flashing gems, now beautifully showcased by his well-groomed brows. His skin looked fresh and glowy too. There was no escaping the fact that, ding dong, he was dishy.

He could literally make me swoon, like a Victorian woman suffering an attack of the vapours. Why had I never realised just how handsome he was? It was as if I had been under a spell. And now I wanted him, he was no longer mine. Now he was with the wicked witch and her spell was well and truly cast.

"You're going to the spa with Jo tomorrow, aren't you?"

Jo? That made my heart break a little more. They were sounding much too familiar for my liking.

"I am, and I'm really looking forward to it."

That was an out and out lie. I was getting so good at fibbing, they just tripped off my tongue like baby ducklings tumbling over each other on an icy pond.

Seb nodded his head.

"I'm so glad. I knew you two would be OK. She really is a nice girl. She's a great listener too, and she even gets on with Adam, and nobody apart from me ever likes him. She tucked into an enormous portion of his home-made shepherd's pie, so she's an absolute star in his book."

I kept silent, but inwardly I was fuming. I knew without a doubt that Jocasta was up to something.

There was a good reason why nobody liked Adam, and it wasn't just his monotonous whine of a voice and his question-able body odour. He really was the dullest chap you could ever have the misfortune to run into. The "yawn of Yorkshire", I had even heard him referred to on occasion. There was only Seb who really liked him, and sometimes I felt even he just tolerated him; but then again Seb liked everyone. It was part of his charm.

Maybe I should have made more of an effort with Adam the few times I had met him. But honestly there was only so much sci-fi chat I could stomach before I wished I had the kinks in my own time machine worked out, so I could escape the monotony of the conversation and transport myself back to a week last Tuesday.

Now, though, I was feeling very different. I wished I hadn't poked so much fun at Seb's beige-based diet and teased him and Adam for being so boring. Now the prospect of enjoying a mash-based meal with Seb sounded just the ticket, even with Adam lurking in the background.

I had always known Seb was a good man. But now he was good-looking one too.

Why had I wasted so much time with younger flings, when the perfect man was right under my nose the whole time? For someone who classed themselves as an intelligent woman, I had really been a fool.

Lottie had always told me that Seb was the right man for me, and I had repeatedly laughed it off, forever thinking my dear friend a little naïve and just an incurable old romantic at heart. She had told me that I was just scared of commitment, and I in turn had quipped back that commitment should only ever be reserved for mental health facilities.

I had maintained that Seb would never be right for me. I needed someone who would challenge me, and the only way I would ever be challenged by Seb was in the sports round at the pub quiz. But I had been wrong all along. And Lottie had been the one in the right. She had even warned me that if I didn't snap him up, then someone else would. I had arrogantly thought that notion ridiculous, but she had been spot on. If only I had listened to her.

I passed by Fluck's office on my way to the main exit. His door was slightly ajar, and I could hear a startling high-pitched squawking noise. It sounded to my ears like a parrot on the loose. Had one bizarrely flown through the open window and landed slap bang on Fluck's desk? But no, it was just the dulcet tones of Jocasta Jennings laughing.

Through the slit in the door, I could just make them both out.

She was sitting across from the old slimeball. He was evidently speaking, although I couldn't quite hear what was being said; then once again Jocasta nearly slid off her chair, convulsed with peals of laughter. I knew that whatever he was saying could never ever be that funny.

I suddenly realised that Fluck was out of his chair and striding purposefully towards the open door. Before I could hurtle through the building's main doors and escape into the world beyond, his door was unceremoniously slammed shut, right in my face.

I felt like a peeping tom caught with my hand gusset-deep in the knicker drawer. My face flamed for a second, and I felt hot tears sting my eyes.

What was happening to me? It must be my hormones or something. I never ever cried, not even as a child when watching *Watership Down*, and boy was that film traumatic for an eight-year-old.

I always took comfort in the fact that I was so tough; but now it appeared I was about as tough as a wagyu steak. I just felt wretched. If this was a competition, then I was definitely on the losing side. It seemed that woman had it all: my Seb, and now the boss too, eating out of her hand like a devoted donkey.

I hated to admit I was jealous about Fluck too, but I really was. I had never been his biggest fan, but at least I felt we had a grudging respect for each other professionally.

We had worked together for years, after all. But seeing him with Jocasta, he seemed so utterly charmed by her: like a delighted little boy at the ice cream van who had been offered a Flake as well as sprinkles on his double cone. And her two scoops certainly seemed to be mouth-watering to men.

As I left the building to deliver the letter, like an office junior, I decided to give Lottie a call. I was keeping my fingers crossed that she would be able to meet me for a drink after work. I could really do with seeing a friendly face. Even if she was going to say, "I told you so."

Chapter 15

I took a deep steadying breath as I entered the establish-ment where Lottie had chosen for us to meet. It was called The Honourable Lawyer, and that title wasn't the only questionable thing about the place.

The smell of damp and despair assailed my nostrils as soon as my leather court shoes hit the sticky floral carpet. The décor was a dismal brown colour, most probably from decades of tobacco smoke clinging for grim life to the ugly flock wallpaper. It clearly hadn't had a freshen-up for many a long year. The jar of yellowing pickled eggs behind the bar looked older than I was, but no doubt better preserved.

It was one of those low rent, spit and sawdust places where you had to wipe your feet on the way out; the sort of estab-lishment my mother would refer to, in a hushed whisper, as "rather uncouth".

It had never moved on with the times, stuck firmly in the 1970s; and from a quick look at the collection of characters propping up the bar slurping pints of dark liquid, that's when most of them had been in their prime.

It was located just around the corner from work, so had been convenient enough to get to, but that was its only saving grace. In all honesty, I would happily have walked much further in my high heels if it meant bypassing this joint and finding somewhere slightly more sophisticated to have a tipple.

Lottie had always had a soft spot for the place. She really had some questionable taste at times. She felt it had "character", and I suppose she was right on that point: it had character going on in spades. In fact, many of the characters looked as if they had just wandered off the set of *Shameless*.

I pulled the collar of my faux fur coat up around my neck, as if I had been hit by a sudden blast of cold wind, even though the temperature in The Honourable Lawyer was far from chilly. In fact, after leaving the frosty street behind and entering the pub, the warm and muggy atmosphere hit me full-on like a blast from an oven.

I just felt a little out of my comfort zone in my vintage spotted coat and four-inch heels; a bit of a fish out of water in a place where the regular clientele all seemed to favour a more relaxed way of dressing: mostly stained T-shirts and tracksuits. Although they seemed to be big advocates of sportswear, I would hazard a guess that none of them had participated in any sports since before the pub had last seen a lick of emulsion.

OK, so my attire might be a little avant-garde for the place, but so be it. I shook off my feelings of discomfort. My mother had always instilled in me the ability to fit in whatever the surroundings, or at the least to try your hardest to give the impression that you did.

I loved my coat and felt a million dollars in it. It was 1950s-inspired, cream-coloured faux fur with large black spots, which I had been delighted to discover in a lovely little vintage shop in Ilkley several years before.

A gruff voice rang out across the bar.

"Oi, Cruella, show us your puppies, love."

My head shot around to locate the owner of the flat vowels. A middle-aged chap at the bar in a zip-up navy velour tracksuit straining over his beer belly and a distinct lack of teeth was winking at me in what I feared was his idea of flirtation. I shuddered inwardly and pretended I hadn't heard him as I studied the row of optics carefully, before ordering myself a large gin and tonic from the bored-looking barman.

Alas, my velour-suited dreamboat didn't seem to take the hint.

"I'm only having a laugh; you look proper champion in your fancy fur coat. Let me get you that drink, pet, I'm in the chair."

I turned to give him a saccharine sweet smile.

"Well, if you're in the chair, let's hope it's electric."

I paid for my gin myself, and with his drinking buddies' laughter still ringing in my ears, I turned sharply on my heel and strode off to find somewhere to sit, as far away from Mr Tragic Tracksuit as was possible. I really prayed that Lottie would hurry the fuck up.

I settled myself at a small round wooden table with a couple of torn beermats under the legs to steady it against the uneven floor and surveyed my surroundings. Apart from my delectable new boyfriend at the bar and his gaggle of mates, only one other table was occupied. A group of surly-looking teenagers were huddled together with bottles of lager clutched in their grubby hands and open bags of crisps being passed around. For the most part they were an unsavoury-looking bunch. Three young men with perpetually angry faces were deep in conversation. One of them looked vaguely familiar to me, but I couldn't quite place where from.

Next to them sat a bored-looking girl, probably only about

nineteen, but already with an air of life having worn her down. Her pasty face was pale under her make-up and mauve-coloured lipstick, and she was picking at a scab on an arm as skinny as a pipe cleaner. She ran a hand through her lank shoulder-length mousy blonde hair with its sapphire blue streaks, the roots darker than the demons I felt she might well be repressing. She stared vacantly into space.

In another lifetime she might have been an incredibly pretty girl. I wondered what had happened to bring her to this grubby bar at 5:47 p.m. on a chilly January afternoon: maybe rebelling against her strict upbringing, or perhaps just a sliding-door effect where if she had just made another choice at another time, she could now be sipping colourful cocktails in one of the up-scale bars in the gentrified part of Leeds city centre.

My heart went out to her. I knew only too well how hard it could be to be a teenager in this day and age. My career had shown me that on many occasions.

Times were not as carefree and innocent as when I had been a girl. We had felt so hard done by back then, but in reality it was the youth of today that really had the short end of the shitty stick: a life lived on social media, never able to escape from the magnetic pull of it, never ever feeling quite good enough.

I inwardly shuddered again in my thick coat. I was so thankful my life had been filled with *Sweet Dreams* fiction novels, *Grange Hill* and listening to the Top Ten on a Sunday night, recording my favourite tracks of the time on radio cassettes. Not like today's youth, recording their every intimate moment in little bitesize, or rather "shitesize", snippets on TikTok, just long enough to keep the attention span of a generation reared on instant gratification.

Despite myself, I felt inclined to say an inward prayer for

this girl. There was just something vulnerable about her that touched me, and I really hoped she would be OK.

I glanced back at her companions, who were now in a heated disagreement about something or other. The shorter one with a shock of curly ginger hair jumped up from his bar stool, giving me a bit of a start.

"OK Doddy, chill, man. I'll get the fucking beers in, even though it's your round. I know you ain't got no money."

He sucked on his teeth noisily and swaggered over to the bar, his fists firmly thrust in the pockets of his scruffy ripped jeans, probably designed to look that bad.

Doddy? Then it came to me in a flash. The reason I had felt a prickle of recognition when observing the youths was that this ratty-looking individual with a razor-cut hairstyle and an even sharper tongue, seated to the left of the girl, was none other than Alfie Dodds. He had been in the same year at school as my son Thomas. Alfie had been trouble back then too, getting expelled in his last year for dealing weed to the Year 8s.

I knew Seb had already encountered him professionally on a few occasions at the firm. I had seen him myself once, lurking sulkily in reception as he waited for his appointment. He was a thoroughly nasty piece of work. Low-level drug dealing, shoplifting and generally disturbing the peace were his favoured ways to pass the time.

I took a large swig of my drink. It hit the spot nicely: just what the doctor ordered. Well, not literally, but then again my GP always had a whiff of single malt about him, so who could tell?

I unzipped my purse to put away the change from my drink. As I dropped it in, I lost grip of the purse for a second and a couple of coins scattered noisily across the table, along with three folded twenty-pound notes.

Although I used my bank cards mostly, I still liked to have cash on me too in case of emergencies. I was old school that way. More like my mother than I cared to admit. She was always pontificating about the "wretched" banks and how anyone with the sense they were born with would have a little something stashed away under their mattress or behind the sofa cushions.

Alfie Dodds had been slouching past my table on the way to the Gents' toilet, but the sound of the coins hitting the table had caught his attention. His ears pricked up like a tatty terrier's, and upon spotting the folded notes his eyes became dark and beady like chips of flint.

He slowly looked me up and down, taking in my silk blouse and expensive necklace. He turned towards me, placing both hands on the table, and shot me a sneering smile obviously intended to rattle me.

"'Ere, darling, give us one of those notes; you look like you can well afford it."

Darling? The cheek of the young whippersnapper. I couldn't believe the nerve of him. He was actually trying to scrounge money off me with menaces.

I eyeballed him, my voice as cold as the ice melting in my drink.

"I don't think so, young man."

He leaned in further, until his face was mere inches away from me. I could smell the pungent odour of cheese and onion crisps on his breath. He laughed in what I've no doubt he felt was a threatening manner, his body language deliberately aggressive.

"I don't think you could stop me if you tried. I could take

anything I wanted from you, just like that."

His eyes roved over my body, and he clicked his fingers to demonstrate his point.

The young blonde girl piped up, her voice wavering.

"Stop it, Alfie, you're not funny. Just leave the lady alone."

"Shut up, Bella, it's got nowt to do with you."

Bella. The girl's name was Bella. It suited her, she really was quite beautiful. Like a faded rose in the manure that was this public house. There were tears in the corner of her eyes as she pleaded with him not to make any trouble.

I was going to have to teach young Alfred Dodds a lesson. An idea was slowly forming in my head. Best buckle up, you impudent little shite. Lila Glover is about to go into full Rottweiler mode.

I met his feral gaze and maintained eye contact, never wavering for a second. It was like a shoot-up in the saloon bar in an old Western film, akin to the ones I would watch with my dad on Sunday afternoons when I was a kid. Only it was our eyes, not Colt .45s that were our weapon of choice. I curled my lip back to match the snarl he had previously given me.

"Really, Mr Dodds, you should think very carefully before you choose your next words."

The shock on his face nearly made me snort with laughter. Not so cocksure now. No, he looked absolutely terrified now, like he might drop a load in his low-slung pants. Clearly, he was thinking how the hell did this posh bird know his name? The anxiety and paranoia from the weed he had smoked earlier beginning to take hold.

I ramped it up a bit, getting more invested in my role. It was probably not very nice of me, but then again, he certainly wasn't nice either.

He spent his days dealing drugs and intimidating strangers. Hardly the best career path for a young man to take. It might prove to be financially lucrative, but it was morally bankrupt, that was for sure.

My words were slow and dripping with ill-concealed threat:

"You want to be careful, Mr Dodds. The last person who threatened me, well..."

I paused for full on dramatic effect.

"Let's just say it didn't turn out too well for them."

I clicked the side of my phone and within a couple of seconds found the photo I wanted. I laid my handset face up on the table. It displayed the image showcasing Jayne's impressive make-up skills: the picture with the special effects make-up, the one that looked so horrifically realistic. Lottie had forwarded all the images to me after our dinner.

The blood drained from Alfie's face. Clearly Jayne was as good as I thought, and he believed the image to be genuine: of some poor sucker who had been beaten black and blue for some personal misdemeanour. His eyes flicked from the picture up to my face and then back again. I could almost hear his drug-addled brain ticking slowly over, trying to figure out who the hell I was.

His eyes darted back to the phone screen.

"Do...do you work for Bulldog?"

I kept silent, my arms folded across my chest and my face serene. I simply tapped the side of my nose. He could read into that gesture whatever he liked.

"Look, missus, I was just having a little joke. I really don't want no trouble. Please tell Bulldog the stuff that went missing I didn't take it for myself; I still have it and I'll get it back to him as soon as I can. He didn't need to send you here after me."

I could only imagine who "Bulldog" was, but my mind conjured up a pretty repellent character. Whoever he was, I was glad I didn't actually know him or in fact work for him.

Dodds turned towards his companions.

"Come on, leave the beer, we're off. We can get a drink at the Red Lion."

He shook his head quickly, obviously thinking better of this.

"Or somewhere else."

He clearly realised it was a bad idea to let me know where they were headed in case I relayed that information straight back to Mr Bulldog or one of his associates.

And with that they left. Bella gave me a small shy smile as she passed by my table, and I returned it with what I hoped was a friendly, not intimidating, wink.

And then they were gone, Alfie leading the way as he dashed out as fast as his baggy jeans and biker boots would allow. They almost collided with a soggy Lottie, who was just making her way through the stiff outer door into the bar, shaking the rain from her multicoloured umbrella.

"Whoa, slow down there, you almost knocked me over!"

She spotted me sitting at the table and gave a brief wave.

"What's going on there? I don't know what their problem is, but that skinny one at the front was running like a skinned whippet."

I tried not to laugh as I shrugged my shoulders.

"I haven't got the foggiest."

Chapter 16

"I love this place."

Lottie breathed deeply, as if she was smelling the sweetest perfume, not inhaling the pong of stale beer and damp decay.

In her chic trouser suit and with her highlighted toffee-toned hair pulled up into a timeless chignon, she looked about as out of place in this joint as I did. But that didn't bother Lottie. She always saw the good in everything. It was one of the things I loved about her. I often wished I could be more "Lottie".

I wrinkled my nose with displeasure.

"I really don't know how you can love this place; it's got all the charm of an attack of dysentery, and if you order a pickled egg from the jar behind the bar that might become a reality."

She shook her head in disagreement.

"It's just so unpretentious, that's charm enough for me. So many of the new bars are just generic versions on the same theme; they don't have the appeal of a real old-style boozer like this."

She settled herself on the rickety stool across from me and unzipped her purse.

"I'll get us a drink."

She peered at my now empty lipstick stained glass.

"What were you having? A gin and slim?"

"Yeah, but actually I wouldn't mind something else. I don't suppose they do cocktails here, by any chance?"

She was out of her seat and heading for the bar in one graceful move.

"I'll see what I can do."

Five minutes later she returned to our table with two glasses of clear liquid with ice, two bottles of what appeared to be blue drain cleaner and a couple of bags of Scampi-flavoured fries clamped between her teeth.

I looked suspiciously at the table as she spread out the wares.

"I don't want to be rude, but I said I wanted a cocktail, and I dread to think what abomination that is."

She dropped the snacks down on the table beside our "drinks" and laughed.

"This is the best I could do in the cocktail department. It's a double voddie each and a blueberry alcopop to mix. Try it, you might actually like it, and the barman said it would put hairs on your balls."

I glanced over at the barman, who raised his hand to me and grinned. Decidedly more friendly than when I had ordered my previous drink. Hairs on my balls indeed? I wondered if he'd heard the exchange I had with young Alfie and been impressed with how I'd handled myself. Maybe thought me a bit more formidable than he'd first imagined.

I mixed my drink together as Lottie had instructed. It was a taste sensation, all right, and definitely not one likely to be repeated any time soon: like cough syrup with a kick. But kick it did, like an angry mule, and after a few mouthfuls it was hitting the spot nicely. So, I wasn't going to complain too much.

I was champing at the bit to talk about Seb. I knew how much Lottie loved her tea, and for once I had plenty to spill. But I was nothing if not polite, so first asked her about her day. It was always best to engage in a bit of small talk before unpacking the box of crap that was my life.

I was keen to spill my guts, not literally of course, but if I had many more of these "cacktails" it might become my reality.

"How are things going with Leo: you two still as loved up?"

I gave her a little cheeky wink, so she knew exactly what I was getting at.

Lottie blushed adorably at the mention of her man, and a little self-conscious smile played at the corners of her mouth.

"Yes, it's just perfect, I've never been happier."

She gave a little contented sigh that I would have found irritating in anyone else, but Lottie got a pass, I loved her that much.

"I have to pinch myself sometimes: I just can't believe this is really happening to me and this is my life now."

I smiled back at her.

"Well, you deserve it, my darling. He was a long time coming, but your prince rode up on his white charger eventually."

She nodded her head in agreement and took a long sip of her blue drink, barely grimacing at all. She was made of stern stuff, that girl.

But my hard-wired Glover nosiness was getting the better of me and I had to pry a little more.

"And the sex? Still as phenomenal as you first thought?"

Lottie's blush deepened and the smile was back.

"Yes, it's incredible. I feel so relaxed and safe with Leo. In truth, I'm doing stuff that I never did with Daniel."

She looked down at the table and picked at the corners of the tatty beer mat.

"Well, you know, Daniel and I barely had a sex life at all for the last few years, and the odd occasion we did indulge, it was only ever missionary."

She paused to take another hearty swig of her drink and I nodded at her encouragingly.

"It's OK, Lottie, I know you find it difficult talking about s-e-x."

She couldn't help but laugh. I had mouthed the letters of the last word with a comically prudish expression on my face. This had always been a quirk of hers −never actually saying the word "sex", but just whispering the letters as if it was a swear word. She would feel cringingly embarrassed whenever the topic arose.

We could be having a fabulous time on a girls' night out, but as soon as anything risqué was mentioned, Lottie would glance around as if she was worried her mother would jump out from the shadows and give her a good old whack with the family Bible.

So, the fact she was sharing her bedroom antics with me now was a revelation. It just showed how confident and liberated Leo was making her feel. It was remarkable the power that being in a good, equal, loving relationship could bring.

"I tell you, Lila, I was the equivalent of a sexual starfish: only ever one position, flat on my back, legs akimbo and barely moving for the whole four minutes it took him to lift my nightie and get the deed done and dusted."

I cringed at this. Lottie really had been shortchanged in the whole Daniel department. Not only had he been a womanising knobhead, but he had treated her like a doormat rather than his wife. And now it transpired that on the extremely rare occasion that they ever indulged in conjugal headboard rattling, it had lasted no longer than the time it took to boil the kettle. And quite clearly never got as hot.

To see Lottie now lifted my spirits. She was blushing, partly from opening up about her sex life and admitting she now actually had one, and partly because of the alcohol. After the lengthy hiatus from all things rumpy pumpy, she was making up for lost time. And to put it politely, it, or rather she, had been a long time coming.

Lottie played with the paper straw in her drink.

"I even like sucking his...you know."

She still wasn't as liberated as I had hoped: clearly saying the word "cock" was just that little step too far out of her comfort zone.

"I never really did that with Daniel. The fact it was called a 'job' I thought was reason enough. It always felt like just another chore I had to do, like the never-ending stack of dishes to be washed or scrubbing the toilet. But it's different with Leo: I can't get enough of it. Everything about him is delicious, even that."

My mind wandered back to my mother's advice to me when I had first started seriously dating, many moons ago. She had taken me to one side and sagely imparted her nugget of wisdom, like she was bestowing the greatest gift a mother could give to her only daughter.

"Only ever go down for diamonds, my darling. That's the best advice you'll ever get."

That had been my mother's opinion on all things carnal. It was simply a transaction between two willing partners, quid pro quo: if he was getting something, you would need to be recompensed for your time and skill. And I liked to feel I was highly skilled in that department. Thank God I didn't hold the same opinions as my mother though. The amount of cubic zirconia I had been gifted over my dating lifetime, I would never have seen any action and there would have been plenty of disappointed men.

Lottie looked at me nervously, her face flushed. I hadn't said anything for a few seconds, and I could tell her brain was working overtime, worrying she had said too much.

"I shouldn't have rambled on so much, should I? I'm blaming the drink. I should have a water next, I'm embarrassing myself."

I hooted with laughter.

"It's me you're talking to, remember. This conversation is barely PG-rated; I don't think you telling your best mate you're a fan of fellatio is going to alert the church elders. Anyway, I'm in complete agreement with you: you just can't beat it with the right man. I don't know if I agree with you on the delicious part, though. I think I would still rather stick to licking an ice cream in the taste department that's for sure."

She sighed, visibly relieved she hadn't overstepped the mark.

I gave her another little cheeky wink, as if I had just stepped straight off the set of a 1970s sitcom. Next, I would be saying "Oooh, a lovely bit of crumpet" or something equally dated and ridiculously un-PC. Instead, I came out with.

"Yep, I love to tongue-tickle the todger now and again, but as ice-cream flavours go, I would never plump for a double scoop of soft serve cock-olate."

Lottie let out a delighted high-pitched giggle that woke up one of the boozers at the bar. He had nodded off into an open packet of cheese and onion crisps, and as he glanced around to see who had woken him from his slumber, he had a few crisps stuck to his face like warts. He reminded me of paintings I had seen of Oliver Cromwell. Only this chap's skin condition was more potato-based than Olly's would have been.

"Oooh, or.... or...."

Lottie was desperately fumbling to think of a "rude" flavour for her favourite ice cream, to rival my suggestion, but it was proving more difficult that she imagined.

"Cocky road or mint choc dick!"

Her face was triumphant, and I couldn't help but laugh. Within a couple of seconds, we were both laughing so hard we could barely breathe, tears running down our faces. It's amazing how when you are with good, true friends, even the silliest little thing can set you off. And the combination of dick-inspired dairy ice-cream flavours and the warty barfly had us in hysterics. Honestly, for a couple of middle-aged women, it was good to behave so childishly. It really blew the cobwebs away.

Eventually I managed to curtail my laughs and wiped my eyes with the back of my hand.

"Well, I know one thing at least: 'vanilla' isn't the only flavour on the menu for you any more."

Lottie raised her blue drink and clinked the glass against mine with a definite twinkle in her eye.

"Amen to that."

I could feel more tears springing into my eyes. But this time they weren't from laughing. I dug around desperately in my handbag, knowing the back of my hand wasn't going to be good enough. I located a tatty tissue and dabbed at my eyes to stem the flow of salty tears. These were sad tears.

Never mind gin for making you weepy and maudlin; it seemed like vodka and blueberry goop was the new Mother's

Ruin. It might be as lethal as petrol to the guts, but it appeared to be gut-wrenching on the emotions too.

"What's wrong, Lila? You...you're crying?"

Lottie's face was visibly shocked. She had never seen me cry before. As far as she was aware, I had never cried. Not like her: she welled up at ads for pet insurance on the TV, but I was usually much more stoic, made of sterner stuff. Stiff upper lip and all that. But just now my lip was wobbling pitifully.

She put a reassuring arm around my shoulders.

"Tell me what's wrong."

I sniffed a couple of times. Not the most attractive of sounds, but considering our surroundings, we were still bringing the glamour, snot and all.

"It's Seb...I've lost him."

She looked confused.

"Seb? What do you mean, you've lost him? You're always out and about together, you two are..."

She registered my expression, and the penny began to finally drop, her eyebrows rising.

"Oh...*you and Seb.*"

Lottie pulled a fresh new pack of tissues out of her own bag. Trust my friend to be so organised.

"Right, start at the beginning."

So that's what I did. I touched on my disastrous date with Mervyn, how I had come to the startling realisation that I had deep feelings for Seb, feelings I had been pushing down for so long. Always trying to protect myself, protect my heart. But if you push things down too much, eventually they're going to pop back up, and often at the worst possible time. And that was exactly what had happened.

I was off crying again, telling my dear friend how I had

lost him to the office floozy, how she wasn't right for him. Uncharitably, I even mentioned that she dressed like a pole dancer in pinstripes. I knew that wasn't kind of me, but Lottie just nodded along loyally.

In Jocasta's defence, I also gave her a compliment: I said she was excellent at multi-tasking; she certainly seemed to be able to help Seb out of his trousers and get into his wallet at the same time.

Lottie was now shaking her head.

"But you didn't really lose him to her, Lila. He was never yours to begin with. He wanted to be, but you were the one who continually friend-zoned him. You were adamant that he wasn't the right man for you."

"I know, I know."

I blew my nose noisily into my soggy tissue.

"But I was wrong, I've been such an idiot."

Lottie was still shaking her head.

"Make it make sense, will you. Is Mercury in retrograde or something?"

I shrugged my shoulders and blew my nose into my now soggy tissue. She pulled another fresh one from the pack and passed it over to me before she continued to speak.

"The thing is you're always 'Lila-ing' around town with younger men. Most of your relationships are 'situationships' and have the shelf-life of a crème fraîche before they start to go bad, and you're forever saying love just isn't for you and you've got a heart like a swinging brick."

I sniffed into my tissue but remained silent. I knew she was right, but I still hated it when she used my name as a verb.

I knew I had been an absolute idiot: forever keeping Seb on the backburner, like a pot of bubbling gravy I could dip into if I ever took the fancy. All these years keeping him at arm's length, and we could have been so happy. I'd been a fool. A big, old, self-absorbed, ridiculous fool.

I had believed I was so independent and strong, parading my young boyfriends around on my arm like they were the latest Chanel bag, when in fact I had a Hermes vintage Birkin under my nose the whole time.

I now knew what I wanted, and that wasn't a message with a dick pic attached from a Tinder beau. No, I wanted one of Seb's cringingly awful sci-fi memes. That would be the thing that would now make my heart flutter.

And after all, a dick pic was only ever fit for the bin, literally junk mail in every sense of the word.

I drained the last of my lurid-coloured drink. I hadn't liked it to start with, but now I was disappointed it was gone and only the empty lipstick-stained glass remained.

"I think I'm so smart."

I hiccuped unattractively before continuing in a voice I could recognise was slightly slurred but unable to stop it.

"But quite clearly I haven't retained the sense I was born with. I should have listened to you about Seb, but oh no, I knew better. I've got a stubborn streak a mile wide, and look at me now: old, bitter and as pissed as a fart."

"Now that's enough."

Lottie's voice was firm but not unkind.

"That's no way to talk about my best friend. OK, you may be as pissed as a fart, but you're still also fabulous. And there's absolutely no point in all these 'what-ifs' and 'what-could-have-beens'. It's a complete waste of time to keep looking at the past, as you're no longer going in that direction. What we need to do is figure this out and what you're going to do now."

I was off babbling again my words spilling over each over in my haste to make my point.

"If I'd just realised earlier that we were meant for each other and I loved him, we would be together now. But the timing is so wrong. I eventually figure it out, and now he's got someone else."

I threw my hands in the air in a gesture of defeat.

"Love...you love him?"

Even through my inebriated haze I could hear the shock evident in her voice. I turned to face her, trying to focus my eyes on her dumbfounded expression.

I thought for a few seconds. Did I love him? I had said it, but did I actually, truly mean it? Or was it the devastating effect on my brain cells from all the alcohol? But no, I realised the stone-cold truth. I absolutely, unequivocally loved Sebastian Young.

Charlotte didn't look overly convinced. Knowing me of old, she was well aware how quickly my head could be turned. How at the drop of a hat my mind could be changed. She had witnessed me covet the latest designer bag for months, but then when I had it finally in my eager hands and was excitedly ripping off the paper packaging, I would begin to feel the first stirrings of regret. All that money, and what had I ended up with? An empty bag, that was what, and it would leave me feeling as empty inside as my bank balance inevitably was. But Seb wasn't a designer bag. No, he was even better than that. He was my future, I was sure of it.

"And you don't think you just want him now because he's dating Jocasta? The fact that you can't have him makes him so desirable. But if he were single, would you change your mind again? Decide that you were only meant to be mates? Move him firmly back into the friend-zone again?"

This gave me cause to ponder for a few seconds. Was she right? Was I just lusting after the unattainable? But no, I knew I loved Seb. I wanted him, no matter what. But was it too late? Had I lost the love of my life to my workplace nemesis?

"I love him, Lottie, that's all I know for sure."

"Well, if you're sure, Lila, then you need to fight for him. You know Seb better than anyone else. If you really think he's the one, then you go get him, girl. Take it from me, love is all that matters in the world. It took me half a lifetime to realise that, but now I know for sure. Be like one of my old screen idols: don your warpaint, throw your shoulders back and battle for his heart."

She was making sense to me. And I had never been one to back down from a battle. I batted my eyelashes at her with fake modesty.

"But darling, you know I never fight; but I might be persuaded to gently tussle."

She snorted with laughter: a sound so unappealing, even the fellow who had tried to tap me up earlier with an offer of a drink now cringed. He clearly had been drinking for most of the day, as with every pint he appeared to be sinking further and further off his bar stool towards the sticky floor.

Lottie's face was determined. Clearly the lady fuel in the beverage was working on her too.

"Yeah, OK, you never fight. That's why they call you 'The Rottweiler' at work, is it? Because you're just such a sweet little pussycat? Well, if you're a pussycat, you've got claws, and you need to use them. It's risk versus reward ratio, when you think about it."

She had seemingly lost her train of thought for a few seconds as she gazed off into the middle distance before continuing her impassioned speech.

"How much would you risk to win Seb back from Jocasta? Figure that out as a starting point and work from there."

I nodded at her in agreement and banged my hand down on the table, making the remaining scampi fries jump up from their packet like startled prawny pillows.

"You're absolutely right. I have to get him back. There's nothing else for it."

Lottie nodded in agreement before scooping a couple of the rogue fries from the table and crunching them down hungrily.

"Bang on, Lila. Do nowt, get nowt. You know sometimes it's easier to apologise than to ask for permission in advance."

Lottie was becoming more philosophical with every second that passed.

She continued thoughtfully chewing on the scampi fries as if they were the finest caviar she was tasting, which they most definitely were not. She had scoffed down the majority of the two packets of snacks. She'd better not blame me for the inevitable heartburn that was coming for her later. When a pub decided to sell those snacks along with the requisite crisps, nuts and pork scratchings, they should really stock Gaviscon shots behind the bar too, along with the Sambuca and Tequila Rose.

Wow, angelic Lottie was really showing a different side to her. Was she actually advising me to pull out all the stops in my desire to be with Seb? Always the Goody Two Shoes, this was not the Lottie of old. In the last year, my friend had really wised up.

But was she honestly telling me to go "balls to the wall" in my pursuit of love? It seemed she most certainly was. And she had still more wisdom yet to impart.

"You can't let the love of your life get away, you just can't. I realise *that* now with Leo. I almost lost him forever, and that would have been the biggest mistake of my life. He even went away to the other side of the world, but thank God we're back together now. Don't make the mistake I did and nearly lose your soulmate. If you're not careful, time goes by so fast that you'll end up old, sad and alone in your ratty dressing gown with only Radio 4 for company and inevitably end up getting eaten by your cats."

Lottie was beginning to confuse me now. When had cats come into the equation?

"But I don't even have any cats. You know I hate cats, superior creatures that snootily look down their whiskers at you. Give me a faithful dog any day."

She wagged her finger at me, millimetres away from my face. Quite clearly, she was now exceedingly tipsy.

"Whatever, just don't leave it to chance, that's all I'm saying. You're my best friend and I love you and you're far too nice and pretty to end up as cat food."

With that she rose shakily from her seat with a little gassy hiccup. The makeshift cocktail and bar snacks had apparently caused quite a commotion in her tummy. She gestured to the empty packs lying abandoned on the table.

"We're going to make a plan for you to win back the love of your life, just as soon as I get us another drink and a couple more packets of those delicious rascals."

Chapter 17

Lottie was good to her word, and within a few minutes she was unsteadily weaving her way back to the table. Like a hunter returning with her spoils, she proudly dumped the snacks down; then expertly mixed our blue cocktails with such finesse, you could have believed she was working in the finest cocktail bar in Monte Carlo.

"The chap at the bar offered to buy these for us; he seems to have taken quite the shine to you."

Her amusement was evident as I glanced towards the guy who had called me Cruella earlier. He was now standing by the ancient jukebox, struggling to feed his twenty pence piece into the slot. He really wouldn't be any use to me. Not that I was looking any more anyway; and even if I was, he really wouldn't have been my type.

Once he finally managed to feed the coin into the music machine and it sprang into life, he also sprang onto the makeshift dance floor: a small area of laminated flooring where he swung his ample derrière in his trackie bottoms to the dulcet tones of the Rolling Stones' *Satisfaction*. As the music rang out throughout the bar, he danced, or rather swayed back and forth to his own personal rhythm, with beer spilling from his pint as he did so, much to the barman's evident displeasure.

Lottie clapped along to the music.

"Oooh, just look, he's got those moves like Jagger."

I rolled my eyes theatrically at this.

"You must be joking, more like moobs like Jabba the Hutt."

"Ouch, Lila, don't be so cruel to your new beau. If you can't have Seb, then you might want someone waiting in the wings, you know."

I shot her a scathing glance, at which she laughed and held up her hands in defeat.

"OK, sorry, just joking. But I can see you're not in the mood for my humour. Go on then, tell all the gory details about your date with Merv the Swerve, because I really could do with a laugh."

So I told her the full sorry story, chapter and verse, and even I was laughing by the time I finished.

Enough days had passed that I no longer shuddered recalling him dashing across the bedroom, loo roll in hand, wearing my stilettos. I could now see how undeniably funny it all was. Well, Lottie certainly seemed to think so, as once again she could barely breathe for laughing.

I felt my spirits lift a little. It was doing me the world of good to be out with my girlfriend, having a confidante to talk to and just to unwind a little. Plus, the more I drank of this turquoise treat, the more delicious it was becoming. Strange, really. One of the great unsolved mysteries in life.

Lottie was shaking her head in disbelief.

"Seriously, Lila, that has to be hands down the worst date you've ever been on, and I know you've had some right stinkers."

I thought for a few minutes: replaying many years of dating mishaps in my brain, like the trailer to the worst disaster movie ever. My thought processes seemed a little sluggish, not as sharp as they should be, quite probably something to do with the few million brain cells we'd zapped in our last few hours of drinking.

"I think you're right, Mervyn the less than magnificent was probably the worst date I've ever been on, but I can tell you it's by the narrowest of margins. I've had my fair share of nutters, and probably half of everyone else's share too; Merv was just number one on the top of a festering dung pile of disastrous dates."

Lottie clapped her hands together in delight. Clearly the subject of my online dating dalliances cheering her up enormously.

"Oh, will you tell me your top five? I'm sure I already know them, but I might have forgotten some of them."

I really was a glutton for punishment. But for some reason I couldn't help but feel that recounting my worst dates of the last few years might actually be a fun way to while away an hour or two. So that's exactly what I did. Like the worst beauty pageant judge ever, I rated them in reverse order; but not like Miss World ranking the worst to best, oh no I was rating from the mildly mortifying to the howlingly horrific.

And so, I began. In place five it had to be the few hours I had spent in the company of Zack. There was no one else who could bring up the rear quite like Zack and considering the amount of time he had spent checking out my arse, it only seemed fitting.

Zack had been a carpet fitter from Barnsley, cue many cringingly bad jokes about having my under felt and getting friendly on the shag pile etc. etc. None of them remotely funny, even under the influence of a couple of glasses of budget vino that I had sunk at record-breaking speed.

Thankfully I had only deigned to have one date with the less than adorable Zack. That had been long enough, well far too long in truth, for me to come to the realisation that he was a complete and utter wassock.

He had felt it appropriate on our first date to impress me by wining and dining me at a rather down-at-heel restaurant chain: all ripped seat covers and stained placemats. He had insisted we order from the early-bird special menu, so we had been seated and food orders promptly given by 6:15 p.m. sharp. In my opinion, this was nowhere near dinner time; in truth, more of a late lunch.

As I picked unenthusiastically at my Icelandic prawn cocktail starter, we engaged in the normal small talk that's a necessity whilst on a first date. I had smiled politely at his chat about polypropylene carpet versus 100 percent wool in stain management, and had even managed to suck down about half my starter, hiding the remainder of the prawns under a limp lettuce leaf that had adorned the startling pink slop. Icelandic prawns, I ask you! I would put good money on the fact that these mushy crustaceans had never swum anywhere near the fjords of Iceland. Unless of course you counted them treading water at the bottom of a freezer unit in the Iceland supermarket in the precinct.

As I failed to eat my starter, Zack had made light work of his cheesy garlic bread. I smiled politely at him as he got progressively more inebriated, breathing synthetic garlic fumes over me like a droning dragon. I was worried the acrid fumes might actually melt my mascara.

Then as he slurped down his fourth pint of gassy lager, belching loudly, he had informed me that I would look so much more appealing, in his opinion, if I dressed in a more provocative way. In fact, he hadn't worded it quite so politely. He had actually dared to utter the words "I was OK for an old bird, but it wouldn't hurt to show a little more skin."

He had then gone on to add to this delightful diatribe by saying I was "pretty fit though, a definite 7.5 out of 10, but with a few cosmetic enhancements I could definitely score a 10".

I had been so appalled by his misogynistic cheek that I had been itching to hurl my cheap plonk all over him. With any luck the alcohol might hit the fire from his rancid breath and reduce him to a smouldering pile of putrid embers. But with more restraint than I realised I possessed; I decided maybe he had a point after all. It wouldn't hurt, I supposed, to show a little more skin. So that was exactly what I did: showed him the skin on the palm of my hand as I slapped him hard across his smug, repugnant face.

And once I had finished describing my date with Zack, it brought me neatly on to number four on my list. And that would be no other than David from Pudsey. Ahhh, what could I say about dashing David? Plenty, as it would turn out.

It had all started so well, though. Cocktails in an extremely fancy bar in the centre of Leeds, and then on to a delightfully rustic French restaurant, where we enjoyed a delicious three-course meal. It had all seemed so promising, until things took a decided turn for the worst when he started quizzing me on my sexual preferences over dessert.

Don't get me wrong, I am not usually shy in discussions in that department; never one to clutch my pearls during mention of anything carnal. I had indulged him with a few juicy snippets of my love life, skirting around anything too graphic, but was beginning to feel more uncomfortable with the way the conversation was heading.

He was enthusiastically describing his own sexploits, in way too much intimate and anatomical detail for my liking. It was not appropriate dinner table discourse over dessert. He was putting me right off my cherry clafoutis. I really didn't need to know what sexual shenanigans he got up to of an evening. It was just all too much for a first date.

I was beginning to feel quite queasy and was becoming increasingly worried that my *coq au vin* might make another appearance, this time unwanted, all over the pressed linen tablecloth.

David had now moved onto talk of the posterior. I had tried at a joke by saying I wasn't the biggest fan of anal. In fact, I had laughed and said it was a matter of steeling oneself and then "touch your toes and up it goes."

He had ignored my attempt at humour and was far keener to move onto the subject of rimming: something he was clearly extremely passionate about, as he went on to demonstrate his technique in great detail with an empty Grand Marnier shot glass as a prop.

This in itself was horrific enough: to witness a man of nearly forty performing such an act on glassware, but the fact that he still had remnants of his chocolate mousse from dessert around his mouth was just a step too far. It was hands down the most disgusting thing I had ever witnessed.

I knew without a doubt that I had to get out of there as fast as my legs would carry me. While he had been distracted taking a call on his mobile phone, I tipped a passing waiter twenty quid to spill a glass of water all over his crotch, in the hope it would cool his ardour somewhat.

So while he was in the Gents' toilet drying his pants off under the hand dryer, I had legged it at full speed.

I was getting into my stride now - nearly as fast as my striding away from David that night. I had actually forgotten just how horrific some of these dates had been, and from the look on Lottie's face, she was enjoying every single second of my trip down repressed memory lane. So, I continued on with my list of lothario losers.

I was now at number three, which had to be awarded to William. Ah, William. He had sounded so perfect on paper, or rather on message, as that was where we had corresponded prior to meeting.

He was tall, dark and handsome. He hailed from Halifax and worked a steady job in finance. He seemed so right, but oh he was so wrong. Unlike with his predecessors, Zack and David, we managed more than just the one date. In fact, it was date four before he had shown his "true" self. William, as it would turn out, was obsessed with babies.

Firstly, there was the baby talk. Don't get me wrong, I don't mind a bit of "lovey dovey" speak now and again, when the mood would take me, but when he turned up at my workplace to give me a big hug and coo that "Little Willy misses his Lila-Wila" it became just a little too much to bear.

And then he was forever banging on about us having a baby of our own. The first time he brought it up, I thought it was the funniest thing I had heard in ages. He must be joking, surely. Unfortunately, it turned out he was deadly serious. I kept telling him I was nearly fifty, and there was a snowball in hell's chance of me ever having another baby, but that didn't stop him.

On our last ever proper date together, he had presented me with a beautiful, gift-wrapped box, adorned with a huge fluffy bow. Hoping it was a silver necklace I had been coveting and had dropped a few heavy hints about, I proceeded to rip the paper off with wild excitement. The box was certainly the right size, flat and square and most definitely bracelet-shaped.

I was so disappointed when I discovered that it was not my bracelet after all nestled in the box, but an intricate carved walnut photo frame. There was no doubt that the frame was exquisite, but what it contained somewhat less so. Smiling out of the frame was an AI-generated image of what our biological children together could look like. Believe me, it was far from heartwarming, in fact the stuff of absolute nightmares. The creepiest-looking kids since *Children of the Corn* stared out menacingly from the frame. Like a cross between Victorian workhouse urchins and a Chucky doll.

I couldn't conceal the look of absolute horror on my face, and William was so crushed. He had thought I would find the present adorable and was hoping it would have pride of place on my desk at work. In turn, I thought he needed locking up where he wouldn't need to mix with the general public ever again.

To be fair, I still have the frame on my desk at work. I replaced the image of our demonic offspring with a lovely smiley picture of a girl's night out with Lottie and the gang. That image was guaranteed to put a smile on my face, the other one not so much.

After the unwanted gift, our relationship had limped on for another few days before inevitably fizzling out for good. I just couldn't bring myself to see him as anything but creepy as fuck. And that is never a good basis for a successful relationship. So without further ado, I had waved "Little Willy" off into the sunset to find himself another baby mama. God help her.

Moving on from the William debacle, and just missing out on the coveted top spot, came Johnny. Johnny was a thirty-four-year-old personal trainer from Ilkley, with the body of an Adonis but, alas, the brain of an amoeba.

He had been lovely to tote around town for a few weeks on my arm, like a new designer handbag. In truth, as handbags go, he had even less personality than a Prada clutch. I managed three dates in total with him. It was a close call even to make it that far.

After listening to him drone on about energy drinks for nigh on forty minutes on the first date, it had been touch and go as to whether there would be a second, or whether we would just be ships that passed in the night. But talking of night and all things nocturnal, I had really fancied a sleepover of the adult variety with him. Call me shallow, and I know I can be, but I was just too keen to discover what was hiding under his designer duds to call it time early doors.

When I eventually got a glimpse at the goods, it was rather underwhelming. I had seen more meat on a vegan menu, and girth-wise it was more chipolata than Chateaubriand in that department. I remember wondering if he had maybe been taking something down the gym to enhance his stamina on the bench press, but reduce his stamina in the boudoir. I didn't know much about steroids, but I believed they could cause some unsatisfactory side effects to the libido.

After our final date, I wondered if they could cause other side-effects too.

We had been out for dinner. I had been keen to try a new Indian restaurant not far from my home and had persuaded Johnny to swerve the gym for the evening and accompany me. He had been quite quiet and was looking a little pale, even under his tan. We had barely got through our poppadoms and pickles when he had excused himself to go "for a quick visit" to the lavatory.

Forty minutes passed and still no Johnny. The waiter had brought our starters out and they were beginning to cool when I received a call from my absent date. When I saw his name flash up on my handset, my heart had dropped like a stone. Was he already on his way home and informing me that our date was over? Did I now live in Dumpsville, the ever ill-fated Lila Glover? But no, the truth was far more horrific than that.

It turned out that while I had been patiently waiting at the table for him, nibbling on my *pakora*, he had been rather poorly in the lavatory cubicle.

In his words, he'd had one "simmering in the saucepan for hours", and when he was finally ready to release the beast, the torrent of explosive diarrhoea had quite taken him by surprise. He had completely blocked the toilet up, and requested that I send someone in immediately with a plunger.

Our waiter, who was as mild-mannered as a Korma, was sent in on the monstrous mission. Ten minutes later, when Johnny and Ajay the waiter had reappeared, Ajay no longer looked Korma-mild. No, now he looked Madras-mad and rather green around the gills.

After that, the relationship had quite literally hit the skids.

And that brought us neatly to the perhaps not so coveted top spot, which had to go to the one and only "Merv the Swerve". On entering his bedroom that night after our successful date at the pub, I had great expectations for what was to follow. Unfortunately, in the dim morning light, it had all turned out to be rather more *Bleak House* than *Great Expectations*. What the Dickens had all that been about? I shuddered as I recounted the tale to Lottie.

I could recall that our night of passion had in fact turned out to be a rather tepid affair, not at all the hot and steamy session I had anticipated. A tawdry tussle of tangled limbs, bestial grunts and airborne fluids.

As it turned out, Merv had been a bit of a sweater, with it dripping off the end of his nose and onto my face at one point in the proceedings. This had horrified me and rendered my lady area drier than the Sahara Desert. He was also a bit of a moaner, though not nearly as much as I was when I copped an eyeful of him in my fancy footwear.

So that was it: Lila Glover's top five worst dates. And I couldn't help feeling a little misplaced pride at just how horrific they truly were. I would always have them to fall back on when conversation at a dreary dinner party dried up, or to scare my grandkids into singledom.

And poor old Toffer hadn't even earned a mention. Not so terrible after all, it would seem. Yes, he was and would always be pretty repugnant, but not nearly as bad as the aforementioned pack of stone-cold weirdos.

Lottie was wiping her eyes again. She hadn't stopped laughing for the entirety of my babbling. Her previously pristine eye make-up was now more than a little smudged and streaked halfway down her cheeks, making her appear like she'd just gone six rounds with Conor McGregor.

"You really should write a book, Lila. I bet it would be a bestseller; it's comedy gold."

"Yeah, a real page-turner, I'd bet, but not so sure about a comedy; more like a horror shocker, to give Stephen King a run for his money. Reading about those pillocks would be sure to give you a few nightmares."

Lottie drained the last of her drink and I followed suit. It really was quite tasty.

My mind wandered back to thoughts of safe, solid, now somewhat sexy Seb. Why, oh why, had I not given us a chance? I had been my own worst enemy for way too long, and that had to change. There was determination as well as vodka coursing through my veins.

Lottie clapped her hands together and jumped off her seat. A strong, confident call to action. Or at least, it would have been had she not staggered back slightly and had to steady herself against a fellow patron who was weaving his way towards the Gents' toilet. It was fortuitous that was his destination, as when Lottie suddenly grabbed the sleeve of his faux leather bomber jacket to steady herself, he nearly shat himself in shock. Clearly, he had not felt the touch of a woman in many a long year, and to be accosted by a pretty yet somewhat pished lovely like Lottie was well out of the norm for him.

"Oooh, sorry, the floor just seemed to wobble there a bit; maybe an earthquake or something?"

The man muttered something inaudible, before putting his head down and dashing into the lavatories, the door swinging noisily shut behind him.

"Whoops."

Lottie giggled and staggered slightly to the side as if there had been a mini aftershock after the earthquake.

"Must have been something I said."

I grabbed her arm and we started heading towards the door, zigging and zagging as we went. We'd both had way too much for a school night. What seemed so much fun now would not be nearly as enjoyable come tomorrow morning, when we would both be experiencing epic hangovers.

Finally, we left the warm, muggy interior of the pub, and after my run-in with in with young Alfie Dodds, it proved to be muggy in more than one sense of the word. We stumbled unsteadily into the frosty air of the street, laughing as we went. I had no idea what was so funny, but laugh we did. After the cloyingly warm atmosphere of the pub, the almost brutal slap in the face from the frosty night air instantly sobered us up somewhat.

Lottie shivered under her coat, which was buttoned up completely wrongly, as if a toddler had fastened it, trying to dress themselves for the first time and failing miserably.

"I'm starving."

Her voice was petulant like a toddler's too.

"I need more than a couple of packets of crisps. Come on, Lila, let's go and get us some dinner. I could really fancy going all out and having a right posh bit of scran. How about *boeuf en croûte* at Brasserie Bleu?"

I nodded my head at my friend in approval. There was a time, not so long ago, when she would never have dared enter the hallowed halls of the chicest French restaurant in town, saying she felt constantly judged by the other diners; wary of the miniscule portions; concerned her chunky butt wouldn't slide gracefully into the fashionable booths; worried she would be wedged in tighter than old Fluck when expected to buy his round at the bar.

That man really was tighter than a gnat's chuff: when he opened his wallet, moths didn't fly out; they had already passed away from old age.

I put my arm affectionately around my friend and steered her down the road towards Brasserie Bleu and some seriously fancy food. I was so proud of her. For her now to suggest the venue as her preferred restaurant was progress indeed. Yes, she had lost weight from her biggest size, but not that much, and truthfully she would probably still be considered "plus sized". But that no longer bothered her.

She had lost some weight, for sure, but what she had gained was far, far weightier than that. She had gained the love and respect of a good man, which was amazing. But even better, she had gained the love and respect of herself. Now the opinion of the rest of the world barely registered. She knew her worth, and it was measured in kindness, respect and self-esteem, not in pounds and ounces.

"OK...Brasserie Bleu it is, Lottie. But I'm telling you, I'm not having the *boeuf en croûte*. When all's said and done, it's just a meat pie with ideas above its station."

Lottie stumbled along next to me laughing, clearly delighted by my silliness and enjoying herself immensely.

Even through the rosy glow of the alcohol, I felt a little despairing tug at my soul. I missed Seb. I couldn't help it; everything made me think of him. Even talk of pastry.

Chapter 18

I didn't wake until midday the following day, and even that took a monumental effort: gingerly opening each eye in turn and blinking desperately like a newborn, trying to focus on my grainy surroundings.

I thought for a second that roadworks were taking place just outside my bedroom window, but alas I soon realised the banging was actually coming from inside my head; just as scary, as if the call from the serial killer was coming from inside the house. My next thought, which is a worry I always have after an exceedingly drunken night on the town, is "Where the bloody hell is my bag?"

I calmed down a little when I spotted it on the floor of my bedroom, kicked unceremoniously into the corner, its contents half spilling out, and next to a half-wrapped bag of chips.

Slowly, memories from the previous night dropped randomly into my fuddled brain. It hurt to think. What I really wanted to do was turn my pillow over to the cool side and sleep for a further ten, maybe twelve hours. But I knew I couldn't, for today was the afternoon trip to the spa with my bestest friend Jocasta. Oh, joy to the world!

The previous night was still a bit of a blur, but I knew that Lottie and I had remained drinking until very late o'clock. We hadn't even got to go for our fancy meal, instead being seduced into a dirty kebab shop a couple of doors down from the pub. The smell of used cooking oil and donner meat had proved too tantalising for us sophisticated gals around town to resist.

Why, after imbibing a gallon of booze, did the mankiest of takeaways appeal so much? I had gobbled down my cheesy chips, extolling the gastronomical virtues of them to everyone in the shop, whether they wanted to listen or not. I claimed they were on a par with the best truffle fries I had ever had, and streets ahead of halloumi fries which, let's face it, had no right to be quite so widely praised and overpriced. They were just fried cheese after all.

My eyes were fully open now. But as my mind recalled me gobbling down a battered sausage with far more enthusiasm than was strictly necessary, I swiftly snapped them shut, hoping this simple act would erase the image entirely. It did not. I could still remember the look of delight on the owner's face to see me fellate one of his foot longs with such frenzied fervour.

I recalled that Lottie had told me through bites of a greyish-looking quarter pounder, the meat as questionable as my floorshow, that she loved to see me like this: much less guarded and more stripped back relaxed, without any airs and graces. Just having fun for the sake of it. It was so refreshing to see me embrace the simpler things in life, not always striving for something better. She was right: I had been less than impressed when I knew we were meeting at The Honourable Lawyer, and even less so at her drink selection, but I had ended up having a simply splendid evening.

That's how I should have been with Seb: not always regarding him as dull and dependable, but realising there could be something marvellous in the mundane.

Why was I so quick to disregard his weekly pub quiz? Haughtily believing it wasn't "my thing" to indulge in half pints of warm lager and "guess the theme tune rounds". No thank you. But my life - the life I had believed was so much more sophisticated and chicer - was in truth an absolute shit show.

I would have been better off with Seb and the sports round all along. These simple things I had scoffed at could have been simply lovely. Even a nice big dollop of shepherd's pie every now and again. I didn't need truffle fries; simple mashed potatoes would do very nicely, thank you. I just needed to let go of my superiority, live a little more simply, out of my comfort zone, even if that meant eating the occasional carb or wandering down the middle of Lidl looking for a bargain.

I shouldn't have to feel the burden on me of always needing to impress. Nobody in life really cared; they were all too busy being caught up in their own worlds. Lottie was right, I was a prisoner of my own vanity. I knew now that was the upshot of it all. And even in my drunken state, that had struck a chord.

I worried too much about things that didn't really matter. There was nothing wrong with Seb. The fault had been with me and my stuck-up pride. I'd been too caught up with what was wrong with him, rather than the countless things that were right.

Chapter 19

When I eventually rocked up at Supreme Serenity Spa, I was feeling neither supreme nor serene. In truth, I was decidedly queasy and green. And on top of that, nearly an hour late. This was the very last thing I felt like doing with a raging hangover and a tongue as dehydrated as cracked sandpaper.

When I announced my presence to the bored-looking receptionist, I was informed that Jocasta was already in her robe and poolside. It took me longer than I had anticipated to get undressed and into my fluffy towelling robe, as any sudden movement was having an unfortunate effect on my gurgling stomach. Nice and gentle movements were the order of the day, it would seem.

I shuffled around slowly, stooped and with my head down, like an old granny in her housecoat who had got lost on her way to the dining room in the nursing home. When I eventually joined Jocasta at the edge of the swimming pool, I was more than ready for another lie down before I fell down.

I sank down gratefully onto the cream padded recliner next to hers.

"Sorry I'm late, it's just been one of those mornings."

I gave her the friendliest smile I could muster in my current state, which she returned with a tight-lipped one of her own.

She was elegantly sprawled on the neighbouring recliner, wearing the most ridiculous oversized sunglasses, designer of course, that made her look like a bug-eyed beetle.

She was sipping a flute of prosecco, and as she turned towards me, her heavy gold necklaces made a clanking sound that reverberated in my brain. I really needed quiet in my current state. And why was she dripping in jewellery anyway? We were in a prefab spa area, attached to the main hotel and golf club, not on a tropical island in the midday sun doing a photoshoot for *Vogue*.

"That's OK."

She raised her sunglasses so I could see from her sharp green eyes that it was clearly anything but OK.

"At least you're finally here now."

She had her toffee-coloured tresses piled on top of her head in a chic updo. I couldn't help but notice she was wearing a full face of slap too. Granted, I had applied a thin layer of tinted moisturiser and the briefest swipe from my mascara wand, but that was just so I didn't scare the neighbourhood children. In my current state, it was fair to say I wasn't looking my best.

But she was done up like a dog's dinner. Much more suited to going clubbing with her girlfriends. It was ridiculous and overly excessive for an afternoon at the spa. All that powder and paint would be sweated off and languishing in her armpits within an hour or so.

She made a sweeping gesture around the perimeter of the pool.

"Just ask one of the attendants milling around to get you a prosecco."

Her voice had a rather bossy, privileged tone to it which set my teeth on edge in my current state.

The thought of more alcohol made my liver contract in terror.

"No, that's going to be a No-secco for me."

I gave a weak laugh and tried to quell the nausea that was threatening to take hold.

"I think I'll just stick with something soft."

She eyeballed me again, her sunglasses perched on the end of her nose now, giving the impression of a haughty librarian – well, one that lurks around the erotica section anyway.

"You do look a bit rough. Maybe get yourself one of their revitalising smoothies?"

I picked up the laminated drinks menu from the table beside me, and cast a glance down the list of health-giving elixirs. There was a Virgin Bloody Mary, but I decided against that, straight off the bat. A Bloody Mary without a good healthy slosh of vodka in it was just a bloody shame.

I decided on the ginger and ginseng smoothie. It sounded just the ticket: ginger for my gurgling tummy, and ginseng for my battered immune system, all swirled together with a gigantic slug of health-giving vitamins in the fruit juice. Just what the doctor ordered. Well, not my own GP, obviously: Dr Webster was more likely to order a nip of whisky, a couple of codeine and a long nap. He had never really bought into the holistic way of thinking, but considering he had been the family GP for decades, he must be doing something right. He was as fit as a flea, even if that flea had a faint whiff of single malt and extra strong mints about it.

I stifled a yawn as I gave my order to the eager waiter. He was dressed in the tightest trousers I had ever seen, but considering that all the other guests dotted around the spa appeared to be women, I figured he must be working on tips. I could clearly see the outline of his tip as it was.

I settled back on my lounger. A nap would be a jolly good idea right now. Perk me up a little and allow the alcohol to sweat out of my pores as I snoozed away. I had just closed my eyelids and felt myself gently drifting off when the waiter was back with my drink.

I took it from him with a smile, determined to look anywhere but at his trousered area. I settled back again and took a long slug of my drink. It really was unbelievably vile. Something that bad must be doing me some good. It tasted like soggy garden in a champagne flute. It was a very unappealing shade of green, like Kermit the frog had gone for a spin in the blender. It also had a few redundant pieces of herb stuck to the side of the glass for effect.

After yesterday and the blue drinks, which were sumptuous compared to this slop, I really had been drinking a rainbow of colours recently. I bravely forced myself to take another little sip of the gloopy beverage. Yes, it really was as bad as I had first thought.

"It's so nice to be away from the office for the afternoon, don't you think?"

In my hungover haze I had briefly forgotten that I was here with Jocasta. Damn it, I was going to have to make small talk with her.

"Yes, it makes a lovely change."

I smiled weakly. It was true that I was glad I wasn't behind my desk in the office at present. The way I was feeling, I didn't imagine I would be at all productive. Unless you counted chucking up into the wastepaper bin a good way to spend the working day.

Neither did I want to be here though. In truth, what I wanted was to be back home in bed with the remote control in my sweaty hand, a serial killer documentary on the TV and my body weight in ultra-processed food for company. Now that would be heaven.

Jocasta giggled in an annoyingly girlish way that just made me want to dump my drink and throttle her. I had long ago realised that I was not the most tolerant of people when suffering with a hangover.

"I'm just so happy that you're here, Lila. I've been dying to talk to you for ages. I've just got so much to tell you."

"You do?"

This was surprising. We weren't exactly bosom buddies. And despite Seb's protestations to the contrary, I still believed deep down that she disliked me as much as I did her.

"You've known Seb a long time, haven't you?"

Oh no. She wanted to talk about Seb. My Seb. I didn't think I would be able to handle it. Not in my current state. I wished I had her sunglasses now, so I could hide my emotions behind them and remain seemingly cool and aloof.

I was worried that if we talked about Seb, there was a real possibility I might start blubbering again like I had last night. And that just wouldn't do. I would rather have talked about work, the weather, anything, even discussed how I still wasn't in Fluck's good graces. She could have teased me about that. How Fluck was still getting stick at his Golf Club about the fashion show fuck up, anything but talk about Seb. I just didn't think my poor heart would be able to take it.

I took a deep steadying breath before answering her.

"That's right, we've been friends for years. He's been my rock at times, someone I could always rely on, and I like to think I've been the same for him when he's needed me."

She smiled. It was tight-lipped and forced and her voice was nearly as sour as my drink.

"Well, isn't that nice? But you don't need to worry about him so much now, as I'll be the one looking after him."

I felt a jolt of apprehension run through me. This was supposed to be a pleasant afternoon, but I felt myself bristle. It seemed as if the warm temperature in the spa had suddenly dropped by a few degrees. I didn't want to talk about Seb, but she did. However, she clearly didn't want to hear what I had to say on the subject.

Jocasta was smiling now, apparently warm and friendly again, but I wasn't convinced.

"I know you two are good friends, so I feel I can open up to you about him."

I sipped my drink again. It was still just as vile, but preferable to speaking. I was worried that words would fail me, or worse still I would fill up again. And I wasn't prepared for this little madam to see me cry. She had Seb, she wouldn't get my dignity too.

"He's an absolute angel, my Seb."

She let out a long-contented sigh and took a delicate sip of her prosecco.

I was beginning to wish I had ordered some hard liquor after all. I felt my heart contract in my chest as if I had been physically punched. Her Seb. It was more than I could bear.

She sighed again.

"He's so dishy now that I've given him a bit of a makeover. Who knew there was such a hottie under all that polyester? He really is a dark horse."

She giggled and pushed her sunglasses down from her eyes so hers could meet mine, clearly keen to gauge my reaction.

"Maybe I shouldn't say this, but that's not the only equine thing about him, if you catch my drift."

She gestured with her hands to show that his package was impressive too.

Oh, I caught it all right. And I wanted to chuck it right back in her smug little face. Her subtlety wasn't lost on me. She was saying that Seb was hung like a horse.

"And let's just say that the man is extremely talented."

She gave a little coquettish wink to let me know exactly what she was getting at.

I didn't know how I was expected to react upon hearing her allude to their hot sex life. I knew she wanted a reaction but I hoped my face was as neutral as I believed it to be, because in reality my heart was breaking into little pieces.

I loved Seb. I knew that with complete certainty. But now, hearing that he was also blessed in the britches and that was something else I was missing out on, it was like rubbing salt in the wounds.

Jocasta made a little zipping gesture across her lips to signal she might have said too much.

"I won't say another word. I want to save any blushes."

I took another sip of my drink. I could barely taste it now. I had a far worse taste in my mouth from what she had been saying.

She gestured to the attendant for a top-up of her prosecco.

"I've booked us in for a nice massage in about half an hour, so we can just chill here for a bit and chat some more."

This was my cue to shut her up.

"That would be lovely, Jocasta, but I've got a bit of a headache so I think I might just close my eyes for a second and hope it passes."

I really didn't want to hear another word about their love life and whatever exploits they got up to in or out of the bedroom. It would just bring my mood down even more, and quite possibly bring my noxious green drink back up too.

So thankfully that was all that was said on the topic of Seb.

It ended up not being an entirely bad afternoon after all. And certainly not the nightmare I had anticipated.

I managed to have a lovely snooze on my padded recliner. It was as comfortable as my divan at home, and I drifted off to the land of Nod in a mere nano-second. And dozing away for a while perked me up marvellously. I would have happily slept for longer, but was alerted to the fact that our massage was due by a sharp poke in my shoulder from Jocasta's manicured finger.

I believe I may have drifted off again during the half-hour massage. The magical hands and the soothing voice of the masseuse worked as well as a big mug of cocoa and a Nytol to send me back off to sleep. I felt so blissfully relaxed and was beginning to feel thankful that I had agreed to the afternoon. It had turned out that my earlier words had indeed been true, and it had made a lovely change.

After the massage we enjoyed a quick dip in the pool, and then some time in the sauna. It was the perfect end to the afternoon for me, as I could literally feel the vodka and toxins from the previous night's festivities sweating out of my pores in rivers.

As I reclined, rosy-skinned and relaxed, in my towel, I sighed to myself, feeling calm and carefree for the first time in ages.

We had chatted at length about her relationship with her ex-husband. He sounded like a particularly nasty piece of work. She had been with him for eight years and he had controlled every aspect of their lives together for most of that time. Even down to what she could wear and who she could see.

He constantly criticised her about her appearance and took pleasure in putting her down whenever the opportunity arose. He clearly felt it was perfectly acceptable for him to live exactly the way he wished, including dating other women.

It had taken enormous courage for her to finally break free from him. But in her brokenness, she had had a breakthrough and come to the realisation that only she could save herself. So, she had picked herself up, dusted herself off and forged a new life for herself without him. That took guts, and I was proud of her for her strength and fortitude.

But then she had met Simon, her recent beau. He had appeared lovely to start but before long had shown his true colours and in truth was not much of an improvement on her ex-husband. He too was a bully and a control freak who took pleasure in treating her like something on the bottom of his shoe. They had only dated for a few months, but he hadn't taken kindly to her calling it a day.

Simon was still hassling her and making her life difficult, any chance he could, refusing to leave her alone, forever lurking in the shadows like the ex-boyfriend bogeyman.

I could hardly blame her for being a bit defensive and prickly at times. She had been through so much. I now saw the woman through very different eyes.

I felt tolerance for her that I had never previously allowed. Us women really need to stick together against those types of men. Men who somehow feel more visible and validated in the world if they are slowly diminishing and destroying another human being. They really are the lowest of the low.

I felt bad for my criticisms of Jocasta's style and way of

presenting herself too; for thinking her too provocative and overtly sexy. Maybe in her mind it had been one way for her to assert herself and take back control.

After the break-up, she had free rein to be her true self once more, and so what if she embraced that with wild abandon? It would be completely understandable that she should want to shake her dowdy wardrobe up after too long living in conservative knee-length styles in shades of beige and grey. It was understandable she might go a little overboard. She was finally free to show off her femininity, and so what if that included thigh-length slits and low-cut tops? Who was I to judge?

In truth, I felt quite ashamed of myself. I had decided that I disliked her pretty much on first clapping eyes on her, and woe betide anyone who tried to change my mind. Both of us had been so combative towards the other. But who could blame her for being guarded after what she had been through? She'd seen other women as competition and not to be trusted.

I was finding myself feeling increasingly protective towards her. Almost motherly. Her story with her ex reminded me of how Lottie's life had been: never feeling good enough; always waiting for the next insult to come; never physically hurt, but attacked by the cruel sting of words, which could often wound like a slap and leave a bruise etched on the soul.

Once we'd talked about her ex until there was not much left to say, we had lightened the mood with general chitchat: what movies we'd seen at the cinema, what books we'd enjoyed, that sort of thing.

And when we eventually said goodbye with a hug, all fresh-faced and rejuvenated, I strongly believed that we were in a much better place. Seb had wanted me to build a bridge with

Jocasta and get over the past; and I knew that we now had. I wouldn't go so far as to say we were the best of buddies, but we were certainly on our way to becoming friends. And that was good enough for now.

It was dark by the time I unlocked the door to my house. The quietness of the interior hit me as soon as I entered. It didn't get me down, though. I was feeling happier than I had when I had hurriedly rushed out a few hours before; in fact, happier and more positive than I had in ages. And it wasn't just the sauna and the massage that had given me such a happy glow.

Overall, I was feeling much more optimistic. I just had an inkling that life was going to get so much better from now on.

Chapter 20

I was delighted that Jocasta and I were in a better place. She really wasn't such a bad old stick, just misunderstood.

She still wasn't right for Seb, of course. That remained unchanged. And I was one hundred percent going to win him back. When all was said and done, he should be with me. It was written in the stars. All's fair in love and war.

After all, Seb and I had been through our own love and war story over all the years we'd known each other: the times of hugs and hardships, tears and triumphs. We had history together; something real and tangible that Jocasta and he simply didn't have. They had barely been together for five minutes. I had pairs of tights that had lasted longer.

Yes, Jocasta and I might be in a better place, and that was good. We would remain there just as long as she didn't fight me for Sebastian. Then the gloves would be well and truly off; it would be bare knuckle brawling all the way.

I was walking past Seb's office towards the kitchen when he called out, which stopped me dead in my tracks. I felt my heart do a sudden quickstep in my chest just to hear his voice.

"So, I hear you and Jo had a great time at your spa afternoon?"

He was out of his office now and striding towards me. So tall and strong. God, he smelled good: like lemons and lust swirled together in a seductive aroma that made me go weak at the knees. That certainly wasn't the old Lynx body spray he used to squirt all over of a morning. He looked lean and lovely in his elegantly tailored suit. It was cut to fit his body perfectly.

I felt a sudden blush rise hotly up my cheek as my gaze dropped unwittingly down to his inside leg area. What Jocasta had said yesterday about his manly attributes was evidently still ringing in my ears. I needed to control my thoughts. My blood pressure was sure to be up, and I was prone to have a "fit of the vapours" as my mother would call it; possibly swoon on the spot and need a doctor at this rate. But Seb, alas, wasn't going to be showing me his stethoscope any time soon, more's the pity. I couldn't help but think that with every day he wasn't mine, he was becoming decidedly less Dr Who and more Doctor Woo-hoo.

I shuffled my feet awkwardly. I needed to concentrate my mind on things more tepid. I tried to recall the droning voice of Fluck as he'd berated me on my wanton waste of office stationery the previous week. He'd pointed at the stained piles of Post-it notes stuck to my desk that I'd been using as coasters for my cup of coffee, then waved his bony finger around while reminding me that "paper didn't grow on trees". He really was a prize pillock.

It seemed to do the trick though. Nothing could quell a lady boner quicker than thoughts of Fluck. They could market him in Superdrug as the anti-Viagra. He could be a veritable goldmine, a surefire passion killer.

I fixed my eyes on Seb's face and smiled pleasantly.

"The spa was good, relaxing, and it gave us a chance to talk."

He nodded, a broad smile lighting up his handsome face. It

was beautiful, like the sun had just broken through the darkest rain clouds.

"Didn't I tell you she was a great girl? She told me last night how well you were both getting on, even the fact that she had opened up about her ex-husband."

His face darkened a little, as if the storm clouds had suddenly returned.

"He sounds like a very unsavoury character, and this latest boyfriend Simon was just like him and Jo's such a sweet girl, and a good friend. It makes me angry just to think about the way some men treat the women in their lives."

I nodded in agreement. He was right there. An image of past Lottie, all sad face and hunched shoulders popped suddenly into my head.

"Yeah, he sounds like a complete arsehole. She did well to find the strength to get away from him."

"Indeed."

He closed his eyes briefly and rubbed the bridge of his nose. He looked tired. It was barely 10 a.m. and he appeared completely shattered. Had Jocasta been keeping him up all night?

I felt a sharp stab of jealousy that almost made we wince. I would bet they hadn't been drinking cocoa and playing board games. And if they had been playing Cluedo, it would probably involve Jocasta in the bedroom in her lingerie with a length of rope to tie Seb to the headboard.

I took a final lingering look at Seb, confident he wouldn't notice as he was checking something on his phone. A look of concern flashed briefly across his face and then it was gone.

How could I have been so blind to how attractive he was? I'd always regarded him as relatively handsome, a bit squidgy around the edges, but not completely unfortunate-looking. But now it was as if a spell had been lifted from me and I could finally see his full appeal. It wasn't just his new wardrobe either; he had always been a looker, even in his zip-up polyester cardigans and corduroy trousers.

I couldn't help but wonder what he thought now when he looked at me. I had always been the stylish one, taking care of my appearance, and I knew he had found me attractive. But did he even notice me in that same way any more? Had I pushed him away one too many times? Friend-zoned him to the point that he would only ever see me as a friend?

Had he really fallen for Jocasta? Did his heart soar when she sashayed into the office in her short skirts and low-cut tops? I still couldn't quite believe she was his type. I'd always thought he preferred a more pared-down look. But then again, what did I know? She was a good-looking woman, there was no denying that; and he was a hot-blooded single male. He couldn't fail to notice her obvious charms.

But did he love her? My heart clenched in my chest. If he did, then surely I had lost him. But no, they had only been seeing each other for a couple of weeks. It was still such early days. But the way that Jocasta had spoken yesterday, in hushed tones and girlish giggles, it sounded like their chemistry was sizzling hot, not something you were likely to find in a GCSE textbook.

Suddenly our eyes met. I could feel a flicker of something pass between us. Like a sudden spark of electricity. Or was it my imagination playing tricks on me? I was so determined to find something where there was possibly nothing that I could no longer recognise the truth. But what I did know was that I needed to get a grip of myself. I was a woman of nearly fifty acting like a love-struck middle schooler, and it simply wouldn't do.

"I...I'm going to make a cup of coffee. Do you want one, Seb?"

He smiled at me, and my heart did another little flutter. I shouldn't be suggesting coffee in my state; a cup of camomile tea would probably be more suitable.

"Sounds perfect."

He glanced down at his watch.

"I've got a meeting in twenty minutes, and I could definitely do with some caffeine. The client is a nice guy, but he has the most droning voice you have ever heard. It bores me to sleep just listening to him, so I certainly need the boost."

I nodded and carried on walking along the hall towards the kitchen. Thinking better of it, I turned back towards him.

"I'll make one for Jo too, and this time I'll make sure I use the right milk."

He smiled at me again.

"That's my girl."

I felt the sharp stab of regret. I had been his girl, but that was in the past. Would I ever be again? And even though the past was gone, what was the future without it?

As the kettle boiled, I busied myself preparing the drinks. Meanwhile I ran through my daily calendar in my head: what meetings I had, what papers I needed to read. It was helping me feel more in control, get my head back into a more professional space.

I then heaped instant coffee into the mugs, careful not to spill any. The big deal was adding the milk: semi-skimmed in Seb's and mine, and a generous slop of Jocasta's milk in hers from the carton with the moronic grinning almond on it. I even remembered to add the sweeteners to her mug.

I could have gone to the trouble of making a pot of fresh coffee, but in truth I just couldn't be arsed. This would just have to do until someone decided later in the day to do a coffee run to the Costa down the road. Meanwhile I patiently waited for the kettle to finally boil. They weren't kidding when they said a watched pot never bloody did.

I glanced down at my nails. I needed a manicure, as my polish was visibly chipped. Then as I leaned down to pull a loose thread from the bottom of my suit skirt, I caught a glimpse of my reflection in the mirrored door of the microwave. I didn't exactly recoil in revulsion, but I couldn't help but notice that I wasn't looking quite as polished as was the norm.

And it wasn't just my nails. Overall, I appeared a little worn out and glum: like a photocopied version of myself when the toner was running out; rather grainy and no longer in sharp focus.

I even had my suit jacket buttoned up wrongly. I hadn't made such a schoolgirl error since Gledhill Primary, when my mother would scold me for traipsing down the path at 3.30 p.m., my satchel dragging along the ground and missing the bottom button on my blazer.

Clearly the last few weeks had taken a toll on me. I had lost my spark. Even shopping didn't hold the same allure any more. My mind was always on something else, or I should say someone else. It just wouldn't do. I had lost my mojo and it needed finding again. And I wasn't going to locate it in the cutlery drawer of this cramped kitchenette, that was for sure.

I sloshed the scalding water into the mugs and gathered them onto the battered tray that was probably older than Fluck. I got ready to pick it up, before making my way gingerly back down the hall to deliver the drinks, when I felt my phone vibrate in my jacket pocket.

I was going to leave it, wait until I got back to my office, but curiosity got the better of me. I pulled it out of my pocket along with a couple of used tissues and a half-empty crisp packet. I must have shoved that in there after my night out with Lottie. More proof I was letting my standards slip.

I squinted at the screen myopically. It was a text from Lottie asking if I wanted to meet her and the girls the following night for a get-together at her house. Bring a bottle, and she would provide the nibbles. I tapped back my reply: I was definitely in. Some female company was just what I needed at the moment. And my friends always had my back.

That was the wonderful thing about having true friends: they would champion you to the world, but behind closed doors would also tell you when you were being a bit of a dickhead. And you would take it on the chin because you knew it came from a place of love.

I was just about to slide the handset back into my pocket when I saw the clearly recognisable blue and white logo of Facebook. I had been tagged into a post. I tapped on the screen, curious to see what it was.

Most probably some random meme from Thomas. My son liked to let me know he was still in the land of the living by sending me random inappropriate memes, usually involving cartoon characters and jokes about bowel movements. He found them completely hysterical, but they never tickled my funny bone in the slightest. It was good to see that university was proving so beneficial in moulding him into a well-rounded productive adult.

But it wasn't a bad taste meme from my son. No, it was something far more disturbing.

Chapter 21

It was Jocasta who had tagged me into a post.

I clicked on it and my stomach dropped like a stone. It was a short video of me from the spa afternoon. And considering I had been less than impressed on seeing my reflection in the microwave a few moments before, feeling I looked dog rough, I now had reason to re-evaluate that opinion.

In the smudged mirrored door of the elderly microwave, I could easily pass for a candidate for *Britain's Next Top Model* compared to this horror show on Facebook.

It was me in all my glory. And it was anything but glorious. I had wanted to relax at the spa, and to be fair I had achieved that. I did appear seriously relaxed: fast asleep on my recliner by the pool and snoring blissfully away. A little river of drool was making its way slowly down my chin and dripping into the crevice between my boobs.

As I snored, my lips parted slightly. I was horrified to see I was sporting a black tooth. Had the cow tampered with the image? A little bit of sly photoshop? But no, it was just a rogue bit of garnish from the smoothie that was wedged "Toffer-style" between my teeth.

I couldn't drag my eyes away from the screen, both horrified and hypnotised by it.

I kept watching as another river of drool began its slow descent down my chin. Or rather I should say chins. From the angle the video had been filmed, I clearly appeared to have three of them.

I was also muttering something in my sleep. I couldn't quite make it out. My voice was low and guttural, like a demon was trapped in my voicebox.

I replayed the video nasty again, trying to concentrate on the low, slurred words. What was it I was saying? My hand flew to my mouth in horror. It sounded like "pleasing hips and muffled cries".

Oh, my fucking hell! I must have been having a saucy dream. I was recalling some shenanigans from a night of nookie with some boyfriend or other, and now it was there for the world to see, hear and no doubt have hysterics at. I could hear my pulse beating in my head with the acute embarrassment of it all.

As the video played for the third time in a row, my breathing slowly returned to some sense of normality when I realised what I was actually saying. It wasn't in fact "pleasing hips and muffled cries" but "cheesy chips and truffle fries". Still embarrassing, but somewhat better than what I had first thought.

I often wondered what I dreamt about at night, as I seldom remembered my dreams. I imagined I travelled to magical faraway places when away in the Land of Nod and had the most wonderful adventures. But sadly, it would appear that in my slumbering state I only travelled as far as the greasy spoon at the precinct. My dreamlife apparently consisted of the thrilling consumption of complex carbohydrates.

I had been too distracted watching my less than perfect self on the video to notice that Jocasta had added a "humorous" caption to it. I was going to bloody well kill her.

"The old dear certainly loves her fried foods. Lucky we're at the spa, so she can get her beauty sleep and work on her cellulite."

She had finished the caption off with two smiley faces. She probably believed this absolved her of all guilt, as it was just meant as a harmless joke.

But it wasn't a joke; it was a complete bitch move. The devious little bint.

It was the unwritten rule between girlfriends that no picture went on social media until everyone had OK'd it first. And of course, the person with the longest arm stretch had to take it and the angle had to be high to avoid the whisper of 'chinnage'. It would be agreed who would be in the forefront of the picture, as they would have to accept the fact that they were going to fall on their sword and be "Sheila fat face" in that shot.

Jocasta must have been lying prostate on the floor to achieve the level of grimness portrayed in the post. I wasn't just "Sheila fat face", I was "Lila lard arse" who looked like she had eaten all the cheesy chips in Yorkshire and possibly County Durham too.

OK, I knew I shouldn't really care. I was nearly fifty after all, and at a stage in my life when I was confident enough not to care a jot about an unflattering snippet of video appearing on social media. I should just have a brief glance, laugh it off and get on with the rest of my day without giving it another thought. But let's get real: this woman was trying to play me, and her games weren't for kids.

So much for me believing we had built bridges and were forging a friendship. Well, this was the stick of dynamite that had just blown that bridge to smithereens.

Seb wandered into the kitchen, his hands shoved in his pockets. He glanced over to the tray of cooling drinks. He must have been wondering what had happened to his hit of caffeine. Before he could utter a word, I shoved my phone screen into his face.

Part of me didn't want to show him, embarrassed for him to see me like that. But I was just too angry not to. Anyway, deep down I knew that Seb had seen me in many embarrassing predicaments over the years, some much worse than me sleeping off the hangover from hell.

He'd witnessed some monumentally horrendous moments; he had even had to hold my hair back on occasion at parties when I had fallen foul of too many dirty martinis on an empty stomach and had needed to dash to the lavatories before I disgraced myself all over the host's cream carpet.

The fact was, I hadn't cared about him seeing me in a state before; but things were different now. Back then, me having no make-up on or not having brushed my teeth wouldn't have been an issue. He was my mate, my non-sexual, non-male mate; a mate that I loved but wasn't in love with. Things were very different now.

He took the phone from me, as I'd pushed it millimetres from his face and he couldn't focus. He watched the video silently, his expression not changing in the slightest.

"To be honest, I've already seen it. Don't worry about it, Lila, it really isn't so bad."

My mind ticked back to when we had talked earlier in the corridor. I recalled he had checked his phone then, and a flash of concern had passed swiftly over his face. No doubt that is when he had first seen me, his friend of many years, in all her grotesque glory.

"It isn't so bad? I'm a flaming laughing stock."

I didn't like the whining edge to my voice. I sounded as if I was going to stamp my foot and have a tantrum. But I needed him to realise that to me this *was* a big deal.

He rubbed my arm briefly to try and reassure me.

"Don't worry about it, she's just trying to be funny and make a joke. I'm sure she wouldn't have done it if she'd thought for a second it would backfire so badly, and you wouldn't see the funny side."

I eyeballed him suspiciously. I knew that Seb could be a little lacking in understanding of the ways of women, but he really wasn't that clueless. He knew that this wasn't just a joke; it was a pretty devious move on Jocasta's part. Seb was just being "Seb" as usual, trying to play the role of peacekeeper. But what I really needed was him to have my back and be my mate.

He was still looking at the screen when a gentle smile flicked across his full lips. He brushed his greying hair back off his face, and I tried to ignore how attractive that move made him appear.

"I actually think you look quite sweet! All your defences are down and you're snoozing away like Sleeping Beauty."

Men really didn't get it. He couldn't have cared less about an unflattering angle in a photo, or anything as trivial as that. For him, the world had many more important things to worry about. But even though I knew that in the big scheme of worldly issues it ranked pretty insignificantly, in this moment and in my life it was still a big deal.

A veritable call to action. A declaration of war.

I snatched my phone back.

"Sleeping Beauty? Are you kidding me? Just forget it, Seb, forget everything. I thought you would have my back. You're my friend. But to be quite honest, I don't know who you are any more. We don't hang out like we used to, I don't feel we chat like we did, and you don't even look the same any more. I miss my Seb in his scruffy old sweaters and his single eyebrow. I miss...I miss....oh, never mind!"

The look of hurt on his face made my heart hurt too. But I needed to get away from him. Get far away before I said too much. And I was hurting too. Stinging with the anger and injustice of it all. I stomped down the corridor on my way to Jocasta's desk. Me and "Miss butter wouldn't melt but cyanide would" were going to have it out.

Chapter 22

I stormed over to her as fast as my fury and high heels would allow.

She was sitting behind her desk in yet another demure outfit. Her skirt looked as if it had been fashioned from shiny black PVC, or possibly a couple of bin bags. Quite fitting really, as the woman was a big bag of trash.

There was a little smile playing on her lips. I knew she had been expecting me. I fantasised about grabbing her by her dirty blonde hair extensions and dragging her around the carpet like a Henry Hoover.

"Delete that post now."

"What post?"

She gave me an innocent little smile before gracefully gliding over to the photocopier with a pile of documents.

It took a battle of wills not to launch myself at her and see how good the photocopy of her forehead would look as I bounced it off the paper feeder.

"You know exactly what post."

I walked over as calmly as I could muster and passed her my phone. From the expression on her face, it was clear she was showing zero shits as to how she had upset me. She was actually making a really bad job of disguising how much she was enjoying it all, and the fact that I might blow a gasket at any moment.

"But it's funny, and look how many reactions it's got already! People are loving it. You're proving to be quite a hit. Honestly, you need to relax a bit, Vera, and not take life so seriously."

Did she just call me Vera? Maybe I had misheard her, because I feared that the continuous suppressing of my fury might be affecting my ability to hear correctly.

"What did you just call me?"

"Oh yes, sorry, it was just a joke. I think Vera suits you so much better, you just seem more 'Vera'. It's my term of endearment for you."

Term of endearment? Who was she kidding? She had about as much affection for me as she would a boil on her arse cheek.

"OK, I won't call you it again."

She held her hands up for a second in mock compliance, and giggled before returning to copying the pile of papers.

"I can see from your face you're clearly unimpressed. You have the same sour expression as when you took your first sip of smoothie yesterday. What did it taste like again? Was it the flavour of unrequited love by any chance?"

The penny slowly began to drop.

I had been right all along, and should have trusted my gut instinct. She really did hate me. It wasn't all in my imagination, as Seb had said. And now I knew the reason why.

There was probably an element of insecurity, because I was senior to her in the firm; maybe she was even jealous of my perceived confidence and skill. But what really got under her fake-tanned, over-perfumed skin was the fact that she was threatened by the relationship I had with Seb. And that threat needed to be neutralised in whatever way she could find.

So here was the truth, finally out: the real reason why she had tried to humiliate me. She was jealous of me, jealous of my closeness to Seb, and she was fighting dirty.

She had probably had her eye on him since the first day she had joined the firm. She'd had to get me out of the way by whatever means necessary: make Seb believe she was this lovely girl, and I was the one with the problem. So she was clearly trying to undermine me at every turn.

She was still speaking as the light from the copier flashed briefly, accentuating her heavily applied make-up. In that light she didn't look nearly as pretty. But then again, maybe that was because until that moment I hadn't realised quite how truly ugly her personality was.

"I don't suppose you can have hated your drink too much, though, as you decided to keep a bit of it between your teeth to have as a snack later."

She giggled again. A most unappealing sound.

"Sorry... sorry, I'm only joking."

She might say she was joking, but she needed to shut her trap. I might not be a comic, but I could happily give her a punchline of my own. And it would be a knock-out one at that.

Chapter 23

So from then on we circled each other like two lionesses primed to attack, our claws barely concealed and ready to roar. We didn't speak unless absolutely necessary; we communicated more with overt hand gestures and looks of withering contempt.

I did a few childish things too that I wasn't exactly proud of, in my quest to feel more in control. Not particularly mature for a woman of my age, but hell, I was only human.

Firstly, I kept moving her stapler around the office to make her think she was going mad. Then I fiddled with the mechanism on the back of her swivel chair so that it ungracefully tipped her out in the middle of an important phone call, and she hit the carpet tiles at speed. I enjoyed that one, even though I felt a slight pang of guilt when she broke the frame of her designer glasses. That said, it was highly amusing to see her walking around the office for the remainder of the day with them held together with botched up Sellotape. Not quite in keeping with the glamour puss look she tried to cultivate. Much more geek than chic.

I even considered substituting her almond milk in its ridiculous carton with cow's milk again and removing all the toilet paper from the Ladies' loo. But even for me, that was a step too far.

If I hadn't been so angry, I would have laughed at just how ridiculous it all was. I had never imagined in my wildest dreams, and let's be fair I now knew my dreams were anything *but* wild, that Seb would be so much in demand as to have two women vying for his attention.

I didn't see much of Seb at all in the weeks that followed. Jocasta made damn sure of that. She was always by his side as if, like her glasses, they were taped together.

And if she wasn't physically with him, she was off fetching him coffee or laughing on the phone at his lame-ass jokes.

And when she wasn't giving Seb her undivided attention, she was with Fluck. She was spending an inordinate amount of time in the boss's office, assisting him with something or other. The door was shut firmly as they discussed "business".

I was beginning to feel the icy fingers of fear creep up my spine. My jangling nerves were getting the better of me. What on earth could they be discussing at such length? I had the distinct feeling in the pit of my stomach that the knives were well and truly out for me. I knew I was still not in favour with Fluck, but did Jocasta actually have enough sway with him to make things precarious for me at work? I wouldn't have thought so.

But then again, she seemed able to wrap men around her little finger with such ease. One simpering glance and a dropped paperclip that she would have to shimmy down to retrieve, like a pole dancer grabbing a dollar bill between their ass cheeks, seemed more than enough to have men eating out of her hands.

There was nothing for it: I just had to get on with things as best I could.

I still wasn't dating; it had just lost all its appeal, and now, like cheesy chips, I just couldn't stomach it. Pointless dates with even more pointless men weren't going to make me feel any better about my situation.

It was true what they said: that you could feel your loneliest in the middle of a crowd. And the truth was that you could feel even worse on a bad date: not just lonely, but willing to poke your own eyes out with your starter fork to distract yourself from the mundanity of it all.

I knew that I just had to learn to live with things. Or even better, find a way to get over it. But the only thing that would make it better was if I could go back in time and fix things between me and Seb. I wished that, like his favourite character, I had a time-travelling Tardis to make that a reality.

My work was suffering too, as my mind wasn't really on it. I had to rectify that. Apart from my friends, my career might be all I had left. Thomas no longer needed me; he was forging a new life for himself, well away from my apron strings.

I busied myself signing a pile of letters that needed to go out in that day's post. I was having another meeting with Mrs Jackson shortly to discuss her ongoing divorce, and wanted to empty my in-box beforehand.

I dropped the letters off on my secretary's desk, and as I turned to walk back to my own office I spotted a man loitering by reception, waiting patiently to be noticed. He was nervously stepping from one foot to the other, desperately trying to catch the eye of the receptionist.

He was a mild-looking man in his early forties, dressed in a beige jumper and corduroy trousers in the same neutral shade. He reminded me of Seb. Well, how Seb used to look.

Eventually Alice deigned to acknowledge his existence. She

was a rather surly woman who had worked at the firm for decades, but always gave the impression she would rather be anywhere in the world than behind her desk.

"Can I help you?"

He cleared his throat awkwardly before speaking. And when he eventually did, his voice was so quiet and unassuming I had to strain to hear the words.

"Would I be able to speak with Jocasta please? I'm Simon."

Alice nodded curtly and buzzed through to Fluck's office where Jocasta and he were having another meeting. Time ticked by, and still no sign of Jocasta. Alice picked up her handbag and made her way outside, no doubt for a quick smoke and to ponder on her unfortunate life decisions.

Simon continued to wait, every so often glancing nervously around his surroundings. He looked like a frightened rabbit; as if the slightest noise might startle him and send him scampering off.

He was certainly a million miles away from how I had expected Simon to be. From what Jocasta had told me at the spa, Simon was a loud, boorish bully who felt the world owed him a favour. That was not at all how this Simon appeared. I knew only too well that first impressions can be deceiving, and many a person was not at all how they seemed. But something just didn't seem right here.

I glanced at my watch. I needed to get back to my office and prepare for my meeting with Mrs Jackson, but something was stopping me. I just felt the need to wait and see what would happen next. OK, I was being nosy, but I felt too invested to leave the scene just yet.

I secreted myself, semi-hidden behind the six-foot artificial plant located next to the reception area. If anyone spotted me,

I would pretend I was dusting the leaves with my suit sleeve. It certainly could do with a good once-over from a Hoover attachment. There was so much dust on it, it looked as if it had been caught in a sandstorm.

Suddenly Jocasta appeared. She looked none too happy to see Simon waiting for her, now seated in one of the old high-backed chairs in the waiting area.

Her eyes narrowed and her body language was confrontational; not at all like that of a victim. And when she spoke, her voice was harsh and laced with contempt.

"And what do you want?"

Simon looked up at her with sad brown eyes.

"I ju...just wanted to talk to you. I couldn't leave things how they were this morning. I had to make you understand how I feel."

His voice wavered a little as his bottom lip trembled.

"Make you see that we just can't carry on like this."

She laughed; a cruel and dismissive sound.

"So, you thought you would turn up unannounced at my workplace, did you?"

She sneered at him, her voice hard and brittle.

"Somehow you believe that *your* feelings were important enough to interrupt my day?"

His head fell like that of a scolded puppy. His shoulders hunched, making him appear even smaller in his oversized sweater.

From my position behind the plant, I began to feel like a voyeur: a dirty old peeping Tom trying to get a quick flash of flesh.

I shouldn't be doing this, spying on a private conversation. I felt bad; ashamed of myself for earwigging. But much worse than that, I felt bad for Simon. Something was seriously wrong here.

"Achoo!"

Oh no. the sneeze was out of me before I had time to try to curtail it with my sleeve. The dust from the plant had made its way firmly up my nasal cavity.

Jocasta's and Simon's heads snapped towards the sound.

I had no choice: I had to show myself. I inched slowly out of my hiding place behind the plant.

"Just admiring the foliage; really amazing what they can do these days, so realistic."

I ran my fingers enthusiastically over the plastic leaves.

Jocasta shot me a look of pure venom before bustling Simon away into an empty meeting room down the hall, where she firmly shut the door, away from prying eyes.

I stood thinking for a few minutes. What had I just witnessed? From my angle behind the fake Ficus, it had certainly appeared that if anyone was the aggressor in that relationship, it certainly wasn't Simon. But surely Jocasta wouldn't stoop so low as to make out she was in a verbally abusive relationship when nothing could be further from the truth? That would just be abhorrent. She wouldn't do that. But I knew without a shadow of a doubt that she would.

The door to the meeting room suddenly burst open and Simon was coming back down the corridor towards the door, his head down; and I could have been mistaken, but were those tears in his eyes?

As he hurriedly left the building, he passed Alice and Mrs Jackson who were making their way in. Alice was rummaging with a packet of mints, no doubt to cover the smell of cigarettes.

I swiftly pushed the worrying thoughts of Simon to the back

of my mind and greeted Mrs Jackson warmly:

"Davina, welcome, I'll take you down to my office now."

I couldn't help noticing that Davina Jackson was looking good. Divorce must be having a positive effect on her. Her grey roots were gone, and she was dressed in a chic navy trouser suit: clearly deciding to spend her settlement in advance. Good for her. Seemed like she hadn't let her bullying ex get the better of her.

The subject of bullies brought my mind swiftly back to Simon. I could be mistaken, but that seemed like a man that was suffering at the hands of his very own bully.

Chapter 24

"Well, maybe you got it wrong."

Lottie was always the one to play devil's advocate in any situation.

I shook my head forcefully. "No, I really don't think so."

We were having a girls' pow-wow at my house the following night; I had summoned the troops together to get their opinions over a Chinese takeaway. With hard liquor and soft noodles, we were going to sort things out. Naturally Lottie was there, but also Jasmine and Jayne had dropped everything to provide their moral support.

They were sipping on gin and tonics whilst listening carefully to make sure they were fully up to speed on the Jocasta fiasco. I couldn't help but note how perfect Jayne's face was. She was so skilled at make-up; it really was a talent.

I smiled to myself, recalling the incident in the pub a few weeks previously. The photo of Jayne's impressive special effects make-up had come in handy to scare the beejezus out of a teenage tearaway who fancied himself as the Yorkshire equivalent to Pablo Escobar.

I handed round a plate piled high with steaming dim sums and spring rolls.

"I know what I saw, and she was not the scared little mouse

she had portrayed herself to be. If anything, he was the one who looked scared out of his wits."

Jasmine helped herself to a vegetable spring roll and dipped it in the viscous orange goop the takeaway provided as an accompaniment.

"But why would she do that? Why make out she's in an abusive relationship when it's a pack of lies? That's a seriously sick thing to do."

"Agreed, but I think she's doing it for the sympathy. That's what she gets off on: everyone feeling sorry for her and wanting to protect poor little Jocasta from her nasty ex-boyfriend, when in truth she's the nasty article and a bully herself."

Jayne was shaking her head, little tufts of springy auburn hair escaping from her messy bun, her clear blue eyes wide with disbelief.

I picked up a dim sum and dunked it in the dip.

"And another thing, I don't even think he is her ex at all. The way they were talking, it sounded like they were still very much together."

Lottie shivered a little in her silk blouse, despite the balmy temperature in the room.

"It makes my blood run cold to think a woman would lie like that about being mistreated, portraying herself to be a victim when the truth is the complete opposite."

I smiled at my friend and rubbed her arm through her sleeve. I knew this conversation would be tough for her. She had been through a lot at the hands of Daniel. To think that a woman like Jocasta could undermine other women when they spoke their truth was a frightening thought for us all, but for Lottie it was even more personal.

"Well, they say the devil takes many forms. I just think that at heart she's an attention seeker, irresistibly drawn to the tragedy of it all, wanting to play the leading role in her own sad little fairytale; and a fairytale is exactly what it is. Only she's not the poor put-upon princess locked in the tower, she's the evil queen."

Jayne reached over to rub Lottie's other arm as a gesture of solidarity, the elaborate bracelets on her arm jangling away merrily, as if to lighten the mood.

"Lila's right: she's just making up shit to get sympathy. It's pathetic; she should be pitied, really."

I agreed with Jayne to a point. But I didn't pity Jocasta; I loathed her. Being in the profession I was, I knew only too well from experience how difficult it could be for a woman to be believed. Jocasta was a real piece of work for behaving the way she had. To play victim only undermined the real victims out there who needed to be heard. It was a really shitty thing for her to do.

Lottie drained her glass, and without a word I reached over and refreshed it for her. I knew she was finding the whole conversation difficult. She sighed deeply, as if she had the weight of the world on her shoulders.

"I'm sorry for doubting you, Lila, and thinking you weren't giving her a chance. It seems like your first impression of her was spot on. I nagged you to give her a break and not be so tough, but you saw through her from the very start."

"Yes, Lottie, but that's because you're so nice, a much better person than me. Unfortunately, I see the world through more cynical eyes. I know that my feelings towards Seb have changed so much but..."

Lottie cut me off abruptly.

"Not changed; you've loved him for years. We could all see it for what it was; there was only you who couldn't. But it's not just about you and Seb now. If he was truly happy with Jocasta, I would tell you to back off and leave him be; sacrifice your own heart to see the man you love happy. But that's not the case. She's not right for him; she doesn't sound like she's right for anyone, to be honest, unless she hooked up with Freddie Kruger perhaps."

We all laughed. Good old Lottie, you couldn't keep her spirits down. She still managed to crack a funny through her pain.

"Or Hannibal Lecter."

Jasmine's brown eyes were sparkling as she got into her stride.

"He loved to cook after all he could make her into a big pan of Bubble and Squeak. You said her high-pitched voice was like a sarcastic squeak that put your teeth on edge. It would be perfect."

Lottie was shaking her head.

"No, Bubble and Squeak is fried cabbage and potatoes. It's vegetarian, you silly billy."

"OK."

Jasmine thought silently for a few seconds before her face brightened and she clicked her fingers together.

"Meat and potato pie then, 'cos she's definitely a big old cow."

She elucidated her point with a lengthy mooing sound at the end.

I was pleased to see that Lottie was still laughing away with us all.

"Seriously though, Lila, you need to make Seb understand what she's like."

"I know, I know, but she's really got her claws into him. I think she realises she's onto a good thing with him. He's an attractive proposition on paper: single man, early fifties, solvent, no dependants, own home, good job etc., etc."

As I reeled off all Seb's attributes, I couldn't help but think his most attractive ones were his kind heart, warm smile and reassuringly broad shoulders. I felt a warm glow come over me just thinking of him.

Lottie took my hand in hers.

"Lila, Seb loves you; you've always been his muse. You're his inspiration in the messy masterpiece that is his life. We all know that, and jerk-off Jocasta knows it too. That's why she's so threatened by you. She's only with him because you never gave Seb a chance. The bloody bitch wants to push you out, or preferably off a cliff, so you need to play to your strengths. The gloves are off, the woman is poisonous. It's no longer about winning Seb back, it's about saving him; saving him from that toxic trollop. You are his best friend. It's time to prove it."

Lottie was making a lot of sense. But even so, I moved the gin bottle out of her reach. It was rare to hear her swear, and she had been letting rip like a sailor on shore leave. But she was spot on, there was no denying it.

I suddenly felt drained and exhausted by it all. But that would have to change. Lila of old needed to waken up within me, like the phoenix rising from the ashes, ready to take flight.

Seb had always been there for me whenever I had needed him, and I had thanked him by taking him completely for granted. Now he needed me, and I was going to be there for him. Even if we never became a couple and he hated me for telling him truth, he was going to listen. He had to.

I held a spring roll aloft as if it were a sword and addressed the room drunkenly.

"By the power invested in me, I shall bring down the bitch. As Lottie said, I am Seb's muse in the masterpiece that is his life, and as such let's get this disaster-piece on the road."

I fell back onto the sofa to the sound of my friends' applause ringing in my ears.

Chapter 25

"Seb, can we talk?"

I had headed him off on his way to the kitchen to get himself his first hit of instant caffeine for the day.

He was looking dapper in his fitted black jumper and slim-legged jeans. He was spending the day catching up on paperwork, no meetings with clients, so was adopting a rather more casual style, embracing the ethos of "dress down Friday".

I doubted whether I was looking quite so stylish. I had barely slept the night before, and probably had eyebags big enough to serve as luggage for a family of four on a package holiday to the sun.

Worried how my conversation with him would pan out, I had counted sheep until the early hours. It was 5 a.m. before I finally nodded off.

But now the time was here, and I was keen to get things off my chest. It needed to be done. I was going to rip the plaster off quick; the wound would get exposed, but then the healing could begin.

He looked at me a little quizzically, probably wondering why I looked so serious for 9 a.m. on a Friday morning.

"Of course we can talk. Just give me two mins and I'll make us both a cuppa to have in my office."

I felt the nerves return, swirling around in my stomach like a toxic soup of adrenaline and Alka Seltzer. It was the knowledge that what I was going to tell him was going to hurt.

At one time I could have told him anything. In fact, I often did. Apart from Lottie and my son, there was no one in the world who knew me better than Seb. All my embarrassing foibles and details that would never be privy to public knowledge he knew. It was the same with him. I understood his strengths and recognised his weaknesses.

For instance, I knew that he had a faint scar on the side of his thumb that he had got from cutting himself with a steak knife when he was eight years old. He had been trying to retrieve an unripe conker from a horse chestnut, too impatient to wait for nature to take its course and open when ready.

I knew he had told his schoolmates that the class bully had bitten him and that's how he had sustained the injury. He had then refused to give away his prize conker – a "sixer" – to the teeny tyrant who had wanted it for himself. He had earned the respect of his peers that afternoon. But now, some forty odd years later, he still felt guilty for telling that fib, especially in the cold weather when even now his scar would itch. Seb was the most honest, truthful person I had ever known. So unlike his current girlfriend.

I was also one of only a few people who was aware of his inexplicable fear of baby lambs, the cutest of all God's creatures. He was fine with slimy crawly things and sharp-toothed rodents, but a gambolling lamb with an adorable bleat was enough to send him running screaming for the hills. The only way he appreciated lamb was in a nice big dollop of shepherd's pie.

That was the thing with a friendship that had spanned so

long: it had history and depth of feelings. But the sad truth was that we hadn't been as close for quite a while now. The easiness between us was just no longer there. I missed it. I missed my friend. But I had something important to do, even if that inevitably meant I wasn't just going to miss my friend, but lose him entirely.

Once inside the smart confines of his office, with its polished wood and neat bookshelves, I took a deep breath ready to get everything off my chest.

"Seb, I want to talk to you about Jo…"

At that very moment Jocasta burst into the room, all bouncy and chipper and dressed like she was off night-clubbing at barely 9.30 in the morning.

She was wearing less make-up for once though, and she looked better for it. However, if she felt she needed a bit more slap, I would be more than happy to give her a nice sharp one around the chops.

"Oh, sorry, Lila, I didn't know you were in here. I just need to borrow Seb for a minute."

I fixed my gaze on her. Her eyes held a warning in them, as if to say, "Watch your step, bitch."

She'd known I had been in here with Seb. Of that I had no doubt. She would have seen see us walk together from the kitchen. She was worried about what I was going to say. And she had good reason to be.

"Sorry, Jo."

Seb gestured to his steaming mug.

"It'll have to wait, I've just made Lila and me a coffee. Give me ten minutes and then you'll have my undivided attention."

Her face took on a sour note, as if she might actually stamp her foot in frustration. However, clearly thinking better of it, her voice took on an irritating whiny pleading edge that was even worse than her normal breathy tone or occasional high-pitched squeak.

"But Sebby, sweetheart, you said you would have a quick look at my catalogue and help me decide what colour dress to choose. You haven't forgotten, have you? If I leave it too long, they might have sold out."

It was clear from his expression that he had indeed forgotten and couldn't give a flying toss about what colour dress she chose. Seb was colour blind; he was the worst possible person to assist in matters relating to colour palettes and fashion.

His voice was pleasant but firm.

"I'm sure another ten minutes won't matter, Jo. Then I'll be with you."

Her smile was as tight as her pencil skirt as she turned on her heel and tottered out of the office, not before shooting me another warning glance that I returned with a grin that would put the Cheshire cat to shame.

Seb blew on his coffee before taking a large gulp.

"So, come on, Lila, what do you need to tell me that's so important? Don't keep me in suspense."

Chapter 26

I told him everything I knew, such as it was. And he let me speak, never interrupting me for a second, just letting me get everything off my chest.

We were sitting opposite each other, as if I was his client. And that's how I felt, like a guilty woman pleading my case. He regarded me with steady eyes and an unreadable expression, his hands knitted together under his chin.

Finally, I was done. I sat silently, my head slightly bowed as the seconds passing excruciatingly slowly while I waited for the verdict.

And then the axe dropped. He was angry. No strike that he was furious. And for someone so perennially placid and easy-going, it was shocking to see.

"I'm surprised at you, Lila, I really am!"

Seb was out of his chair now and pacing around his office.

"I know you're mad at her, but to say she's been lying about her ex is too much, Lila, even for you."

Even for me? What the hell was that supposed to mean? I knew I could be a little tough at times, but I was always fair. And I never lied. OK, I might occasionally exaggerate about a couple of inches in length to massage a man's ego, or insist a girlfriend's arse looked good in a dress when in truth it was so huge it could be seen from space like the Great Wall of China. But I would never ever make up something like this.

Maybe I had been wrong about Seb, and he didn't really know me at all.

"It's true, Seb! I saw her with him yesterday, and he wasn't the brute she'd led us to believe. In fact, she was the one that was treating him like dirt; she was talking to him like he was a piece of shi…"

Seb held up his hand to silence me, as if I was a naughty schoolgirl that needing scolding. And not in a good way.

"Enough, Lila, I don't know what you think you saw, but you were wrong. Jo wouldn't lie about something like that. She's really opened up to me about how bad their relationship was, and how frightened she was. She was genuinely upset when she confided in me as her friend. You just can't fake that."

Can't fake that? That was a laugh. The woman was as fake as a wristwatch on the Mona Lisa. Faking a few tears was nothing to her, I was sure of it.

I knew that Seb always saw the best in people, but this time I knew he was wrong. Jocasta had pedalled the same sob story to me at the spa, and I'd fallen for it hook line and sinker too. But I knew better now.

I knew what I had seen yesterday, and I might be pushing fifty, but my eyesight was as sharp as my wit. That was no abused woman beaten down by a man.

"But Seb, I know what I saw."

His expression was steely.

"You've clearly got an issue with Jo, and you're seeing things that aren't even there. Wanting to think the worst of her. She's told me how she thinks you've got it in for her."

He sighed deeply before continuing.

"I don't like to say this, Lila, but she's of the opinion that you might be a bit jealous of her, being as she's younger and..."

His voice trailed off and he looked down at his shoes with obvious embarrassment. He clearly didn't want to hurt my feelings.

Too late. It wasn't that my feelings were hurt, they were bloody eviscerated.

How fucking dare she. The cheek of the little moo, telling all and sundry that I was jealous of her. I had an issue with her. And now Seb thought I would pedal a false narrative, just to make her appear bad. Poor little put-upon Jocasta. Don't make me laugh.

I wanted to know what else she'd said, though. I was nothing if not a glutton for punishment.

"And what else did she say, Sebastian?"

His eyes darted away from me for a second. He knew I was angry with him when I used his name in its entirety. When his eyes returned, they met mine and they locked for a few seconds.

The blueness of his irises were intense, and suddenly I felt I might drown in them. Unexpectedly a woozy feeling came over me, like the oxygen was being sucked out of the room. I worried I might faint, but he continued to gaze deeply into my eyes, not breaking contact for a moment.

"She said that you had a problem with her because you wanted me for yourself. She said she thought you might be in love with me."

I was holding my breath now, my heart beating hard in my chest so hard I felt sure he must be able to hear it.

His eyes dropped down suddenly, breaking the spell.

"I told her not to be ridiculous, though. You're not interested in me, you never have been."

It was my moment. My time to tell him. To speak my truth and spill the contents of my heart and hope he would gather up the broken pieces and put it back together. Make it whole again. To sweep me up into his arms in a passionate embrace.

But instead, I just laughed. A cold and hollow sound.

"Yeah, totally ridiculous."

My back was to him, and I marched out of the room as quickly as I could, pleased he couldn't see the tears that were collecting in my eyes.

Chapter 27

I decided to stay late at work. In truth, I had nowhere better to be. It was Friday night and I was looking at a long weekend stretching ahead of me, filled with nothingness. All my friends were busy, I had no intention of seeing my mother and I didn't know my neighbours particularly well. I had lived next to them for years, but only the week before had mistaken the chap from next door for the Amazon delivery man. I really needed to start making more of an effort with people.

I glanced at my watch: 7:10 p.m. I yawned deeply and rolled my shoulders back, listening to the muscles crack in protest. They felt tight and unyielding, as if they had been clenched for eternity.

It was time I called it a night and headed home. Sitting at my desk, staring into space with only the dim overhead light for company wasn't doing me or my mood any good. I had stopped being productive hours ago.

I could hear the distant hum of Greta the cleaner's vacuum as she worked away in one of the offices down the hall.

She was singing along tunelessly to Dolly Parton as she hoovered. She always had her big pink earphones clamped to her head, holding her mass of grey curls firmly in place.

She was endlessly cheerful and happy with her lot in life. I wished I could channel Greta more. She had once told me she could be anyone and anywhere when she escaped into her music. She had a point. I might have to crank up the radio on the drive home. A few good tunes might drown out the thoughts circling in my head; maybe a bit of hard rock would silence them altogether. Unlike Greta, I wouldn't be listening to Dolly Parton or the like; too many heartfelt nostalgic songs about liquor and lost loves. Greta really was the world's biggest country music fan, unlike Jocasta, who I now knew was just the world's biggest cu...next Tuesday.

Little Miss Perfect had left work at lunchtime. She had claimed to be poorly, suffering with Lie-abetes, no doubt. I had been glad to see her leave the building, hips swinging and her hair bouncing in the breeze in time with her bosom.

She had attracted an appreciative wolf whistle from a couple of men smoking outside their office. Morally I felt affronted by their crass behaviour, but in all honesty it also irked me just how easily she could turn men's heads.

I slid my tired feet into my high heels, which I'd kicked off hours earlier, pushed my swivel chair back under the desk and turned off the light.

I was going to treat myself to a takeaway on the way home to cheer myself up. Something tasty and teeming with trans fats. There was no point watching my waistline any more. I might as well get fat: single, fat and about to turn fifty. God, that was a depressing thought.

It was probably high time I got some cats after all. And if they did end up eating me like Lottie had said, at least if I was fat, they wouldn't go hungry.

I would watch a horror film too: some crazed maniac hunting

down his poor victims with a chainsaw, or such like. It might save me from feeling like the unluckiest person in the world for approximately ninety minutes.

Greta was now in reception. I heard her well before I saw her, noisily emptying Alice's wastepaper bin and grumbling about the spat-out wads of nicotine gum in it. I could hear her scraping them off as she sang tunelessly to *Country Roads Take Me Home.* I couldn't agree more: it was time that I was out of here.

I was proud of myself for staying late, though. At least I had managed to catch up on some admin, and it would show Fluck that I was willing to put in the hours when necessary. He wasn't to know that I had spent the last couple lost in my own thoughts. More lacklustre than litigation. But that was going to change. From now on I was going to be back on my A game. My clients deserved it, and after all, my career was all I really had.

The building felt rather oppressive and gloomy with the dim emergency lighting illuminating my way. Once I had left, only Greta would remain. But she didn't seem bothered in the slightest at being in a creaky Victorian property on her own. She had now moved on to cleaning the kitchen, and I could hear the strains of her singing along to Glen Campbell's *Dreams of the Everyday Housewife.*

I had my hand on the door handle in readiness to leave Fluck, Young & Glover for the night and head out into the vast world beyond, when a sudden noise startled me and stopped me dead in my tracks. It was a faint scuffling sound, and it appeared to be coming from the vicinity of Fluck's office.

There was only me and Greta left in the building, so what could the noise be? I heard it again, a little louder this time.

My mind shot back to the night at Merv's house and the rodent under his bed. Or at least what I had believed was a rodent. It certainly had looked like roadkill when it has been languishing on his bald pate.

Maybe a rat had been living in the old walls of this building and felt somehow drawn to Fluck's office. It was the King Rat's lair after all.

I knew Greta was oblivious to the noise. I could hear her happily singing away, completely oblivious. Her song choice had now moved onto Joe Nichols and *Tequila Makes Her Clothes Fall Off*. True words indeed.

I was in two minds what to do: ignore the noise and head off home, or morph into Miss Marple and play the 'shero', doing a little investigating of my own. Curiosity got the better of me, and with a sigh I turned back to walk down the corridor to my boss's office.

I knew Fluck was not one for working late nights. He felt he was of an age and position in the firm that he could set his own hours. He was often teeing off at his golf club when he should really have been behind his desk. For him to stay at work beyond 4.30 p.m. was completely unheard of, especially on a Friday.

My hand was on his office door handle when I head the scuffling noise again, this time accompanied by a definite squeak. My blood ran cold. It was a rat after all. Seb might have a fear of wee woolly lambs, but it was rats that terrified me. Their sharp teeth and beady eyes plagued many of my nightmares.

My first impulse was to run away, find a stool to leap on, clutching my skirt and wailing, like you would see in an old episode of *Tom and Jerry*. But no, I was going to be brave. I was going to have to learn how to be a little braver in life, so why not start now?

I grabbed my heavy tote bag off my shoulder, ready to whack Mr Ratty around his furry face if needs be, and burst into the room.

I really wished I hadn't. What I saw was far worse than a hundred rats. I really longed to turn the clock back to five seconds prior. I was going to need to bleach my eyeballs after this.

Fluck was sitting back in his office chair with a contented look on his face and his eyes firmly shut. At first glance I had worried he was dead, but that was not the case. As he leant back further, and a contented sigh escaped his ancient old mouth, the chair squeaked slightly under his weight. That explained the noise: it probably needed a quick squirt of WD40.

I still had the door handle in one hand and the strap of my bag wrapped tightly around the other, ready to attack. It was clear that he hadn't heard me come in. Neither had Jocasta, who was knelt on the carpet in front of him. I had been wrong about her leaving early for the day, as quite clearly she still had a job to do.

It was like one of those really scary moments in a film when you're desperate to look away but can't, as morbid fascination keeps your eyes glued to the screen. The last thing I had expected to see this evening was Jocasta Jennings flossing her teeth with Fluck's greying ball hair.

They still hadn't seen me. Fluck's expression was one of pure rapture, Jocasta not so much. She also had her eyes shut, but looked about as happy in her work as when I had asked her to descale the kettle.

I slowly backed away and out of the room, letting the door

silently close. I was on autopilot as I made the short walk to retrieve my car from the multi-storey car park. As soon as I was safely away from work, I began to doubt what I had actually seen. It seemed too horrendous to be true. But true it was. There was no mistaking what I had witnessed, and that was Jocasta giving our boss a blowie.

There was no way that could be explained away as innocent. She wasn't just picking up spilled pens from the floor. No, it was his penis that was about to spill. I felt queasy at the memory of it, worried that my lunch might make a sudden reappearance. But considering I hadn't had any, that would have been quite a feat in itself.

I shuddered in my coat and wrapped it a little tighter around myself. I wasn't going to bother with a takeaway after all. My appetite had well and truly gone.

I had always known that Jocasta was a wrong 'un, but this was on another level. OK, I realised it could be some women's fantasy, sex in the office with the boss. But when that was portrayed on screen or in a book, it would be with the gorgeously grumpy boss, who just happened to be infatuated with his underling and was a billionaire into the bargain. Now Fluck wasn't short of a penny or two, and he was certainly grumpy. But gorgeous? Give me a break. There weren't enough paper bags in the whole of England to make that man shaggable.

Fluck was no billionaire dreamboat. He was the stuff of nightmares. Giving him a gobble was like fellating Nosferatu with nostril hair.

"You actually saw it?"

Lottie sounded as stunned as I expected her to be.

"Oh yes, I saw it all right, in high definition and technicolour splendour; and believe me, it was a video nasty. I may never sleep again."

"You have to tell Seb."

I had phoned Lottie as soon as I got home. I hadn't even bothered to take my coat off in my haste to speak to my friend, dialling the number I knew by heart.

"I can't tell him, Lottie, I just can't."

The firmness in her voice was evident over the phone line.

"You have to, Lila, you've got no choice. He's your friend; you owe him that much."

"But he'll hate me for it. He already thinks I made up, or at least exaggerated, what I saw with her ex, he's going to think this is just me stirring it again. He's never going to believe it; I barely do, and I saw it with my own eyes."

I shuddered at the memory.

"I wish to hell I could unsee it."

I felt a chill run through me and walked briskly to the thermostat in the hall to crank the central heating right up.

"That's a chance you just have to take. He needs to know,

and you're the one who has to tell him. You can't let him carry on seeing her; she's making him into a laughing stock."

I knew she was right, but I also feared this would be the end of Seb's and my friendship forever; and the thought of that was even more horrendous than what I had witnessed this evening. Hard to believe, but true.

I could hear Lottie still speaking, so forced myself to concentrate on her words.

"And he's got a wife too, poor... what was her name again? Deidre?"

"Dinah."

"Yes, poor Dinah, I know you've always said she's got the personality of wet lettuce, but she needs to know. He's betraying her in the worst possible way. Believe me, I know how that feels, you need to tell her too."

I let out another lengthy sigh, but I knew in my heart that Lottie was right. There wasn't only Seb going to be destroyed by this; there was Fluck's wife to consider too. Dinah always looked like misery personified whenever she was near her husband, but even so she would no doubt be devastated to discover his infidelity. They had been married for over thirty years. I was sure this was going to break her heart.

I carried the phone with me into the kitchen and stuck my head in the fridge, looking for something chilled and alcoholic to blur the edges of the day. There was a half-opened bottle of Pinot Grigio, that would do the job nicely.

I poured myself a hearty glass and filled a small bowl with cashews to serve as my dinner, then returned to my spot on the settee in the lounge. I might as well get comfy. This was where I planned to be spending most of my weekend. I put the glass bowl of nuts down on the oak coffee table. My mind returned to when I had bought it. I had dragged Seb along to get his opinion on it, as it was a bit of an investment buy. He had taken one look at the price ticket and shaken his head in disbelief.

"Distressed furniture, I ask you? I'm bloody distressed after seeing the price."

God, how I missed him and his Yorkshire charm.

Lottie's voice was persistent on the other end of the call.

"So, you will tell Seb, Lila. You must."

I sighed deeply to myself. I knew she was right. I just couldn't face it now. I would do it face to face first thing Monday. And like I had as a child, I hoped the weekend would last forever and the new week would never come.

Chapter 29

I barely felt I'd blinked before Monday was upon me once again. Mondays were always ghastly by nature, but this one was the most horrendous yet. I was going to have to speak to Seb, and I was absolutely dreading it.

My intentions were good. I was going to march straight up to him in his office, tell him I needed to speak to him in private and it couldn't wait. Then I'd unpack the shit tsunami that was living rent-free in my head and hope his head didn't spontaneously explode.

But I bottled it. All went well as I marched on rather wobbly legs into his office first thing, where I discovered him sitting behind his desk, engrossed in some reading.

He looked up, briefly surprised to see me standing there. His eyes appeared to brighten slightly, the blueness of them quite beautiful, but then again that might have just been the early morning sun hitting him through the sash windows.

"Lila, how are you? How was your weekend?"

I shifted nervously from one foot to the other, just as I had as a child when summoned to see the headmaster for some misdemeanour or other: pulling a girl's pigtails or claiming I couldn't hand in my homework because the dog had defecated over it.

"It...it was good, thank you. Quiet, just stayed in and watched some films, read a little. It was chilled."

That wasn't true. My weekend had been far from chilled. Well, apart from the wine, that is. It was fair to say I had indulged in a little too much of that which had then inevitably led onto a family size bag of Chilli Heatwave Doritos. When I had eventually retired to bed Saturday night, I was drunkenly sporting orange tipped fingers and red wine fangs. Not my best look.

I had spent much of the weekend fretting over this very moment and had barely been able to concentrate on the TV or the books I had picked up. As a rule I loved a good lengthy thriller; my taste in books was rather like my men: I enjoyed them girthy and a crowd-pleaser. But I couldn't concentrate at all on my current paperback and was struggling to even get past page one.

He smiled up at me, still standing there awkwardly across from him. That lopsided grin of his that always gave him a rather boyish charm was threatening to render me weak at the knees. I worried I might faint.

"Stayed in? You're telling me that Lila Glover, party animal extraordinaire, stayed in all weekend with a good book of all things? Should we alert the elders? The world might spin out of control."

I smiled, despite myself.

"Oh, I don't know. I just haven't felt like going out much lately; it hasn't had the same appeal."

We locked eyes for a few seconds then, and I felt as if time stopped in that very moment. I really needed to get a grip of myself. I was beginning to act like one of Lottie's heroines in her old romantic movies. It must be my hormones playing up.

I must go back and see my GP, get myself on HRT or some such.

Seb stretched back in his chair. His shirt moved up a few inches, exposing a smooth, flat stomach. Much flatter than it should have been for the amount of complex carbohydrate and potato-based meals he consumed. I forced my eyes away, feeling like a voyeur.

"Well, I had a great weekend myself. Adam and I went to this sci-fi event at the Town Hall; it was fantastic."

His face lit up as he recalled his day. He looked young and happy and absolutely adorable. There was no way on earth you would guess he was in his fifties. It just showed that if you were a nice person on the inside, it really showed on the outside. The skin care companies should really take note.

"And then on Sunday Adam and I met up with some of the other guys and did the whole *Lord of the Rings* marathon. Twelve hours it took us in total, an epic day, possibly one of the best ever."

I couldn't help smiling at this. We really did come from two very different worlds. But what in the past I would have found annoying about him was now strangely endearing. Maybe the adage had been right all along, and opposites really did attract.

"So, you didn't see Jocasta this weekend then?"

He looked a little confused by this.

"Jocasta? No, I didn't see her. Why, was I supposed to?"

I stared for a few seconds at his puzzled face. This was my moment to tell him. To speak my truth. But the words simply wouldn't come. He looked up at me expectantly, after a few seconds his expression changing to one of concern. No doubt because I was standing there with my mouth wide open, gaping at him like a startled pigeon.

"Are you OK, Lila? What's the matter?"

I couldn't tell him. I just couldn't. I snapped my mouth shut. At least I wouldn't risk catching flies any more.

"Nothing, I'm fine. I'll go back to my office. I've got a hell of a day today. I really need to get working."

He nodded his head slowly, the quizzical look still evident on his face.

"OK, well, I'll see you later."

I nodded my head briefly and scurried out of his office, just desperate to get away.

I scolded myself inwardly on the short walk down the corridor. I really was a wimp. I owed it to Seb to tell him the truth. But strong, formidable Lila Glover just didn't have the lady balls to get the task done. I felt ashamed of myself. My mobile phone vibrated from the confines of my coat pocket, and I reached in to retrieve it. It was a text from Lottie.

"Have you told him yet?"

I stopped walking so I could concentrate on typing my reply. *"No! I just couldn't."*

Immediately my phone buzzed again. I clicked on the message: a sad-faced emoji from her. I knew she was disappointed in me. I was disappointed in myself.

I hadn't realised that Jocasta was standing slap bang in front of me until her voice nearly made me leap out of my skin in shock.

Now that was a woman who really should be ashamed of herself. But that was not how her face appeared. In fact, she looked full of the joys of spring for a winter's morning. Full of smiles and her cheeks were positively glowing. However, that was more than likely down to the heavy make-up she had applied that morning. To impress who? I wondered.

She appeared like she might possibly be wearing the entirety of the Estée Lauder range. She wasn't trying to achieve the "less is more" approach today, that was for sure. There were at least two layers of undercoat and a thick coat of emulsion, and that was just her base. Her pouty lips she'd painted scarlet, and her eyes had more cut creasing and contouring than you would expect to see on a teenager at a prom.

She had an air of superiority about her that was testing my last nerve. She must believe that secretly shagging the boss gave her some sort of cachet. It really didn't. It just gave me the massive ick.

"Hello, Lila, good weekend? It must have been incredible! I've got to say you look bloody knackered."

She gave me another one of her trademark winks, to show she was only joking. But I knew there was a grain of truth in it. No doubt I looked exhausted. But there was no need for her to be quite so vile. She really was a walking void of a human.

I was finding her so-called "jokes" about as funny as a turd in a porcelain teapot.

She didn't wait to see if I would reply, just trotted away on her taupe stilettos. But not before I had the chance to glimpse the smug expression on her overly made-up face.

Chapter 30

I dumped my briefcase on my desk in fury. She really was an obnoxious little witch. I knew I shouldn't let her annoy me; after all, that was just playing right into her hands, and my hands desperately wanted to be wrapped around her scrawny little neck.

I knew I should keep my distance, get on with my work since there was enough of it to keep me drowning in paperwork for the foreseeable. But before I could stop myself, I was marching back down the corridor towards her desk.

She was sitting behind it, thumbing through a large stack of papers and noisily sucking on a mint. I couldn't help but wonder if she was trying to get a certain nasty taste out of her mouth.

Standing in front of her desk, I suddenly felt unsure of myself. I really didn't want to let her know I was aware of what she had been up to. I didn't wish to show my hand too soon. I had aces to play, after all. But the truth was that I had always been a lousy poker player. Much too emotional.

Her head snapped up suddenly, aware of my presence. Maybe the atmosphere had altered slightly, my outraged aura crackling like static electricity. Inside I was a thunderstorm brewing, but outwardly I was calm personified. I smiled sweetly at her, a monumental effort on my part.

"I didn't get a chance to ask how *your* weekend was, Jocasta?"

She looked at me suspiciously, clearly thinking she could just hurl her barely concealed insult at me like a missile and then trot away on her ridiculous heels as if no harm had been done. She'd never expect the explosion brewing on the horizon.

"Er...it was OK."

She put down the pile of papers she was holding and looked directly at me. Her green eyes were captivating yet somewhat cold, like a reptile.

"Actually, it was amazing. Seb had this sci-fi thingy to go to, so I didn't see him. But I went bowling with some friends Saturday afternoon, and then nightclubbing until the early hours."

Well, if that were true, she definitely hadn't been with Fluck. Nightclubbing really didn't sound like his cup of tea. I would bet the last time he had strutted his stuff in a discotheque, John Travolta would have been shoehorned into his white suit and gyrating to the warbling of the Bee Gees. And as for bowling, unless it was Crown Green, I doubted very much whether that was his thing either.

I smiled at her pleasantly, like a cat cruelly toying with a baby mouse.

"That sounds nice."

I could see from her face she was confused as to why I was being so convivial towards her. After all, she had been a massive cow to me so she expected me to be a mardy arse in return. She couldn't work out what I was up to, and that wasn't sitting well with her.

She let out a little awkward laugh. It sounded more like a

petulant squawk in my opinion.

"I suppose you think bowling and clubbing is a little childish, not something you would do."

I shook my head emphatically.

"No, not at all. I like to go clubbing myself every now and again, and there's nothing wrong with enjoying yourself and letting off some steam. It doesn't make you childish in the slightest."

A slyness settled over her features.

"Yeah, but I guess when one gets to your age, you've not been considered childish for over forty years. You wouldn't know half of the music playing in the clubs these days anyway, Madonna would be much more your style or Grandma-donna I should say."

She laughed at her joke, as if she was the world's best comedian; not realising that the joke was actually on her.

My hand flew to my mouth in ill-feigned shock, as if I was mortally wounded by her words.

"Ouch, that's a bit mean, Jocasta. You're not that young yourself and hardly *Like a Virgin*, or had you forgotten you were no longer in your twenties and not a million miles away from the big 40."

Her expression darkened, as if someone had turned down the lights. Oh, how I would love to turn her lights off permanently.

I smiled pleasantly at her, my expression suggesting I had just necked a sedative and a large Sauvignon Blanc. Looking for the whole world as if I were so chilled out and relaxed, I wouldn't notice if my arse was on fire.

"I know you think your little jokes at my expense are funny, but they're not. In fact, it's all rather tedious. I get it you don't like me, but there's no need for you to be such a complete fucking bitch, is there?"

To elucidate my point, I let out an exaggerated yawn, as if it was all beneath me and not worthy of my time or effort.

Her eyebrows shot up, well, as much as her Botox would allow. They now resembled two startled slugs against their fake-tanned backdrop.

"Well, I was only having a little joke. You don't need to resort to language like that."

"Oh, pardon me, I do apologise for the coarseness of my words. I should have realised that nothing so uncouth would ever come out of your mouth."

I smiled pleasantly at her and lowered my voice a little.

"Or go into it for that matter."

She stared at me blankly, not having a clue what I was getting at.

I waited patiently for the penny to drop. It didn't take long, and when it did, like those old coin fall machines in a seaside arcade, it brought them all tumbling down. Jackpot!

Her face still bore a look of confusion, but the arrogance she had previously conveyed had slipped away. As quickly no doubt as Fluck had slipped away on Friday night after she had completed her "overtime": back to his wife for a home-cooked meal and a cozy night in front of the telly.

She studied my face carefully, confused but cautious, not quite sure what I was getting at, but worried all the same. After all, how could I know? They had been all alone in his office on Friday, hadn't they? Or so she believed.

She laughed nervously.

"Well yes, I try not to swear too much. I just find it rather crass. And as for my mouth, I do eat healthily wherever possible."

She gestured to the half-opened packet of mints spilling out over her desk.

"I really don't eat these all the time, just as a one-off. And I do tend to crave sugary things when I'm stressed."

I nodded at her as if impressed by the wiseness of her words. I was really getting into my stride now and beginning to enjoy myself immensely.

"Oh, I agree, it's all about balance when it comes to diet: not too many sweets, a good amount of protein, and you can't beat a nice big portion of meat and two veg when you get the chance."

I think she might have actually stopped breathing for a second or two in shock. When she did eventually take in a deep breath of air, she choked on her mint.

I was only too happy to dash around to provide my Florence Nightingale support, giving her back a jolly good whack to try and dislodge it.

She grabbed desperately for the bottle of mineral water on her desk and commenced gulping it down, red-faced and with her eyes bulging. She was no doubt worried I might try and administer the Heimlich manoeuvre on her next and crack a couple of ribs.

When she had recovered from her coughing fit, she addressed me with wary, watery eyes. Her voice still raspy.

"Is there something you want to say to me, Lila?"

I shrugged my shoulders nonchalantly.

"About what? And your voice sounds terrible, by the way. You might need some deep throat spray, if that's what you're accustomed to."

She started coughing again, tears running down her face and mixing with her make-up. She was beginning to resemble a circus clown, literally and figuratively. The patchy mess that was now her face looked for all the world like a primary school watercolour class. Less Warhol and more asshole.

"Oh, I don't know Lila, it's just you're acting a little odd and I wondered if you'd heard something...I don't know...some silly gossip or...or something."

I had to lean right in to make out what she was saying, as she had lowered her voice so much.

I suddenly realised, as she had, that Alice had been watching our exchange with mounting interest. She would have witnessed Jocasta's choking fit and wondered what was going on, even though Alice's desk was situated far enough away from hers that she wouldn't have been able to make out our every word. But it was clear from the expression on the older woman's face that her interest was piqued. She was now regarding the pair of us with an expression of curiosity on her weathered face.

"No, I've heard no gossip."

I had dropped my voice now so that it was as low as Jocasta's.

"I think you'll find this is a professional place and everyone has better things to do than gossip. It's not the epicentre of rumours and lies that you may think, just a well-regarded law firm with *decent* people working for it."

She scowled at me and reached over to grab a handful of mints, not bothering to offer me one before shovelling them into her gob. Clearly something was stressing her out.

I continued speaking over the loud crunching sound coming from her direction.

"Or at least it was respectable. Now there's more drama going on here than an episode of *The Real Housewives of Yorkshire*."

Alice was out of her seat now, packet of cigarettes clenched tightly in her hand and making her way to the front door. Obviously, curiosity over our conversation was not a strong enough pull against the lure of Madame Nicotine.

When she was safely out of the building and the heavy wooden door had closed behind her, Jocasta was out of her seat and marching around, her fists clenched.

"Stop playing with me, Lila. If you've got something to say, just spit it out."

Now I was going to give it to her both barrels, and I was going to enjoy every second.

"Is that what you did? Spit it out all over his golfing shoes? Noshing off the boss when you thought everyone had left for the day?"

I paused for a moment to appreciate the look of utter shock on her face. She was stunned, like she had been slapped resoundingly around the face. It was a satisfying sight indeed. I remember reading once that it took forty-two muscles to frown, but only four to reach out and slap someone. Well, I wasn't the one frowning now, and I hadn't even had to move a single muscle.

"You're such a cliché, Jocasta. It would be funny if it wasn't so tragic. Blowing old man Fluck, that's hands down the most disgusting thing I've ever seen, and I've cleaned a teenage boy's bedroom."

Jocasta's lips were moving but she was unable to find a word in her defence she just kept staring at me as if she was face to face with her worst nightmare. Well good, because I sure as hell had been faced with mine when I had seen her and Fluck together *in flagrante.*

"If I could give you a little advice Jocasta it would be to go and see your doctor, clearly you need a checkup from the neck up if you consider Mr Fluck a suitable lover."

I gave an exaggerated shudder that quickly turned into laughter.

And boy did I laugh. All those jibes she had made at me. The video she had uploaded to social media, and more importantly what she had done to Seb. She finally had her comeuppance, and it hadn't come a moment too soon. But I still had one parting shot.

"It's all just so horrible, seedy and pathetic, and if I can be brutally honest almost as ghastly as those hideous shoes you're wearing."

Chapter 31

What a time to be alive.

It's amazing how exhilarating finally getting something off your chest can feel. After my less than friendly exchange with Jocasta, I spent the rest of the day in my office with the door firmly shut. I had back-to-back meetings with clients, and plenty of other admin tasks that needed my attention and would keep me out of any more trouble.

I felt cleansed. Almost as if I had been back to the spa again for a detox, but this time it had done me the world of good. I was refreshed, invigorated and even better, nothing was going to be shared on Facebook.

The only downside to it was that I still needed to tell Seb. But that could wait for a while. I would see what Jocasta's next move would be first. No doubt she was currently weighing up her options and, like a chess Grand Master, deciding what piece to move.

She would be wondering if I would tell Seb everything. She knew that we were good friends, and obviously my loyalties would lie with him. Let's face it, I couldn't give two flying shits about her, absolutely no love lost between us. There was no girl code. Well, not unless it was Morse code and lengthy sighs, rude hand gestures and tutting were our way of communicating.

Let's face it, we pretty much despised each other. And that had been fine, until now when it wasn't. The time had come when people were actually going to get hurt.

Would she try to get to Seb first? Brazen it out. Try rolling shit in glitter. Make him believe that there was no truth in it at all and she was completely innocent. Turn the waterworks on again to gain his sympathy.

Try to paint me as a jealous menopausal woman who was prone to exaggeration, if not full-blown fibbing and definitely not to be trusted. She might even consider that I would keep the juicy nugget of gossip to myself, not wanting to give rise to out-and-out war in the workplace.

And if she did speak to Seb and convince him that nothing had happened, somehow spun the tale that she had taken an innocent stumble off her kitten heels and had fallen open-mouthed onto Fluck's open fly, well, if that was the case, then I was just going to have to live with it.

I had come face to face with the crusty Casanova myself that morning. Fluck had popped his head into my office to collect some documents regarding a new client, and I had found it difficult to make even civil conversation with the man. I just had the image of him slumped in his swivel chair while Jocasta gave him her undivided attention. It kept playing over and over in my head like the worst horror movie trailer ever. *Night of the Living Dead* with Fluck as the rotting corpse.

He was completely oblivious to the fact that just looking at him was making me want to gag, and not for the same reason Jocasta might.

Normally such a miserable old duffer, he was in a surprisingly good mood. Had a spring in his geriatric step. But then again, after what I had witnessed, maybe that wasn't so surprising after all. He looked refreshed, as if he had had the cobwebs blown away. On second thoughts, maybe he had. I could only imagine what had been lurking in his saggy Y-fronts.

"Just the file for Smithson, please, Lila."

He furnished me with what I assume he considered a pleasant smile.

I returned his smile with a rictus grimace of my own and handed him a pile of paperwork and the file he had requested.

He took them from me with a brief nod and thankfully started to make his way out of the office. He stopped briefly as if thinking better of it. He laughed. It was not a pleasant sound, in fact it could have scared children worse than the Bogey Man while trick or treating on Halloween.

"It really was quite amusing what happened at the fashion show, when you think about it."

He smiled again, showing off a row of neat white teeth like a creepy china doll.

"Now I've had time to calm down, I can see the funny side of it. All those fine young women tumbling over themselves in their fancy frocks, it was like a comedy farce. Obviously, the sign ripping like that was unfortunate, but no harm done in the long run."

Well, that was certainly a turn-up for the books. Where had Fluck gone, and who was currently residing in his flaccid grey skin? There must have been an invasion of the body snatchers, because he was being far too nice. And Fluck simply didn't do nice. Jocasta must have been blowing fairy dust up his dick to make him this delightful.

He was heading out of the door again before he threw a final comment over his shoulder.

"By the way, Jocasta has had to go home. Apparently she's dealing with a personal emergency, so bear that in mind if you had given her any work to do."

Interesting. So, Jocasta was avoiding me and avoiding work. Fluck didn't seem to be nonplussed by her absence, so clearly he didn't know that their little secret was out.

Alice cornered me on my way to the loo. She was heading out of the building for yet another ciggie break, but dashed over to me keen for any tidbit of juicy gossip I might be able to provide. But I was resolute and kept my trap firmly shut. I had been tempted to say "when in doubt keep snout out" but I had managed to stop myself.

Instead I had told her I had no idea what Jocasta's "personal emergency" was. Why would I? Alice slunk out of the door in disappointment, bracing herself against the gust of cold winter air that met her in her quest to get her nicotine hit.

I didn't speak to Seb at all. I was avoiding that conversation, the way I avoided horizontal stripes. Anyway, I think I'd had enough confrontation for one day, thank you very much. Any more would seriously compromise my composure.

I spied him on several occasions through the open sliver of his office door, and he appeared fine, no cause for concern. He certainly didn't look as if his life had been well and truly ripped apart by a flame-haired harlot.

All in all, it was a strange workday. Not as bad as it could have been, but unsettling all the same.

The initial adrenaline rush I had felt after the showdown with Jocasta slowly ebbed away to the inevitable come-down, and now I was left feeling empty and low.

She had clearly run away, no doubt ashamed of her actions. But I couldn't run away so easily. No, I was going to have to deal with the fall-out before she returned. I would speak to Seb. I would also find a way to be in the vicinity of Fluck, without wanting to throw up all over the Axminster. We would all get back to some sort of normality. We just had to.

I wasn't going to stay late in the office tonight. No, tonight I was going to be off quicker than Fluck's checked golfing slacks.

Talking of which, he had already left for the evening. Something about an awards ceremony at his golf club that he simply had to attend. He would no doubt already be sipping his first single malt of the evening. I hoped he was telling the truth, and he wasn't using his wood with Jocasta tonight, deep in her bunker and putting his little heart out.

On the drive home, I decided to make a little detour and pick up something for dinner. I had a hankering for some fish and chips: not my usual go-to for my evening meal but I knew it was one of Seb's favourites, and just having them would make me feel slightly connected to him, even if it was in such a small way.

If I'd been a schoolgirl, I would have been writing his name in ink on my pencil case with a big red heart around it. I had called Jocasta the cliché, but I was turning into quite the cliché myself.

When I entered The Cod's Pollocks, the smell of fried fish and chips assailed my nostrils immediately. That familiar aroma of frying batter and vinegar was so evocative. I had to admit it smelt bloody lovely, reminding of when I was a little girl and my dad would bring me out to our local takeaway to get fish and chips when my mother was working late.

We would eat them in the car straight out of the newspaper,

and they tasted divine. After we had munched the final chip and disposed of the evidence, Dad would give the car upholstery a quick spritz with his Brut aftershave so my mother wouldn't have a clue what we had been up to. It was our little secret.

I had loved my dad so much. He had died five years earlier from cancer, leaving just me and my mother Veronica behind. I loved my mum too, but she was quite a formidable woman, a little prickly and hard to get close to. My husband Duncan had called her "The Cactus", and as our marriage progressed, he told me I was becoming the same, a chip off the old block.

I always laughed that off and told him he was being ridiculous. I was nothing like my mother. There was a much softer side to me, I believed. I wasn't so structured and single-minded as my mother could be. But maybe he had been right all along, and I was just a bit of a "cold fish" too.

And talking of cold fish, I eventually made it to the front of the queue. I stood facing the frazzled-looking young woman, in her white uniform and hairnet, looking as if she would rather be anywhere than in The Cod's Pollocks on a chilly January evening.

My mind went blank. What was it I wanted? Traditional fish and chips, or maybe throw caution to the wind and have me a stodgy mince and onion pie and a potato scallop? But no, I decided I was having what I would have done when I came with dad: battered cod, small chips and a large tub of mushy peas. The caviar of the North, as Lottie always called them.

I took my bundle of wrapped food and held it close to my chest, protecting it like a newborn baby.

I passed a group of fierce-looking women on my way to the car. They eyed me with suspicion, and I feared they might make a grab for my goodies. I was starving, and really looking forward to my fishy feast; I would fight to the death to protect it. But they passed by me, one of them making a comment I couldn't quite catch, and they all laughed. Then they were gone, a group of cackling hags into the night.

My food parcel was warming me nicely in the cold winter air, the heat radiating right through to my La Perla bra. Cosy and comforting like a fried food hug. Maybe this is what was meant by comfort food.

As I placed the wrapped food gently onto the passenger seat, my mobile phone buzzed in the pocket of my coat. I nearly ignored it. I had had enough of people today and was just keen to get home to the safety and solitude of my home and stuff my face. What if it was more drama? I just didn't think I could deal with any more of that.

But my curiosity got the better of me and I fished it out of my pocket and checked the screen. It was from Seb.

"We need to talk."

Chapter 32

My heart sank like a stone, straight into my stilettos. What did this mean? What did he know? Or more to the point, what didn't he know?

As if by magic my appetite had gone, completely disappeared like a fart in the wind. The Jocasta Jennings diet should really be patented. Dealing with the drama that woman caused could drop the weight off you quicker than a dose of dysentery.

With shaky fingers I tapped out a reply to him.

"OK, when?"

I watched the bubbles on the screen, knowing he was replying and desperate for the message to appear.

"Can I come to yours? I can be there in an hour."

I was in two minds. Was this a good idea? Part of me wanted to see him, but the other part was terrified of what it could mean.

I began to type my reply: to tell him that I was tired, it had been a long day, and I would just see him tomorrow. But something stopped me, and I deleted what I had written. I owed him more than that. Plus, I had decided that I was going to be more decisive, seizing the day even though it was evening. Less Carpe Diem and more Carpe Noctem.

I typed just two letters.

"*OK*".

I fretted the entire drive back to my house. It only took twenty minutes, but as I pulled up into my drive it felt like no time had passed at all.

I grabbed my handbag and the bag of wrapped food off the passenger seat, and on unsteady legs made my way up the path and into the house.

Seb, as always, was true to his word. Exactly an hour from his message being sent, there was a sharp knock on my front door which nearly made me jump out of my skin, like a housecat when you turn the vacuum cleaner on.

I had been sitting stiff-backed on a dining room chair. The room was silent. Just me and my thoughts. The fish and chips were still wrapped and abandoned on the kitchen counter: I still had no appetite. It was at times like this that I almost wished I smoked: something to do with my hands and keep them from shaking, taking the edge off my anxiety.

I might not smoke, but I did have other vices. I had poured myself a large glass of white wine. I had to stop myself from finishing the entire bottle, but I felt it best to be nearly sober when he arrived.

I nearly knocked my glass over when I heard the knock on the door. My nerves were jangling like a windchime in a hurricane. I had changed into a pair of jeans and a long-sleeved T-shirt, but everything about me felt stiff and uncomfortable, like I was wearing clothes two sizes too small. It must be all the tension I was holding in my body.

I felt my feet dragging as I made my way to the front door, like a condemned woman walking to her fate. Once there, I took a deep breath and pulled it open, steeling myself for whatever would come next.

He was standing there, framed in the doorway: tall and handsome and with an unreadable expression upon his face. It was impossible to guess what his mood was. I could tell he was tired, though; he just exuded weariness. I had an overwhelming urge to reach out and grab him, to pull him into a hug and never let go. But I wouldn't do that. That just wasn't my way.

"Hello, Lila, thanks for letting me come round."

I smiled at him. It felt forced and unnatural to me.

"Of course, Seb, come in. Can I get you a drink? I've got white wine open, or I might have a beer kicking about if you would rather."

He shrugged his broad shoulders non-committally.

"A glass of wine will be fine, thank you."

I nodded briefly and made my way into the kitchen to retrieve the opened bottle from the fridge and pour him a glass, topping up mine at the same time.

He followed me in to stand with his back against the black granite worktop. He had changed into more casual attire too: a pair of navy jeans that gripped his long legs perfectly and a cream jumper that gave him the air of a catalogue model from the 90s, all country gentleman chic.

His hair was rather unkempt, as if he had been worriedly running his hand through it, and there were little crow's feet etched around his eyes. I couldn't help noticing his eyes had never looked a more intense shade of blue than they did in that moment. If I hadn't known better, I would have sworn he was wearing coloured contact lenses, they were so brilliantly vibrant.

I passed him his glass without a word, and he took it with a wary smile. He drained a good third of it in one go while I waited patiently for him to finally speak. My nerves stretched to breaking point in anticipation of how the conversation might go.

"I'm sorry, Lila."

My head snapped up and I looked at him, confused. What was he sorry about? Was he sorry our friendship was over? Was that what it was?

I shook my head at him.

"What, Seb? What are you sorry about?"

He sighed deeply and put his wine glass down on the counter, his handsome face looking troubled.

"I should have believed you from the start; I've known you for so long, I ought to have known you wouldn't just make things up. I've let you down and for that I'm so very sorry."

He looked down at the floor as if ashamed to meet my eyes.

"What you told me about Jocasta's boyfriend: I should have just believed you. I don't know what I was thinking, accusing you of lying. I suppose I just wanted to see the best in her, didn't want to have to face the fact that she had been leading me a merry dance all along. Didn't want to admit to myself that someone would be capable of making up such horrible lies."

I nodded, not trusting myself to speak yet, and took another sip of wine.

He ran his hand through his thick, dark hair. That explained why it was sticking up in such random tufts.

"Lottie told me."

My ears pricked up suddenly at this. *What exactly* had Lottie told him?

"She told me what you saw in Fluck's office on Friday evening. How you couldn't bring yourself to tell me, because

I hadn't believed you before, and how you'd been right about her all along, saw through her act."

I think I was actually holding my breath at that point. I feared I might pass out from lack of oxygen.

His eyes were pleading with mine now.

"I'm so sorry, Lila, really I am."

All the tension I had held in my body up to that point seemed to instantly fade away. My muscles were suddenly fluid, and I was glad I was sitting down at the kitchen table as I feared my legs wouldn't hold my weight.

His eyes were still searching mine, but I looked down, fixing them instead on the kitchen floor, focusing on the small Bolognese stain that remained from my culinary attempts some nights before.

I spoke quietly, still not trusting my own voice.

"It's OK, Seb, I just didn't want to hurt you. I knew how close you two were and I didn't want to break your heart and cause you pain. I care about you too much to see you devastated."

A look of confusion settled on his face now.

"Devastated? Why on earth would I be devastated? Disap-pointed, yes, but devastated, that's a bit extreme don't you think?"

He wasn't the only one who was confused now. I was shaking my head, not understanding things at all.

"Because you've been seeing each other for weeks. Aren't you a couple?"

He laughed for a second as if I had cracked a joke, but it died in his mouth upon seeing my serious expression.

"No, I haven't been seeing Jocasta. We hang out as friends now and again, and she's been an asset at the pub quiz on occasion; well, on the rounds about popular culture and fashion anyway. But seeing each other that's just daft"

He let out another laugh as if the notion of them dating was completely ridiculous.

"Yes, she's a good-looking girl, but we wouldn't go out together. She's not my type at all, and I'm pretty sure I wouldn't be hers in a million light years either."

Well, I knew for a fact that wasn't true. Seb always had such a low opinion of himself in the attractiveness stakes. His self-deprecation was always part of his charm: his inability to see what others could. But I knew exactly how Jocasta had seen him, and she'd had her sights set firmly on him.

"But I don't understand: she took you shopping, changed your wardrobe…"

Seb interrupted me.

"Yes, as a friend she did those things, she helped me. You've been telling me for years to smarten myself up, and finally I listened. And I must admit it feels good to take pride in my appearance. But I always had you in mind when I tried on any new clothes: what your opinion would be, what you would think of them."

He paused for a second to give a small, embarrassed shrug.

"I guess I was doing it all for you."

I felt a lump settle in my throat. Like an olive from my martini that I just couldn't budge.

So, they hadn't been together after all. I thought over all my recent conversations with Seb, and it was true he had never once said they were dating. In fact, he had only ever referred to her as his friend. But why had she gone to so much effort to make me believe that they were an item? Even eluding in a non-too subtle way to their satisfying sex life and his obvious charms in the trouser department.

But I didn't need to be Einstein to figure it out. It was because she wanted him, and she was threatened by me. Maybe it had never really been about Seb, and it was more about getting one over on me all along.

She was competing with me, in any which way she could. And she knew that Seb carried a torch for me. It had been the worst kept secret in the workplace, after all. So, to win his heart would have given her such a boost.

Or maybe I was giving myself too much credit and I didn't feature that much in it at all. Maybe it was all about Seb. And I now knew what Jocasta did, that he was an amazing catch. Like I had said to the girls, he really was good on paper: great job, solvent, in fact just the whole package. But whatever the reason for her wanting him, he had never wanted her.

That knowledge meant everything to me. My heart was suddenly light. I felt like my nine-year-old self again when I had received the Fun Time Barbie for Christmas that every little girl in my class had coveted. I'd felt completely on top of the world back then. Just like I did now.

Seb was staring deep into my eyes, and I felt my heartbeat quicken in my chest.

"It's you, Lila, it's always been you, pretty much from the first moment I clapped eyes on you all those years ago. Standing at that drinks party by the punch bowl, looking so bored I worried you might drown yourself in it. All the men in the room wanting you, but you happy to ignore them and just talk to your girlfriends. I loved you from that moment, and I love you now. I've never stopped, never will."

It took him precisely four seconds to walk the distance across the kitchen and gather me up into his strong arms.

When his lips touched mine, it was electric. Like the air was alive and fizzing with it. But sweet too, and tinged with so much longing. A year ago, if someone had told me I would be kissing Seb in the middle of my kitchen, I would have laughed it off, thought them certifiable. But now it just felt the most natural thing in the world. There was no weirdness about it, like I had always assumed. No, now it was just fabulous, pure and simple. Just perfect.

And the man could really kiss: just the right amount of pressure to make me go weak at the knees. I felt my whole body liquefy with lust as he ran his hands smoothly up and down my back and our kiss deepened.

He broke away for a second and looked deep into my eyes. His pupils were darker than before and full of yearning, the depth of his emotions evident.

"I love you, Lila."

I reached up and took his face gently in my hands my eyes searching his.

"And I love you too, Seb."

Suddenly his face broke into a smile so bright it could have illuminated the whole of West Yorkshire.

"You love me?"

He suddenly looked much younger, almost like a little boy and it made my heart glad.

"You can't know how long I've dreamt of hearing those words. I feel like running out into the street and shouting it from the rooftops for the whole world to hear...Lila Glover loves me!"

I was laughing now.

"Please don't do that! Mr Dick, two doors down, is perfectly named and would probably call the police and have you arrested for disturbing the peace."

I gave him a seductive smile.

"But you can kiss me again if you like."

Seb returned my smile, his eyes full of longing. "Now *that* I can definitely do."

I don't know how long we stood in the middle of my kitchen smooching like a couple of lovestruck teenagers. It could have been minutes; it could have been hours. I simply had no idea. Time seemed to stand still in that very moment. When he eventually pulled away, his voice was deep and throaty.

"Does this mean we're officially dating now? That we are a couple?"

He looked at me, his eyes hopeful and full of meaning.

"Yes, I think it's fair to see that's exactly what we are, and I think we'll make a fabulous couple...touch wood."

And with a sly smile, I reached over and grazed my hand against the obvious bulge in his tight jeans.

"And I don't mind if I do."

And as my hand caressed the bulge in the denim my excitement quickly grew. It seemed that there was one thing that Jocasta hadn't been lying about. Just a lucky guess on her part.

Chapter 33

The next morning, I couldn't quite believe what had happened. I almost pinched myself to check I wasn't still dreaming. But no, it was true. We were in love. And it was bloody fantastic!

The night had been nothing short of amazing. I had always prided myself on my ability to have sex without attachment in the past. To see it for what it was: a mutually beneficial arrangement between two consenting adults. As a lawyer, I understood only too well the concept of a contract. But all those romantic Mills and Boon novels that my granny had devoured when I was a kid, a big mug of tea in one hand and her novel clutched in the other, had turned out to be true. She would tell me, her glasses all steamed up, I never knew whether from the tea or the steamy pages she was reading, that I had to wait for "the one".

Even as a child, I had laughed that off. In a world of nearly eight billion people, how could there be "the one"? And how likely was it that they would just happen to be living in the same town as you?

I had thought her books were unrealistic and cheesy and just incredibly uncool. But maybe they had been spot on all along, and there really was "the one". Now I'd found that sex when you were in love, truly in love, was the biggest thrill of all. And I knew in my heart this was the real thing with Seb.

I once believed I loved my ex-husband, truly loved him, for the longest time. But like the yogurt residing in my refrigerator, it turned out that our love had a limited shelf life. And when it finally turned sour, well, it was nothing short of rancid.

We had made the best of things for a while. But unfortunately, the remnants of our love that remained were not enough to weather the storm of life. And the bitterness that had set in had been like a rot, just too corrosive to our relationship.

I had hated Duncan so much for cheating on me, but if I was totally honest with myself, it had given me a reason to boot him out on his arse. In some ways I should have thanked that girl. She did me such a favour.

But even in our best times, the love I had for my ex-husband was nothing compared to this. I couldn't believe I had denied my feelings for so long: always believing myself a strong, independent woman who was best on her own. Confident I knew what I wanted, I damn well made sure I got it. But nothing could have been further from the truth, because if I'd really been true to myself, I would have realised that what I'd wanted all along was Seb. And now I had him, I wasn't going to let him go.

My past half-life of lack-lustre liaisons and hedonistic endeavours was behind me. All I needed now was Seb: his sci-fi socks, his shepherd's pie and his...ahem...light sabre. I smiled just thinking of what I had been missing for all those years. It sure made me glow.

We didn't just get intimate in the boudoir, though we talked for hours too. I'd believed I knew everything about him, but in the afterglow of our passion, we opened ourselves up fully to each other, our souls completely bared. And it was beautiful.

What we hadn't done, though, was eat. And after all that energy had been expended, we were completely ravenous. So in lieu of shepherd's pie we microwaved the abandoned fish and chips and shared them between us.

Never had there been a meal that tasted quite so divine. You could keep your champagne and your finest oysters from now on. Reheated fish and chips eaten under the duvet with the man you loved just couldn't be beaten. They were manna from heaven.

And looking at Seb now, dozing on the pillow next to me, the shafts of sun streaking through the linen curtains and illuminating his face like a golden kiss, he looked every inch the angel that he was.

Chapter 34

Time passed so quickly. A month went by in the mere blink of an eye with us barely noticing. We were lost in our love. And that love was just going from strength to strength.

It was Valentine's Day, and I couldn't get enough of it. In the past I would always roll my eyes at the most pointless day in the calendar. I would inform anyone who cared to listen that Valentine's was just a capitalist construct and anyone who bought into all that nonsense was a complete nincompoop. Well, who was the nincompoop now? Oh yes, that would be me. Because I was bloody loving it! Bring it on. All of it. I just couldn't get enough, from the padded hearts to the horny red devils and all the other cheesy nonsense in between. I was in love, and that was to be celebrated every day, but especially on February 14th.

So tonight, to celebrate Valentine's, we were going out for dinner with Lottie and Leo. Although we were loving time on our own, it was great to be able to do couply things now too. Like going to the pub quiz with Adam and his friends. It turned out I actually quite enjoyed the simpler things in life. I had even forgone my normal white wine or vodka martini to try a half pint of the local ale, and it really wasn't too bad. Not likely to be my preferred tipple of choice, but OK once in a blue moon.

I proved invaluable on the "guess the famous face" round, being the only one surrounded by sci-fi fanatics who hadn't the foggiest who Kim Kardashian was. I surprised myself by how much fun it was. Even Adam wasn't as bad as I had first thought. I was ashamed of myself for never giving him more of a chance. I'd felt he was the dullest man on God's green earth, and believe me, he was still deadly dull with his monotone voice and talk of all things animé, but he was a good soul and he was a great friend to Seb. So for that reason I would tolerate him and make things nice.

Lottie was completely over the moon at how things had turned out. She boasted that it was her part in playing match-maker and intervening, when necessary, that had finally got us together. I couldn't deny the part she had played in it all, and I would be forever grateful.

Lottie had left it up to me to decide where we should book our meal. So, I let Seb have the deciding vote. Needless to say, it was going to be somewhere where fine dining was frowned upon and where half the menu was designed to be eaten with fingers and a napkin stuffed under your chin to catch the inevitable drips. But that was fine by me.

I had learned that a good relationship was all about give and take: even if that meant giving your Spanx a good old workout and taking a pack of Rennie's with you in your handbag for the inevitable heartburn later.

I sat across the table at The Fat Belly Deli, and smiled lovingly at my man.

He was looking particularly gorgeous in his new shirt and jacket. We had gone shopping that afternoon and bought him a few new bits and pieces. Of course we'd got some items for me too. I still hadn't lost my passion for fashion, now that I had discovered other passions could be great fun too.

I suppose I had Jocasta to thank for persuading Seb out of his rut, style-wise. For he certainly scrubbed up well now. He was far more delicious than anything described on the restaurant menu. And the 28-day well-hung beef had nothing on him.

Seb was in heaven. The restaurant was the type that sold meat by the pound: half a cow cooked to your liking with a mountain of chips on the side. You could pick whatever sauce you wanted to drizzle on your hunk of beef, ranging from the delicious-sounding red wine and shallot to the frankly stomach-turning chocolate and bacon bits.

Seb had carefully chosen the 24 oz cut of beef to come with a hearty side of mac and cheese, onion rings, skin on fries and corn on the cob. His preferred sauce, after much deliberation, turned out to be the rather sedate creamy mushroom.

He looked at his food with almost as much adoration as he lavished on me. I didn't mind, though. I was just happy that he was happy. And anyway, it meant that next time we dined out it would be my choice, and there was a lovely new sushi restaurant I was dying to try. Seb was not a fan of sushi; he preferred his fish big and battered. He had once told me that raw fish was not for dinner, it was for scraping off the bottom of a trawlerman's boot.

I watched him tuck into his food with gusto, and I felt a little wave of emotion sweep over me. I really adored him. How could I feel such tenderness while watching him eat a corn on the cob with butter dripping down his chin? But I did.

"Good choice for restaurant, Seb."

Leo commented with obvious approval.

He was nearly as enamoured with his food as Seb, having also plumped for the steak, slightly smaller than Seb's, but with a plethora of side orders and a blue cheese sauce accompaniment.

Lottie smiled at him affectionately. I couldn't help but notice the look she gave her man was akin to the one I had just given mine. It was fair to say we we'd both been impaled by Cupid's arrow.

She, like me, had plumped for a lighter option and was having a chicken dish with a medley of winter vegetables. Neither of us wanted the meat sweats later. She did, however, dunk a carrot spear into Leo's cheese sauce to liven it up a little.

"So, what happened to Jocasta then?"

I looked to Seb to answer.

He paused from wolfing down his meat. Something I also hoped to be doing later.

"In all honesty, we don't really know. She left immediately after Lila dropped her bombshell, claiming there was a family emergency, and we haven't seen hide nor hair of her since. It's fair to say that Fluck is hopping mad. It's left the firm seriously understaffed."

"Yes, and possibly left his staff seriously over firm."

I couldn't help making a joke out of it.

After Jocasta had made like pigeon shit and hit the road, many things had come to light. Firstly, the fact that Fluck and his wife were no longer together. The surprising part was that it had absolutely nothing to do with what he had been getting up to with Jocasta on his swivel chair.

It seemed that dreary old Dinah wasn't quite as beige as we had all thought. In fact, she had walked out on Fluck with her bags neatly packed, well over a month ago. She was now to be found in and around Vietnam with her new boyfriend, photographing the near extinct snub-nose monkeys for a wildlife magazine.

We had discovered from someone Seb knew that worked at Leeds Leads that Mrs Fluck had run away with their lead photographer after she had met him at the fashion show. Once he had fulfilled his brief and snapped all the images he needed, plus a couple of lucky ones, namely the tattered sign and Fluck's bony enraged face, he had retired to the bar for a quick drink before returning to work.

That was when he met Dinah. They had felt an instant connection between them. They struck up conversation, and as they say, the rest is history. Or rather geography and Southeast Asia, it would appear.

Fluck had never noticed his wife's interaction with another, much younger man. It was fair to say he was as mad as a meat axe that day, and raging to all and sundry that he was going to be a laughing stock at his golf club. But then again, he barely acknowledged her at the best of times. His eyes were never fixed in her direction.

But once she had gone from his life, maybe never to return, all that had changed. Now his eyes had been truly opened. The truth was that he missed his wife and regretted all the years he had taken her for granted. He was lost without her. He became a sad shambolic shell of the man he once was. And that was really saying something, because he had always resembled an extra from *Zombie Apocalypse* as it was.

Once we had discovered this bizarre plot twist, it put a slightly different spin on things. Yes, it was still seriously gross that Fluck and Jocasta had been getting up to fiddly diddly in the workplace after hours, but at least he hadn't been cheating on his spouse. And maybe due to what had happened in his personal life, a serious error of judgement could be somewhat excused.

Even when he had been in my office acting unusually cheerfully, it had been his way of dealing with the grief at the breakdown of his marriage. While I thought he was strutting around like the cat who had got the cream, he was in fact putting on a show for the world. Giving the impression that all was good, when in fact he was crumbling apart inside.

But that left Jocasta very much still in the frame. She was the undeniable villain of the peace. For one thing, she was the one claiming to be single, but I knew that was a big fat lie. Fluck was in fact the single one. I really couldn't fathom out her motives.

Leo's voice interrupted my thoughts. He was holding the solid menu in the air and looking around the table expectantly.

"So, are we all too stuffed, or is there a bit of room left for pudding?"

Seb leaned back in his chair, his normally slim physique looking a little rotund in the gut area from the sheer amount he had scoffed.

He let out a barely audible groan.

"I don't know if I could, I'm fit to burst. But pass us the menu, Leo. It wouldn't hurt to have a little look."

Leo passed it across the table to Seb, and once he had it in his hands his eyes lit up like a pinball machine, obviously impressed with the range of sweet treats Fat Belly Deli offered.

"Oooh, I might just be able to squeeze a sliver of jam roly poly in, though."

He shut the menu with a decisive snap.

"It's my favourite, after all, so it would be rude not to."

Lottie shot me an amused glance, which I returned.

My phone beeped on the table next to me. I quickly moved my paper napkin away as it was concealing half of the screen. It was a text message from a number I didn't recognise.

"I know it's a lot to ask, but would you meet me tomorrow for a coffee, 10am Gourmet Delights? I really need to talk to you… Jocasta"

Chapter 35

How had she even got my number? But then I remembered I'd given it to her when we'd been arranging our spa afternoon.

"Are you going to meet her?"

Seb questioned over toast and coffee the next morning.

He was looking adorable, with little crumbs stuck to his upper lip. I brushed them off gently. At one time I would have found this image of domestic bliss completely cringey. But not any more.

"I don't know, I haven't decided yet."

That wasn't exactly true. I had decided. I had made my mind up when I was buttering his toast. I *was* going to meet her. My curiosity was pricking at me just too much not to.

So, I was going to have a late start at work this morning. First, I had a meeting with a spiteful floozy for a flat white, and possibly a fat slap if she didn't behave herself.

At dead on 10 a.m. I marched into Gourmet Delights as cool as a cucumber, but looking as hot as a jalapeno. I was certainly dressed to impress. I had taken Coco Chanel's words to heart: *"Dress like you are going to meet your worst enemy today."* And that was exactly what I had done.

I saw that the same guy was serving behind the counter, but I no longer felt embarrassed. All that seemed a million years ago, as if it had happened to a different person. I was a different person now. And I was glad.

And now that I was happy in life again, I was seriously looking my best. While I was pining over Seb, my *joie de vivre* had deserted me faster than a toupee in a tornado. But I was back on form and my most fabulous self once more.

I was decked out in a new knitted dress that I had bought when shopping with Seb. It was figure-hugging and fantastically chic and in the most beautiful shade of vibrant scarlet.

And on the subject of scarlet women, I spotted Jocasta sitting at a small table off from the hustle and bustle of all the other customers. There was a large cup of coffee cooling in front of her. And as I made my way over to greet her, she lifted her eyes to meet mine and gave a weak smile that didn't quite reach her eyes. She looked nervous. And so she should.

I was shocked by her appearance. Firstly, she was not dressed at all how I was used to seeing her. Her appearance was much more demure and dressed down, in a simple crisp white crew-neck T-shirt and jeans. Her blonde toffee-streaked tresses were swept back into a high ponytail, and she wore the bare minimum of make-up.

That in itself was shocking, but there was much worse. Above her left eye there was a nasty-looking bruise. It was maybe a few days old and had begun to yellow slightly around the edges. It still looked nasty, though. I winced, just looking at it.

Maybe I had been wrong all along and she was in an abusive relationship after all. The thought that I might have misjudged things chilled me to the bone.

I sank down into the chair opposite her, concern swelling in my chest.

"Lila, I'm so glad you came; I wasn't sure you would. I really think if we could talk, we…"

I cut her off mid-sentence.

"Did Simon do that to you?"

Her hand flew to her head, and she gently touched the bruise, a look of regret sweeping across her face.

"After everything I've lied about, it would be the easiest thing in the world to blame this on Si. But no, he didn't do this to me."

She gave a nervous laugh.

"But like I said, I'm really glad you came today."

"I wasn't sure I was going to, but here I am."

I laughed wryly and fixed the younger woman with a suspicious stare.

"I must be a glutton for punishment."

She glanced down nervously at her hands. I could have been mistaken, but I was pretty sure a fleeting look of shame crossed her features. She played with the handle of her cup; it was clear that this wasn't easy for her. But I had little sympathy left to give.

She touched the yellowing bruise again and winced slightly.

"I did this in a changing room, believe it or not."

She laughed and shook her head slightly as if not quite believing it herself.

"I was trying on a pair of tight satin trousers, and I got my foot caught and fell out of the cubicle and hit my head. I think my pride was hurt even worse than my noggin. I had my arse exposed to half the shop, and I was wearing granny knickers too. That'll teach me for loving such tight clothing. It was almost like karma was giving me a little kick for the way I've been behaving lately."

I looked at her in surprise. This was not like the Jocasta I had known and disliked intensely over the last few months. The fact that she admitted to wearing granny knickers was shocking enough, but this woman was softly spoken and self-deprecating. In fact, the complete opposite to the Jocasta Jennings I had grown to loathe.

Her eyes looked up and there were unshed tears in the corner. I felt torn. The expression on her face was so forlorn and genuine, I felt instantly moved. But I knew she could turn the waterworks on at the drop of a hat. She had done it when talking about her ex. Those crocodile tears had seemed so genuine then too.

She wrung her hands together and let out a nervous laugh.

"I don't know where to start, it's all such a bloody mess."

"Why don't you start at the beginning. Just, please, can we have the honest version this time. If I want a work of fiction, I'll get my Kindle out of my handbag."

So that's what she did. We sat opposite each other at that little table, and for the most part she talked and I listened.

She told me how she had been intimidated by me at work. That I always seemed so poised and professional and that made her feel less than. Like she was a rather uncouth and unsophisticated country bumpkin, and she worried she would never reach my level.

This took me completely by surprise. This was never the impression I had got from her.

She admitted she had crippling low self-esteem, and to combat that she would often go on the defensive. And her best form of defence was to attack. And that meant attacking me. Trying to undermine the person she felt overshadowed by. She had believed that if she belittled me, it would make her feel much better about herself. Like, somehow, she would be winning.

"But what about your Simon? You made us believe he was this controlling bully of a man, but that wasn't at all what I witnessed at work."

She had the grace to blush and drop her head.

"I know, I don't know why I did that. I suppose I just thought that if people believed the worst about him, they would see the best in me. The truth is that Si is a lovely guy, too lovely if anything. He never stands up for himself, and even when I'm in the wrong, it's always he who ends up apologising."

She drained the last of her coffee, which must have been cold by now. I caught the attention of a passing waitress and ordered two more. I hadn't had a cup yet, too engrossed in what she had been saying.

She dabbed at her eyes with a napkin to stem the flow of tears that freely flowed now.

"I know I treat him badly. I hate the way I am with him. When I'm mean and put him down, he looks like a little whipped puppy. But sometimes I just can't help myself. I want him to be more of a man, to stand up to me, but he never does."

I shook my head at her.

"But he *is* a man. A strong man in fact, to take all that from you and still hang around and never retaliate. He must see something in you that's worth staying for."

She laughed bitterly.

"I don't know what. I do love him though, I really do. I suppose it's the fact that I don't love myself that makes me the way I am and treat him as I do. Si is such a good man; his family and friends love him; no one ever has a bad word to say about him, whereas I have no one. I think sometimes I'm jealous of him. I've driven all my friends away with my toxic ways, and most of my family don't even speak to me any more."

At least she seemed to understand that the problems lay with her.

She twisted the napkin around her fingers.

"We're going to see a counsellor together. It was Simon's idea but I'm fully on board with it now. I truly want us to make it as a couple. I know there's a lot of work to be done, but I'm willing to put in the effort. I'm just so glad he hasn't given up on me."

"That's good. But why did you tell everyone he was your ex? That's what I don't understand. And why did you make me believe that you were in a relationship with Seb?"

She played with the silver teaspoon, now trying desperately not to meet my eyes.

"I suppose I saw the good in Seb, and the fact that he worshipped you made him the ultimate prize. I could see you liked him, even though you wouldn't admit it, so I thought that if I could get with him, I would have somehow made it. I didn't really think it through properly. He was never interested. If he had been, I don't know what I would have done about Simon."

She laughed bitterly and shook her head.

"I like to think I would have finished with Si if I had got with Seb, but who knows? I probably would have seen the two of them behind each other's back."

At least she was being honest. I had to give her credit for that. Although hearing how close I could have been to losing Seb stung a little.

"Seb was fun to be around. He was so nice and decent, it made me feel better about myself. I loved helping him pick out smarter clothes and getting to know his friends. I could be a better, nicer version of me when I was with him. More the person I knew I should be. I realised he wasn't interested in me as a girlfriend, but I couldn't help making you believe we were. I got a kick out of seeing the hurt in your eyes when I talked about him. You tried to act so casual, like you weren't bothered in the slightest, but I could tell the truth. I know that makes me a horrible bitch, and I'm so, so sorry."

More tears were flowing now, and I truly believed they were genuine. I had been fooled before, but I chose to trust my instincts now. I rested my hand over her pale one and gave it a gentle, reassuring squeeze.

"But what about Fluck? You couldn't have actually fancied him...could you?"

She shuddered slightly.

"I know you might not believe me, but that only ever happened the once. It was like an out-of-body experience or something. I had flirted with him a bit before, I admit that, when we had our meetings. It was just a bit of banter, or so I thought."

She stopped for a second and dropped her head into her hands with a deep moan.

"He even confided in me about his wife. I suppose that made me feel superior, that I had this information that no one else did. Made me feel somehow important. We ended up talking about Dinah leaving and how cut up he was, and that toxic trait in my personality just reared its ugly head. I suppose I saw myself sitting at your desk, enjoying the power and position that went with it, and in my ridiculous brain I thought that pleasing the boss might be my way to get there. You're right, I'm the worst cliché there could possibly be. I know how badly you must have thought of me."

I smiled gently at her.

"Well, for one thing, I thought you had a very friendly vagina; that kitty was prowling all around the office like she was on heat."

Despite herself, she laughed. And I was glad. Anything to lighten the mood a little. But there was something important I needed to say.

"Jocasta, I've worked my arse off for many years to get to the position I'm in. And believe me, I'm no prude. But not once have I ever had to prostitute myself to get on in my career."

She was nodding her head.

"I know, I know, I'm so ashamed of myself. I've spoken to my doctor about why I act the way I do. He thinks I've got serious self-esteem and anxiety issues, so we're working on it together."

"Well, that's good, it sounds like you're dealing with it in a positive way. "

"I know I've been horrible, done the worst things, been the worst person imaginable. But I'm going to change. Simon has been offered this new job in Manchester, and I'm going to go with him. It's going to be our fresh start. Where we do things right this time."

I worked out how far Manchester was from Leeds: 45 miles. Yes, that should be far enough. I was warming to the woman, but I still knew we would never be friends.

"You've left us all in the lurch at work, just walking out like that. Mind you, in the circumstances I think Fluck will be able to overlook it."

She relaxed visibly, her shoulders appearing less hunched.

"I just couldn't set foot back in there, once I knew what you'd seen. I was so ashamed. I idolised you, even though I never showed it, and to imagine what you would think of me, it was all too much. I really have been the sort of woman I usually hate. I've been horrendous. That horrible Facebook message, spilling coffee all over your gorgeous shirt. I must be the biggest bitch in Leeds, possibly the whole of Yorkshire."

The coffee! I knew I had been right all along. Suddenly I felt vindicated.

I smiled at her kindly and tried to lighten the mood.

"Well, it's fair to say you've been fairly divisive, and about as charming as cracker crumbs down one's cleavage. But the biggest bitch in West Yorkshire? My dear, you clearly haven't met my Auntie Maud."

She laughed then. A little snot bubble escaped her nostril with a tiny high-pitched whistle. It was fair to say the sexy *femme fatale* look she had cultivated of late was well and truly gone.

"I'm sorry, Lila, I just wanted you to look up to me the way I did to you. But I know I went about things completely the wrong way. Will you ever be able to forgive me for being so vile?"

I gave her a small smile as the waitress placed our steaming mugs of coffee down in front of us.

"Well, put it this way, why don't you order us a couple of those gluten-free cakes from this lovely lady, and we'll call it a peace offering."

Chapter 36

Well, that was all a right turn-up for the books. It was only 11:30 a.m., but I felt wrung out and ready to return home for a much-needed nap.

That said, I was still glad that I had met Jocasta. It was fair to say we would never be friends. And I was glad that she and her wardrobe of low cut blouses and tight pencil skirts would soon be sashaying their way Manchester-bound.

I no longer felt any animosity to her, though, and that was a positive. I felt I understood the workings of the woman a little better now. She wasn't at all happy in life, and she hadn't known how to deal with it. She had tried to gain control by manipulating situations, feeling that if her life could go in a different direction, it would suddenly make her happy. But life just didn't work like that. You couldn't lift yourself up by bringing others down.

I wished her well, I really did. I believed that everyone was capable of redemption. We were all broken in our own way and the pieces could, in time, be put back together. Either by ourselves or with the help of others. I truly hoped she was getting all the help she needed. It sounded like she was receiving a lot of support. I kept my fingers crossed that her story would find its happy ending, as mine had done.

As I pushed open the heavy door into Fluck, Young & Glover, I noticed there was someone sitting quietly in reception, their head slightly bowed.

Alice waved her hand as soon as she spotted me, desperate to get my attention.

"Lila, this young lady wants to see you, but she hasn't got an appointment. I told her I didn't know what time you were arriving, but she was adamant she would wait."

I turned my head to see who was so desperate to speak to me. A pretty young girl was sitting nervously on one of the high-backed chairs, appearing anxious and seriously out of her comfort zone.

She looked vaguely familiar, but I couldn't quite put my finger on it. She smiled timidly, her eyes wary.

"Ms Glover, I'm hoping you can help me."

I looked expectantly at the young woman. Slowly my brain clicked into gear, and I realised how I knew her. She was the girl at the table with Alfie and his mates at the pub when I was waiting for Lottie a few weeks before.

She looked so different now. She had put on a little weight and there was a rosy glow blooming in her cheeks. Her hair, which had looked matted and in need of a good comb, was now hanging in glossy blonde waves down her back. The blue streaks had gone, and it was shining like spun gold.

I tried to recall her name. I knew it began with B, but what was it? And then it came to me in a flash.

"Bella, isn't it?"

She looked delighted that I knew her name.

"Yes, I'm Bella. I recognised you straight away when I saw you in the pub. I was in the year under Thomas at school. I remember he was such a nice boy, and I remembered you too.

You always looked so glamorous and important when you came to the school, with your suits and your briefcase. You seemed so different next to all the other mums."

I smiled to myself. But the smile hid a little sadness. In truth I hadn't been so glamorous back then. It was just that I often had to rush to the carol concert or prize-giving evening straight from work, so was still wearing my suit.

I had always been working. There were so many things I'd missed when Thomas was growing up: all the awards nights and coffee evenings. I wished I could go back to those days and don my jeans and trainers and get involved more. But I couldn't change that now. Those days had sadly gone.

That was the lot of being a woman, though. We never thought we were enough, no matter what path we chose in life.

"Well, it's lovely to see you, Bella, and you're certainly looking really well. But what is it you want?"

She looked up at me, her wide blue eyes filling with tears.

"I really need your help. I'm in a lot of trouble, and I don't know where else to turn."

The End

About the Author

I always wanted to write. I remember as a child I would look forward to getting home from Middle School so that I could write my stories and get lost in my own little worlds. Sadly, as I grew older, I lost my courage to write, put my notebook away and there it remained for many decades.

After being diagnosed with cancer for a second time I knew if I was going to make my childhood dreams a reality, I would really need to get my skates on! Not literally of course as I have two left feet and could trip over my own shadow.

After writing the successful "Playing with Fire – The True Story of Fireman Scam" with my twin sister, detailing a very difficult few years in our lives I knew writing was still what I really loved to do.

A children's book I wrote at ten years of age is being faithfully recreated (some 40 years later) and is due to be published soon. I'm so excited by this, it will be amazing for children everywhere to get to know "Humphrey" after all these years.

The first novel in my "Teapots and Tequila shots" series is "The Reinvention of Lottie Potts." This series will concentrate on strong female friendships. Women in their thirties, forties

and older encountering all the ups and downs of modern-day
life. With plenty of tears, tequila, and cheeky humour along
the way.

Two thirds of profits from the sales of "The Reinvention of
Lottie Potts" and a portion of profits from sales of all further
books in the series will be donated to Great Ormond Street
Hospital and Epilepsy Society.

You can connect with me on:

🌐 https://www.klcrear.com

Also by K L Crear

The Reinvention of Lottie Potts

Lottie Potts is happy enough - or so she thinks. Her life is slowly ticking away as she spends her days watching old films and daydreaming about another, better, version of herself. But Lottie isn't one for change. That is until a blonde bombshell blows into town and knocks her husband Daniel completely off his feet.

Lottie is forced to take a long hard look at herself. She is fat, in her forties and thoroughly fed up. Does she fight for her husband and the safe predictable life she knows? Or is revenge, like her favourite ice cream, a dish best served cold?

With her trusty circle of girlfriends and a surprising return from a charming face from her past, Lottie embarks on a transformative journey. Buckle up for the rollercoaster ride of laughter and tears as Lottie navigates the twists and turns of her reinvention, discovering the genuine essence of life along the way.

This is the first book in the "Teapots & Tequila Shots" series

Evelyn Weaver is a Later Life Diva

Evelyn Weaver has lost her spark. In fact, it has dimmed to a mere flicker. Her life is boring her senseless and she has taken to living vicariously through her soap operas. Her usual activities of the bridge club and supermarket shopping just aren't cutting it anymore.

She may be in her seventies but is this really all there is? Must she just shuffle along for the remainder of her life in her fluffy slippers with knitting at hand. Or could there be more? Could there be one final love affair waiting for her if only she dared to be brave enough?

Join Evelyn as she flips the script on her life completely. There are dating disasters, plenty of drama and surprising new friendships along the way.

In a tale that is both heartwarming and hilarious Evelyn proves that growing old is inevitable but thinking old, well that's a choice. And sometimes life's best chapters are still to be written.

This is the third book in the "Teapots & Tequila Shots" series

Playing With Fire: The True Story of Fireman Scam
"In my 23 years of policing, I have never encountered a man as manipulative as Greg Wilson... a compulsive liar who has shown absolutely no remorse... If somebody wrote this as a script for Coronation Street, it would be too outrageous."
– Detective Constable Chris Bentham

Coleen Greenwood was overjoyed to meet James Scott, a heroic firefighter and man of her dreams. Little would she know her dreams would soon become a nightmare as his web of lies started to unravel.

The astonishing true story of one man's lies and a family's fight for justice.

This is the full untold story that was made into the BBC Sounds podcast series "Love-Bombed with Vicky Pattison" which reached No1 in the UK Apple podcasts playlist within the first week of its release. Features as an episode of "Red Flag" on UKTV Play.

A portion of profits from sales of this book will be donated to Women's Aid - www.womensaid.org

Healing From The Burns: Life After Fireman Scam
"The background to this offending shows frankly jaw dropping
arrogance and cruelty in the way that you so persistently and
wickedly deceived your victims, particularly Coleen Greenwood."

- Judge James Adkins

Greg Wilson is now in prison. Finally, it is over for Coleen and
Karen. They can now move on, take time and heal. But is it that
easy? Or is there still much more of the story to come? The
uplifting follow-up true story to "Playing with Fire." How after
the darkest days have ended, light will always break through.

A portion of profits from sales of this book will be donated to
Women's Aid - www.womensaid.org